"Well," he breathed.
"You do honor your bets."

Though he no longer touched her, it was as if the kiss hadn't ended. He was still so close. Ai Li stumbled as she tried to step away and he caught her, a knowing smile playing over his mouth. Even that tiny, innocent touch filled her with renewed longing.

In a daze, she bent to pick up her fallen sword.

"Now that our bargain is settled—" she began hoarsely, "—we should be going. You said the next town was hours from here?"

He collected his sword while a slow grin spread over his face, and her cheeks burned hot as she forced her gaze on the road ahead.

She had to get home and warn her father. Ai Li had thought of nothing else since her escape, until this blue-eyed barbarian had appeared. It was fortunate they were parting when they reached town. When he wasn't looking she pressed her fingers over her lips, which were still swollen from that first kiss.

She was outmatched, much more outmatched than when they had crossed swords.

* * *

Butterfly Swords
Harlequin® Historical #1014—October 2010

Author's Note

The Tang Dynasty has always held a special lure for me. This was a time when women rose to the highest ranks as warriors, courtesans and scholars. Anyone with the will and the perseverance to excel could make it. The imperial capital of Changan emerged as a cosmopolitan center of trade and culture. The most famous love stories, the most beautiful poetry and the most elegant fashions came from this era.

The Silk Road which connected East to West was at its height during the eighth century and the empire embraced different cultures to a greater extent than ever before. I wanted to know what it was like to wear silk and travel to the edges of the empire during this golden age. And I wanted sword fights!

When *Butterfly Swords* was awarded the Golden Heart® 2009 for Historical Romance, I was overcome. It was a dream come true to receive recognition for writing a story that encompassed everything I loved.

In *Butterfly Swords,* you'll find historical fact and a little fantasy, of course. I hope you enjoy the drama and sensuality of the Tang Dynasty as much as I do.

Butterfly Swords
JEANNIE LIN

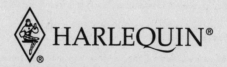

TORONTO • NEW YORK • LONDON
AMSTERDAM • PARIS • SYDNEY • HAMBURG
STOCKHOLM • ATHENS • TOKYO • MILAN • MADRID
PRAGUE • WARSAW • BUDAPEST • AUCKLAND

Recycling programs
for this product may
not exist in your area.

ISBN-13: 978-0-373-29614-9

BUTTERFLY SWORDS

Available from Harlequin® Historical and
JEANNIE LIN

Butterfly Swords #1014

This is Jeannie Lin's debut novel for
Harlequin Historical, but look for

The Taming of Mei Lin

a Harlequin Historical Undone! eBook
that links into

Butterfly Swords

and is available now.

To my little sister Nam,
my "evil" twin, my ideal reader—
Thank you for the tough love, for telling me
which darlings to kill, for reading all the ugly
drafts, for everything. I made a promise to dedicate
my first book to you, and here it is—
more than twenty years later.

Heartfelt thanks to my agent, Gail Fortune, for her
stubborn dedication. To Anna Boatman and
Linda Fildew for making this story even bigger
and better. And to Barbara, Elaine, Dana and Kay
for all the love and guidance.

Chapter One

❧❧❧

The palanquin dipped sharply and Ai Li had to brace her hands against the sides to stay upright. Amidst the startled cries of her attendants, the enclosure lurched again before crashing to the ground with the splintering crack of wood. She gasped as the elaborate headdress toppled from her lap and she was thrown from her seat. A tight knot formed in her stomach, and she fought to stay calm.

What she heard next was unmistakable. The clash of metal upon metal just beyond the curtain that covered the wedding sedan. Sword-strike, a sound she woke up to every morning. With her heart pounding, she struggled to free herself from the tangle of red silk about her ankles. This skirt, the entire dress, was so heavy, laden with jewels and a hundred *li* of embroidery thread.

She fumbled behind the padded cushions of her seat, searching frantically for her swords. She had put them there herself, needing some reminder of home, the way another girl might find comfort in her childhood doll.

Her hand finally closed around the hilt. She tightened her

grip to stop from shaking. From outside, the sounds of fighting grew closer. She ignored the inner voice that told her this was madness and pulled the swords free. The short blades barely fit in the cramped space. She had no time for doubt, not when so much was at risk. With the tip of one sword, she pushed the curtain aside.

A stream of sunlight blinded her momentarily. The servants scattered like a flock of cranes around her, all posts abandoned. Squinting, she focused on the hulking figure that blocked the entrance and raised her blades in defence.

A familiar voice cried out then, *'Gōngzhǔ!'*

Old Wu, the elder lieutenant, rushed to her while she faced the stranger. Her armed escort struggled against a band of attackers. In the confusion, she couldn't tell who was who.

Wu pulled her behind the cover of the palanquin. The creases around his eyes deepened. *'Gōngzhǔ*, you must go now.'

'With them?'

She stared at the thugs surrounding her. Wu had been a bit too successful at finding men to pose as bandits.

'There are clothes, money.'

Wu spoke the instructions and the head 'bandit' grabbed on to her arm. Instinctively, she dug in her heels to resist him. Everything was unfolding so quickly, but she had known there would be no turning back.

The stranger relaxed his grip, but did not release her. An act, she reminded herself, fighting the panic constricting her chest.

'There is no more time,' Wu pleaded.

'Your loyalty will not be forgotten.'

She let herself be pulled through the trees, stumbling to keep up with the ragged band. Who were these men Old Wu had enlisted? When she looked back, he was standing beside the toppled sedan, his shoulders sagging as if he carried a sack of stones. The secret he'd revealed to her two days ago weighed heavily on her as well. Ai Li hoped that she could trust him.

* * *

God's teeth, the scent of cooking rice had never smelled so sweet.

Ryam's stomach clenched as he stared across the dirt road. An open-air tavern stood empty save for the cook stirring an iron pot over the fire. The establishment was little more than a hut propped up in a clearing: four beams supporting a straw-thatched roof. Bare wooden benches offered weary travellers a place to rest between towns and partake of food and drink.

Travellers with coin, of course. The only metal Ryam had touched in months was the steel of his sword. He was nearly hungry enough to eat that.

The proprietor perched at the entrance, whip-thin and wily in his black robe as he stared down the vacant trail. Nothing but wooded thickets in either direction. A single dirt road cut through the brush, leading to the stand.

Ryam pulled his hood over his head with a sharp tug and retreated into the shade. He was too big, his skin too pale, a barbarian in the Chinese empire. *Bái guǐ*, they called him. White demon. Ghost man.

He wrestled with his pride, preparing to beg if he had to. Before he could approach, a mottled shape appeared in the glare of the afternoon sun. The proprietor jumped into motion and waved the newcomer into the tavern.

'*Huānyíng, guìzú, huānyíng,*' the proprietor gushed. His head bobbed as he bowed and bowed again.

Welcome, my lord, welcome.

Four men followed the first traveller inside and tossed their weapons with a clatter onto the table. Their presence forced Ryam back beneath the branches. A heartbeat later, he realised what was bothering him. That was no man at the centre of this rough bunch. Not with hips that swayed like that. He was wrong about many things, but there was no mistaking the instinctive stir of his blood at the sight of her.

The woman wore an owl-grey tunic over loose-fitting trousers. A woollen cap hid her hair. With her height, she could have passed for a lanky youth. She affected a lofty confidence as she addressed the proprietor. Behaviour appropriate for a male of superior status.

Ryam knew the rules of status. As a foreigner he was the lowest creature on the ladder, a hair above lepers and stray dogs. It was one of the reasons he skirted the back country, avoiding confrontation. The promise of a hot meal had tempted him into the open. The sight of this woman tempted him in another way. Beneath the formless clothing, she moved with a fluid grace that made his pulse quicken. He had forgotten that irrational pleasure of being distracted by a pretty girl. Blind masculine instinct aside, the determination with which she carried on with her ruse made him smile.

He wasn't the only one paying such careful attention to her. The proprietor cast a scrutinising glance over his shoulder while he spoke to the cook, then donned his previously submissive demeanour as he returned to the table, balancing bowls of rice soup on a tray. Apparently, the woman overestimated the effectiveness of her disguise.

The proprietor set down the last bowl before his customers, then looked up. His mouth twisted into a scowl the moment he saw Ryam across the road.

'Away with you!' He strode to the edge of the stand. 'Worthless son of a dog.'

Ryam let his hand trail to the sword hidden beneath his cloak. He had become a master at biting his tongue, but today the sun bore into him like bamboo needles and the ache in his belly felt all the more hollow. Under normal circumstances, he wouldn't think to use his weapon against this fool, but he seriously considered it as the verbal abuse continued. It was like being pecked to death by an irate rooster.

He gritted his teeth. 'The old man does not own this road,' he muttered.

At least he hoped he said that. All the years on this side of the world and the only phrases he had at his command were bawdy insults and a smattering of pillow talk.

The rooster ducked inside, only to re-emerge with a club bigger than his arm. Ryam straightened to his full height with a warning growl. From her seat, the woman craned her neck at the disturbance. The men around her turned in unison. The four of them pinned him with their cold stares. He was making a wonderful impression.

'Leave him, Uncle.' The woman's voice rang clear across the road, lowered in an attempt to further her pretence. 'He means no harm to you.'

The proprietor backed away, muttering about foreign devils. The woman rose then, and Ryam stiffened with his back pressed against the tree. Now was the time to leave, but pure stubbornness held him in place. Stubbornness or reckless curiosity.

He focused his attention on her boots as she came near. The hilt of a weapon teased over the edge of the tanned leather. He wondered if she could wield it with any skill.

'Are you hungry, Brother?'

She held her bowl out to him, extending her arm with great care as if approaching a wild beast. The steam from the rice carried hints of ginger and scallions to his nose and his stomach twisted in greedy little knots.

He was well aware of how he must look to her. Another one of the hordes of beggars and vagrants roaming the empire since the collapse of the old regime. Against his better judgement, he lifted his head and for the barest second, forgot that he was stranded and that he was starving.

Her eyes widened as she met his gaze. Hazel eyes, like the turning of autumn leaves. How anyone could mistake her for a man was beyond his understanding.

Now that she had seen who he was, he assumed she would recoil in fear or disgust or, even worse, pity. Instead she regarded him with curious interest. Next to kindness, it was the last reaction he expected.

'*Xiè xie.*' He mumbled his thanks as he took the food from her slack fingers. Any words he knew would be inadequate for this moment.

She nodded wordlessly and backed away, still staring. Only when she had returned to her companions did she take her eyes off him. By then the rice had gone cold. He gulped it down in three swallows and set the bowl on the ground before pausing to steal a final glance.

Inside the hut, the group finished their meal with little conversation and tossed a scatter of copper coins onto the table. A sense of desolation fell over him when she turned to go, but she did look back. He nodded once in farewell. They were both in hiding, after all—he in the shadows and the woman behind her disguise.

Once she disappeared down the road, he scarcely had time to straighten before the old man returned with his club and his viper tongue. Ryam presented his back to the stream of insults.

He trudged westwards, as he had done for the last month. The last remnants of their legion remained in the marshlands outside the north-western border. Perhaps he would no longer be welcome, but he had no other place to go.

Five years ago, they had fought their way across the silk routes to end up at the edge of the Tang Empire. The Emperor had tolerated their presence, but Ryam's last blunder had likely destroyed any hope of a continued truce.

A hundred paces from the tavern and his feet began to drag. He swayed, caught off guard by the lurch in his step. A tingling sensation stole to his fingertips and toes. This feeling was all too familiar. Heavy headed, off balance, tongue thick in his mouth.

He was drunk.

Not drunk, drugged. The little beauty had drugged him and then abandoned him…. But that didn't make any sense. Cursing, he shook his head to clear the fog in his skull. Thinking was becoming an even harder task than moving.

The woman had given him her food…which meant the drug was meant for her.

He reached for his sword, then froze with his fingers clenched over the hilt. This was the sort of impulse that had almost got him killed. His head spun with whatever they had slipped into the rice. He grappled with the odds. He was an outsider. He knew nothing about her or her bodyguards.

But those startling eyes had looked at him as if he was something more than an animal.

To hell with it.

Lifting one leaden foot after another, he forced himself around and drew his sword, lumbering back towards the tavern. The old proprietor shrieked when he saw him. The stack of bowls he carried crashed to the ground as the man scrambled for cover. Ryam ran past him and continued on the road.

He heard shouting in the distance and tore through the undergrowth in pursuit of it. Branches snapped against him, scraping over his arms and face. He stumbled into a clearing and everything slammed into his head at once: the pound of footsteps and the flash of steel. A dozen bandits armed with knives surrounded the swordsmen from the tavern. Ryam blinked through the haze clouding his eyes and searched for the girl.

She stood her ground at the centre of the swarm, wielding a blade in each hand. The swords flew in a whirl of motion. Rushing forwards, Ryam slammed his shoulder into one of her opponents and then struck the hilt of his sword against the man's skull. The bandit crumbled to the ground.

One down. With an air of satisfaction, he swung to face her, grasping at the proper words. 'I'm a friend—'

Her boot slammed neatly into his groin.

Pain exploded through his entire body. Nauseatingly bad pain. He should have left her to the wolves.

Without mercy, she came at him with the swords while he was doubled over. He hefted his blade up and parried once and then again. God's feet, she was fast. He shoved her aside roughly. His body begged to sink to the dirt.

'Here to help,' he ground out.

Her arm stopped mid-strike as she focused on him. Another one of her companions collapsed as the drugs took effect and the bandits circled closer. She swung around, swords raised to face the next attack.

The battle continued for him in bits and pieces. He struck

out again and once again he connected. In minutes he would be useless. He grabbed the woman's arm.

'Too many,' he forced out.

She hesitated, scanning the field before going with him. More bandits gave chase, but he drove them back with a wild swing of his blade. Then he was running. Tall grass whipped at him while his world tilted, strangely yellow and dark at the edges. He blinked and when he opened his eyes the surroundings were unfamiliar. The woman had pulled ahead and she was shouting something at him. He stumbled and the next thing he knew was the smack of solid earth against his chin.

The muddled taste of blood and dirt seeped into his mouth. Spitting, he rolled himself over, his arms and legs dragging. He could no longer feel them. He could no longer feel anything.

The swordswoman hovered over him, her lips moving soundlessly. He fought against the blackness that seduced his eyelids downwards, but the ground felt really, really good. Unable to resist any longer, he let his eyes close. He hoped he'd have a chance to open them again.

The foreigner lay on his back, denting the wild grass while his breath rumbled deep in his chest. Taking hold of one shoulder, Ai Li shook him as hard as she could.

The man was built like a mountain.

With a sigh, she looked back at the line of the trees, head tilted to listen. No footsteps. No one chasing after them. The dense undergrowth provided cover, but if they found her she was lost. She did not know who the attackers were, but she hoped they were merely outlaws. She prayed they weren't men sent to take her back to Li Tao.

The men could be tracking her through the trees, but she couldn't abandon the barbarian while he was helpless. Wiping the sweat from her brow, she turned back to him. At first glimpse, his pale skin and sandy hair had shocked her. When he spoke her language, she had fled like a superstitious peasant, but up close he was no ghost or demon. Just a man. A wild-looking, possibly crazed man who had saved her.

He slept lion-like in the grass. A tawny growth of stubble roughened his jaw, making him appear as if his face was chiselled out of stone and left unpolished. Emboldened by his slumber, she reached out to push away a lock of hair to get a better look. Her fingertips grazed the edge of a scar above his ear. She recoiled and looked once more to assure herself that he was asleep. Then, with morbid fascination, she traced the line of the old wound.

When she first noticed him skulking by the roadside, her heart had gone out to him. Here was one of the unfortunate souls forced to wander after the recent rebellions. Now she knew he was the sort of man who could rush into the thick of battle without a trace of fear.

His hand remained curved about the hilt of his sword. A web of nicks and dents scored the blade. Her father would have called this a sword with a past, one that deserved respect. With her brothers and the men under her father's command, she had been around warriors all her life. A fearsome swordsman like this would have to be desperate to beg for food like a peasant.

He had come to her rescue despite his troubles. To leave him now would be dishonourable, no matter that he was a barbarian. Picking up her swords, she rose to stand guard. Her ancestors would expect no less of her. Even Fourth Brother's spirit would understand.

She twirled the blades restlessly, trying to attune herself to the rustle of the leaves and the scatter of bird song. The woods stretched on forever, and it seemed she would never get home. She had never done anything so wilful in her life, but Father had promised her to a man he considered an ally. He didn't know that Li Tao was false. Not only had he been plotting against them ever since the former Emperor had died without an heir, but he'd done far, far worse. As soon as the stranger woke up, she would need to hurry home.

The sun had slipped low to wash the grove in amber light when the barbarian finally stirred. Her long shadow fell over him as his eyelids flickered open. With a startled sound, he grabbed his sword and sprang to his feet.

She brought her swords up defensively. For the ox that he was, the barbarian was unexpectedly agile. She had to remember that.

'Who are you?' she demanded. 'Why do you risk your life to save a stranger?'

He peered at her, struggling to focus. Then he sank back to his knees and pressed the heels of his palms to his eyes. 'Please. Slowly.'

The side of his chin had been scraped from his fall. With a lost look, he surveyed the barrier of trees, oddly vulnerable despite the sheer strength in him.

Cautiously, she slid one sword back into her boot and searched through the knapsack slung over her shoulder. She held out a waterskin, then watched in fascination as he took a long drink, his muscles gliding with every move. Centuries-old writings proclaimed the Great Empire of the West as a land of tall, powerful giants. For once, it seemed the accounts hadn't been exaggerated.

'You stayed,' he said with some surprise as he handed the skin back to her.

'I owed you a debt.'

The corner of his mouth lifted crookedly and his blue eyes slid over her. 'To see you is payment enough.'

She must have been confused by the mix of dialects and his atrocious inflection. A man wouldn't use such sugared tones when she was disguised this way.

She squared her shoulders. 'Where did you learn how to speak?'

'Why?'

'You sound like you were taught in a brothel.'

He exploded, his broad shoulders shaking with laughter. 'Can't deny that,' he said with a grin.

The words of his native tongue sounded jarring to her ears, but she recognised them. 'I can try to speak in your language,' she offered.

'You know it?' A deep frown appeared over his forehead. 'Few in the empire do.'

She clamped her mouth shut, biting down on her lip. 'My father is a tea merchant. He travels far outside the empire along the trade routes.'

The explanation seemed feeble at best, but his expression relaxed. 'They call me Ryam.'

'*Ryam.*' She tested the sound of it. 'What does it mean?'

He remained seated in the grass, his arms dangling carelessly over his knees. 'It means nothing.'

No mention of a family name as was the custom. She didn't ask about it for fear of being impolite.

'My name is Li, family name Chang. You can call me Brother Li.'

'*Brother*? Anyone can see you're a woman.'

Her hand tightened on the sword. Suddenly she didn't like the way he smiled at her at all.

'I'm not going to harm you,' he said quickly, holding up his hands, palms out. 'I ran into a horde of men waving knives to help you, remember? You kicked me pretty hard for all my trouble.'

She blushed, remembering exactly *where* she had kicked him. 'My name is Chang Ai Li,' she relented.

'Ailey. That's a pretty name.'

She ignored the compliment. 'What is a foreigner doing so deep in the empire?'

'What is a woman doing travelling alone with a group of men?'

His eyes met hers without wavering, as if she were the strange one. She was becoming more curious about him with each passing moment, but it wouldn't do to linger out in the woods with a barbarian.

'I see now that you are not hurt.' She spared him a final glance. 'Farewell then.'

'Wait, where are you going?'

He shot to his feet and her breath caught as he stretched to his full height before her. Her gaze lifted from the expanse of his chest to meet his eyes. They were so pale, like clear, cloud-less skies.

'I—I need to get back to my bodyguards,' she stammered, her throat suddenly dry. 'They will be looking for me.'

'Are you sure you want to do that?'

He continued to block her path. With his size he could overpower her easily, but the look on his face showed nothing but concern. Something told her he wasn't the sort to use his strength against a woman.

'What do you mean?' she asked.

'That rice was meant for you. Whatever was in there, it was enough to smuggle you out of the province before you woke up. A face like yours would fetch a high price in the pleasure dens.'

A sickening feeling twisted her stomach. 'My guards would not betray me.'

'How long have you known them?'

She fiddled at the collar of her oversized tunic. Old Wu had hired those men under desperate circumstances, but she knew that loyalty could not be bought. Not with all the gold on this earth.

'It's nearly sundown,' he said, glancing at the sky. 'You had better stay here in case any of that scum is still about.'

Stay the night here with him and no one around for miles? Her heart thudded as if trying to escape the tight cloth bound around her breasts. He had rescued her. She should have nothing to fear from him, but there was something primal and dangerous in him. Masculine. *Yang.* He stood too close, close enough for her to catch his scent—an enticing mix of leather and the autumn smell of the woods that invited her to tempt fate. She couldn't let her guard down.

With a steadying breath, she stepped back. 'How can I be sure it is safe here?'

'You don't want to face those smugglers alone.' He regarded her with a half-smile. 'Unless you intend to fight off all of them with those knives of yours.'

'They're not knives. These are butterfly swords.' She shoved the second blade away.

'You can get back to the road in the morning,' he said. 'I won't touch you if that is what you're afraid of. I'll start a fire.' He moved away to gather kindling, allowing her space to consider.

Everything he spoke of made sense. Her guards had fallen too easily. Someone among them had betrayed her. Once Li Tao discovered she was gone, he would send his men in a black swarm over the area. Instinct told her she needed to keep moving, but to where? She was stranded in the southern province with night nearly upon them and no road to guide her. She laced her hands together and lowered her head in thought.

Her gaze drifted to the sword at the foreigner's belt. The blade was larger than the ones used among the soldiers of the empire. A weapon designed to cleave armour and crush bone. He had wielded it with obvious skill.

More importantly, he didn't recognise her.

A new plan started to form in her head. Father would call it reckless. Mother—her mother would expend much more than a single word to describe her foolishness. But what could she rely on out here besides her butterfly swords and her instincts? Even though her instincts had proven wrong with the hired guards, she had a sense of *yuán fèn* about this swordsman. That she would meet a barbarian, of all people, on this journey—what could that be but fate between them?

And she had no other choice.

Ailey paced as he gathered fallen twigs. She circled the clearing once, hands on her hips. The tips of the yellowed grass brushed over her calves. With each movement he caught hints of her shape beneath the drab clothing: tapered waist and gently rounded hips that would fit perfectly into a man's hands. He had glimpsed the edge of the cloth wrapped tight around her breasts just below the neckline of her tunic. Already his imagination ran wild with the thought of her undressed and unbound before him.

With one knee set on the ground, he sparked the kindling with flint and steel. His mind could wander all it wanted where Ailey was concerned. Thoughts were harmless, even heated thoughts about pretty girls lost in the woods. As long as he kept his hands where they belonged.

The grass rustled behind him as she approached. Already he was acutely aware of her every move, his senses reaching out to search for her.

'You decided to stay,' he said over his shoulder.

She was looking down at him with sudden interest. Unfortunately, it wasn't the kind of interest he usually sought from a woman.

'You handled yourself well against those men,' she began.

He shrugged dismissively. 'Common thugs.'

'And you were outnumbered and drugged as well.'

She took a step closer. Her teeth clasped over her lower lip uncertainly while her eyes shone with hope. She had no idea what that look did to a man.

He blew out an unsteady breath. 'Anyone would have done the same—'

'I need your protection to help me return home,' she interrupted in a rush.

An immediate refusal hovered on his tongue. 'Where do you live?' he asked instead.

'Changan.'

The imperial capital. A good week's journey from here and in the opposite direction of where he needed to go. The area surrounding the city would be littered with imperial soldiers who would be overjoyed to see him.

'I can pay you,' she said when he remained silent.

She pulled a silk purse from her belt and threw it to him before he could respond. The coins rattled as he caught it.

'Open it.'

The weight of it told him what he'd find before he pulled at the drawstring to reveal a handful of gold and silver. He closed it and tossed it back with a flick of his wrist. The purse landed in the dirt at her feet.

'I can't.'

Her eyebrows shot up, puzzled. 'You do not know how much this is.'

'I know how much it is,' he said through his teeth. 'I don't want your money.'

She lowered her tone. 'I have offended you.'

He straightened, avoiding her eyes while needles of guilt stabbed at him, sharp and unrelenting. She didn't know what she was asking.

'I can't go to Changan no matter what the price. And don't go throwing your money around—what the hell are you doing?'

She had her hands clasped together in front of her, palm to fist, head bowed humbly.

'I am beseeching you as a fellow swordsman. I need your protection.'

'We're not fellow swords*men*,' he growled. Raising a hand to the back of his neck, he pinched at the knot forming there. 'You don't even know who I am.'

'I know we are strangers and this is an unspeakable imposition, but I must get home and I cannot make it alone.'

Now it was his turn to pace. He could sense her hovering nearby, waiting for an answer as if he hadn't already given it. His inability to help her tore at him. He couldn't be responsible for Ailey. His last mistake was the deadliest in a long, winding chain of them. Whoever had decided he should lead other men must have been either drunk or daft. At least while he was alone, no one else could get hurt.

'What are you doing so far from home, anyway?' he demanded.

'I help my family with our business.'

'Selling tea?'

'Yes.' She paused. 'Tea.'

'No respectable merchant would send his daughter out here unprotected. The imperial army no longer guards these roads.'

'I was not alone,' she insisted. 'I was with bodyguards.' Her voice trailed away and she pulled the cap from her head in an agitated motion. A single braid tumbled over her shoulder, black as ink. Unbound, it would frame her face like a dream.

No. He was not going to be swayed.

'If I go to Changan, I'll be hanged,' he said with forced coldness. 'Is that the sort of man you want to be travelling with?'

She tensed, but refused to back down. 'What did you do? Did you steal something?'

'No.'

'Did you kill someone?' Her voice faltered.

'*No.*'

She shouldn't look so relieved. He wasn't a thief or a murderer, but he wasn't much better. Anger and regret flooded him all at once. 'I made a mistake.'

A half-witted, disastrous mistake. He should have never taken that command. He wasn't fit to lead others. He could barely keep himself alive. The fire crackled and sputtered as it began to die.

'I'll take you to the nearest town,' he said, tossing more wood into the fire. 'You can find someone else to take you home.'

After a long silence, she settled in the grass beside him and pulled her legs to her chest. She didn't argue with him, but he could see the stubborn determination in her eyes.

'I want to help. I'm just not the right person to do it.'

'I know you're a good man.'

The firelight danced in her eyes, reflecting a spark of gold within the irises. His gaze strayed to her mouth despite his best intentions. Desire blindsided him, heated, unbidden and greedy.

'I'm not,' he muttered.

Ailey shouldn't have been alone out there, as trusting as she was. A man could easily take advantage of her. She would be silk and moonlight in his arms. A couple of hours of forgetfulness.

He was a savage to even consider it. She was stranded and desperate. She had begged for his help and he had refused after she had shown him the only touch of kindness he'd known in a long time. The first since he had woken up in a hovel a month ago, the gash on his head still healing.

He struggled to find something civil. 'You're pretty good with those swords.'

'My brothers and I would practise together. I have five—had five.' An unmistakable look of sadness crossed her face.

'Where in God's earth are they?'

She grew quiet, scraping the toe of her boot against the dirt. 'They're scattered to different corners of the empire.'

'I can't believe there is no one nearby who can help you. An associate of your father's or the town magistrate.'

'There is no one.'

She raised her chin stubbornly. His hands itched to stroke the graceful line of her neck. He could almost taste how sweet her mouth would be, innocent and untried. Grabbing a twig, he snapped it in two and threw it into the flames. Apparently he did have some principles after all. Her faith in him, misplaced as it was, humbled him.

He drew his sword. She started at the sound, her lithe body coiled and ready. Fighter's reflexes. The kind that took time and practice to develop.

'I'm laying this down between us,' he explained.

Her eyes lit up. 'May I?'

His attempt at honour seemed lost on her. She wrapped her slender fingers around the hilt with careful reverence. Her arms sank under the weight.

'It's quite heavy,' she murmured.

'It belonged to my father.'

What had compelled him to tell her? It had been years since he'd spoken of his father. Her gaze roamed over the guard and down the length of the battered steel. The scrutiny felt so much more personal than if she had looked him over with the same admiration. Suddenly it bothered him to be sharing this moment with a stranger, this odd girl who liked swords.

Without a word, he took the weapon from her hands and placed it between them. She regarded him with a confused look before withdrawing. Hugging her arms around her knees, she scanned the darkness. The whir of cicadas filled the night. For a moment the look on her face was so vulnerable, the need to protect her overwhelmed any other urge. They were both stranded out here with no idea what the next day would bring. He wagered she wasn't as accustomed to it as he was.

He undid the clasp of his cloak and tugged it from his shoulders.

'I've got thick skin,' he said when she protested.

That earned him a faint smile. She thanked him and wrapped the cloak around her, disappearing into the wool. Seeing her in it sent another wave of possessiveness through him.

He lowered himself to the grass and tucked his arms behind his head. 'It's not far to the next town.'

'Did you just come from there?'

'Yes. They chased me away with shovels and axes.'

She blinked at him, not understanding.

'Someone will help you there,' he amended.

She pulled his cloak tight around her, as if shielding herself from the night. 'I know you have done all you can.'

A grunt was all he could muster in response.

If she knew any better, she'd have never asked for his help. Even the soft sigh of her breath seemed like seduction. He dug his nails into his palms, using the sharp bite to distract him as he stared at the outline of the trees against the sky, black on black. There was nothing he could do for her and he hated it.

'I should tell you something,' he said.

The grass shifted beside him as she turned onto her side. Only her face was visible from under the hood. The fire cast a deep shadow beneath her cheekbones.

'You do not know how to lie.'

She frowned. 'I don't lie.'

'You carry a sword and have five brothers trained to fight. Why would your merchant father be raising a small army?'

When she said nothing, he knew he'd hit his mark. She had the look of a cornered fox ready to flee.

'What does it matter? You will be gone by tomorrow,' she said.

The dwindling fire crackled in the ensuing silence. He let his head drop back against the hard ground. Apparently, he'd made the right decision not to get involved.

'You're nobility. Warrior class.'

She didn't answer. She didn't need to. Nobility or not, Ailey was not for him. He was a barbarian in this land and always would be. Her sword-wielding brothers would castrate him if they discovered him alone with her. And then they'd kill him.

Chapter Two

Ailey woke with the first hint of daylight, blinking up at the sky in disbelief. It took a moment before she had enough command of her muscles to sit up. Though she couldn't see any stones now, she had sworn there were a thousand of them beneath her during the night. All digging sharply into the parts of her that were most sore. It was better to wake up on the cold, bare earth than shackled in Li Tao's wedding bed, but she didn't want to think of how many more days and nights there were between here and the capital. She had journeyed for over a week by palanquin, escorted by the wedding party. Now she was alone.

Not completely alone.

Ryam slept beside her with his arms huddled over his chest, his chin tucked close. His sword still lay between them and the heady scent of his skin permeated the wool around her. The boyish look of him in sleep sparked some nurturing instinct. She untangled herself from his cloak to lay it gingerly over him. The material barely covered the expanse of his torso. With a muffled grunt, his long fingers curled around the wool to pull it up around him.

Fearsome warrior indeed.

Now that she was more accustomed to him, his features didn't appear so harsh. She could even see how his strangeness might be considered handsome…if one looked long enough. She turned away as a disturbing awareness fluttered in her chest. Best to let him sleep.

The atmosphere hung damp and heavy, and a sheen of morning dew covered the grass. She stood and raised her arms over her head, letting the blood flow through her languid muscles. The stir of the breeze between the branches greeted her from the woods. A whooping call of a bird in the distance was the only sign of any living creature other than the two of them.

She had only told him part of the truth about her family the night before. Ryam was an outsider who wasn't likely to have any ties to their enemies. She couldn't tell who was loyal any more. She lifted her swords and paced towards the centre of the clearing. Restlessly, her right arm directed its blade in an attack pattern. Perhaps she could think of a way to persuade the foreign swordsman to stay with her. The left blade followed out of habit, echoing the same precise movements.

If she was at home, Grandmother would be watching over her as she went through her daily practice. Her grip remained easy as she let the butterfly swords circle in front of her. She tried to conjure Grandmother's voice. *Better. Now again.* The familiar exercise held no comfort. She might never see her grandmother or the rest of her family again.

All her life, she'd dreamed she would leave one day to marry. Part of her had always dreaded that moment, but only with the usual sadness of any daughter leaving the comfort of childhood behind. She never imagined she'd defy her betrothal to flee back home.

It was shameful. *Dishonourable.* The echo of her parents' disapproval resounded deep within her, louder than any true sound could ever be.

But how could she marry a murderer? Old Wu had told her that her brother Ming Han's death wasn't an accident. Li Tao was the one responsible.

'What is that you're doing?'

Ryam's presence broke through her sorrow, shattering the stillness like a pebble tossed into a pond. He stood outside of arm's reach and his gaze followed the path of her swords.

She stared at her hands as if they were no longer her own. 'First sword form,' she replied, at a loss.

Had he been watching her? She had been going through the motions to try to focus her thoughts. Her technique must have been unforgivable—what a strange thought to have at that moment! Her pulse hammered under his scrutiny. She was used to Grandmother watching her with the eyes of a hawk. This was so very different.

'I was…I was practising.'

'This is how you practise?'

He folded his arms over his chest and cocked his head as he circled her. The intensity of his gaze flooded her with heat. It was a wonder she didn't cut herself with her own swords.

'All those elaborate patterns,' he murmured. 'Does that help in fights?'

'In combat, your body falls into what it has done a thousand times before. A perfect harmony between instinct and thought.'

Her throat felt dry as she recited the words. Her elder brothers were commonly praised for their skill, but never before had a man shown such interest in her. She drew out an intricate pattern with the tip of one sword in three neat swipes, as if wielding a calligraphy brush. It gave her something to do as he stepped closer. All of the air around her seemed to rush towards him whenever he drew near.

'Your brothers taught you this?' he asked.

'My grandmother.'

His laughter filled the clearing. 'Your grandmother?'

'Grandmother was a master.'

The next pass of her sword sliced a scant inch in front of him, taunting. He stood his ground and his smile widened.

'So do you want to try it?'

Her swords froze. 'Try it?'

'My barbaric head bashing against that beautiful sword work of yours.'

A duel. Her heart was already pounding with the promise of it.

'No,' she replied.

'No?'

'You are far more experienced than I am.'

The meaning had been clear in her head as she spoke the words, yet another, more suggestive meaning loomed between them. A well of heat rose up her neck. She blamed this barbarian language.

He placed a hand to his chest with mock passion. 'But you got the better of me yesterday when I was drugged. Don't I deserve a chance to redeem myself?'

She was certain there was something not quite proper about a strange man offering to spar with her the day after they met. Yet this foreigner treated her with such directness and familiarity, like her brothers. He continued to taunt her with laughter shining in his eyes and the curve of his mouth hinted at an irresistible wickedness. Her stomach knotted in response.

In truth, not like her brothers at all.

'I should get some advantage since you are so...' she looked him up and down '...big.'

'What do you have in mind?'

With a household of five brothers she knew how to pick her battles. Ryam had had more training than she and his sword could cut her in half, but its weight would slow him down. And the terms were yet to be negotiated. With a good plan, she could defeat Fourth Brother and occasionally, even Third Brother.

'I attack first. Ten attempts. You can only defend,' she proposed.

'You do this often, don't you?'

His irises shifted to storm grey, the laughter in them transforming into something dark and unknown. He held her gaze while the woods faded around her.

'What do you say to a wager?' He unsheathed his sword in a seductive whisper of steel. 'If I win, you give me a kiss.'

Barbaric. But she saw her opening.

'If I win, you take me to Changan.'

He let her heart beat on for ever before answering.

'Agreed.'

Her palms began to sweat, and a fever rose beneath her skin. Up until then, she truly believed she could defeat him. She had been running strategies through her head, but suddenly she found herself staring at the rough stubble over his jaw and wondering if it would tickle. It was the sort of daydream that would send Grandmother's bamboo switch stinging over her knuckles. The sort of thought that would have Mother beseeching their ancestors to bring her back to sanity.

'After the first round—' She ran her tongue over her lips. For all her negotiation, she had the sinking feeling this duel had slipped out of her grasp. 'If you do not defeat me after ten attempts, you should honourably forfeit.'

'Of course. Twenty moves?' he asked softly.

Deep breaths, she reminded herself. Mind, breath, body. 'Or first blood.'

He raised his sword in salute. The smile remained on his face as he backed away, setting the starting distance.

Ryam couldn't resist the promise of a kiss to keep him company on the cold journey back to the frontier. It might even be worth the risk of facing imperial soldiers again—not that he intended to lose.

Ailey stood across from him, poised and still. She shook the hair from her eyes with a slight toss of her head and her braid whipped over her shoulder. When she focused again on him, the young woman disappeared and a warrior stood in her place.

The fight started here, at the moment of decision, long before his sword ever reached striking distance. Ailey radiated more determination than many a seasoned fighter. She bowed formally, bending slightly at the waist with her eyes trained on him. He considered, for a brief moment, whether Ailey had been bluffing all along.

'Ready?' he murmured.

She flew at him.

In a flash of silver, the butterfly swords cut tight lines through the air. He deflected in two sharp clashes of steel, surprised by the strength behind the attack.

'I thought this was a friendly match—'

The next swipe of her blade whistled by his throat.

Ailey pushed inside his defence without fear, without caution. For a second she darted within arm's reach. He considered simply grabbing her and wrestling her to the ground. Pin her beneath him. The image lingered dangerously. Definitely not honourable.

He had to jump back to avoid her knee as she drove it upwards.

'I can't take you to Changan if you kill me.'

He twisted her next attack aside only to have her spring back, eyes dark with intent, a hint of green sparking within them. She left no room, no time to recover. His heart pumped hard as instinct took hold of him. According to her rules, he could only defend and not attack. He side-stepped and angled the strikes away. Ailey knew what she was doing, keeping him close so he couldn't use his reach against her. She danced around him with deadly elegance, matching him toe to toe. The rhythm of it almost sexual.

Better than sexual.

'Ten,' he announced.

'Show me what you have,' she retorted. The fight had sparked quite a fire in her.

Once the rules changed, he expected her to go on the defensive and hold out for the forfeit, but that wasn't her way. She kept at him, carving up the space around him until they were breathing hard. Precise angles, perfect placement. There was considerable training there. Discipline. But he could read by the clean control of her patterns that she had never been forced to use these skills where there were no rules.

He brought the hilt down against her wrist and followed it up with a wide arc of his blade that sent her stumbling backwards. Brute force over grace. This was his fight now.

She dodged away to search for an opening. He left none. The next chain of attacks crowded her against a tree. The force of each block resonated through her. He lifted his arms and brought his sword down, forcing her to cross blades with him. Metal grated in a harsh shriek of sound. It was a blow that could cleave through armour if he hadn't held back.

Their blades locked and she braced against his strength, her arms straining under the pressure. Her chest heaved with each breath, lips parting, and her skin glowed with the exertion. Beyond lovely.

He looked down upon her as she struggled. 'You're good—for a girl.'

'How very clever,' she snapped.

She kicked at his knee and attempted to slip away. He allowed her to advance. Unable to resist the slightest opening, she cut at his shoulder. At the last moment he stepped aside and grabbed her wrist, pinning her arms against one another. With a gasp, she dropped her swords.

He grinned. 'Surrender.'

Her eyes narrowed defiantly.

'I don't even need my sword any more.' He stabbed the point of his weapon into the ground and left it standing. 'You know, it would serve you to be more cautious, being half my size.'

'I am not—' she twisted in his grasp like a rabbit in a snare '—half your size. Let go.'

He relaxed his hold and she stepped back, massaging her wrists. The exhilaration of the fight throbbed in his veins.

'We agreed to some terms, I recall,' he said.

Her lips pressed together in what was suspiciously close to a pout. 'I honour my bets.'

He moved in to claim his prize and she went completely still. Changan or no Changan, he would still be risking life and limb to get her back to civilisation. He at least deserved one kiss for it. Her mouth parted in silent invitation and her hands curled uncertainly by her sides. He revelled in the soft catch in her breath as he leaned closer. Then he stopped just shy of her. Her eyes clouded with the unspoken question.

His mouth curved into a smile. 'The deal was *you* were supposed to give me a kiss.'

Every muscle within her pulled tight, poised on a knife's edge of anticipation as she stared at his mouth. He had planned this. His eyes flickered with amusement, reflecting sunlight and shade. The rough beard on his chin gave him a wild, dangerous look. Stiffly, she lifted herself onto her toes, bracing a hand against his shoulders. He was steel beneath her grasp.

Did he have to watch her so intently?

She closed her eyes. It was the only way she would have the courage to do this. Still he waited. It would be a brief meeting of lips. Nothing to be afraid of. If only her heart would remember to keep beating. Holding her breath, she let her lips brush over his. It was the first time she'd ever kissed a man and her mind raced with it. She hardly had a sense of his mouth at all, though the shock of the single touch rushed like liquid fire to her toes.

Her part of the bargain was fulfilled. It could be done and over right then. Recklessly, after a moment's hesitation, she touched her lips once again to him. This time she lingered, exploring the feel of him little by little. His mouth was warm and smooth and wonderful, all of it new and unexpected. He still hadn't moved, even though her knees threatened to crumble and her heart beat like a thunder drum. Finally he responded with the barest hint of pressure. The warmth of his breath mingled with hers. Without thinking, she let her fingers dig into the sleek muscle of his arms. A low, husky sound rumbled in his throat before he wrapped his arms around her.

Heaven and earth. She hadn't been kissing him at all. The thin ribbon of resistance uncoiled within her as he took control of the kiss. His stubble scraped against her mouth, raking a raw path of sensation through her. She could do nothing but melt against him, clutching the front of his tunic to stay on her feet.

A delicious heat radiated from him. His hands sank low against the small of her back to draw her close as he teased her mouth open. His breath mingled with hers for one anguished second before his tongue slipped past her lips to taste her in a slow, indulgent caress. A sigh of surrender escaped from her lips, a sound she hadn't imagined she was capable of uttering.

His hands slipped from her abruptly and she opened her eyes to see his gaze fixed on her.

'Well,' he breathed, 'you do honour your bets.'

Though he no longer touched her, it was as if the kiss hadn't ended. He was still so close, filling every sense and thought. She stumbled as she tried to step away and he caught her, a knowing smile playing over his mouth. Her balance was impeccable. She never lost her footing like that, just standing there. His grip tightened briefly before he let her go. Even that tiny, innocent touch filled her with renewed longing.

In a daze, she bent to pick up her fallen swords. Her pulse throbbed as if she had run a *li* without stopping. In her head she was still running, flying fast.

'Now that our bargain is settled…' she began hoarsely '…we should be going.'

To her horror her hands would not stop shaking. Brushing past him, she gathered up her knapsack and slung it over her shoulder. 'You said the next town was hours from here?'

He collected his sword while a slow grin spread over his face. She couldn't look at him without conjuring the feel and the taste of him. Head down, she ploughed through the tall grass.

'A good match,' she attempted.

He caught up to her easily with his long stride. 'Yes, quite good,' he replied, the tone rife with meaning.

Her cheeks burned hot as she forced her gaze on the road ahead. She could barely tell day from night, couldn't give her own name if asked.

She had to get home and denounce Li Tao. Warn her father. She had thought of nothing else since her escape, until this blue-eyed barbarian had appeared. It was fortunate they were parting when they reached town. When he wasn't looking she pressed her fingers over her lips, which were still swollen from that first kiss.

She was outmatched, much more outmatched than when they had crossed swords.

Chapter Three

It was supposed to be one little kiss. The sort of meaningless flirtation he'd engaged in many times over. She would slap him afterwards, as he deserved, but it would be worth it. He hadn't counted on his hunger at the first taste of her. Or her willing response.

Too sweet for words.

Ailey forged ahead, bundling up her thick braid to shove it under her cap. She could chop off all her hair and dress in rags—she would still heat his blood to a boil. Her hands trembled faintly and the scoundrel in him couldn't help gloat at the sign that she was just as affected.

He hooked his thumbs into his sword belt as a reminder to keep his hands where they belonged. Conversation came slowly in fits and starts as they walked along the stretch of open road. They stopped after an hour on foot, resting beneath the shade at the side of the road.

He nodded towards the bruise forming at her wrist. 'Sorry for that.'

'You hit hard,' she said, not really complaining. She rubbed at the spot before pulling her sleeve over it.

'You were coming at me like you meant it.'

He let his gaze wander over her face as she took a drink from the waterskin. This girl wielded swords like an avenging angel, then kissed him with her eyes clamped shut. Yet her mouth had moved against his with the same bold instinct with which she fought.

Heat flooded his body anew. He forced himself to ignore it. 'How long have you been training with those swords?'

'Since I was a child. We would spar in the training yard.'

'You and your brothers?'

'And the soldiers in training.'

Sword-fighting. The topic was neutral enough. There was a forced casualness in her tone and she avoided his eyes as they started on their way again, but he caught how she passed the tip of her tongue over her lips and pressed them together, as if to recapture the fleeing sensation.

Kissing Ailey had been a mistake. A gloriously wonderful mistake.

'Suddenly the boys stopped fighting seriously,' she went on. 'Instead they would tease me, acting like monkeys.'

'They must have realised one day that you were a girl.'

And enticing enough to make any boy act the fool. Or any man, for that matter. He tried to imagine where she had come from, the well-bred daughter of a military official who studied how to fight instead of embroidery or whatever it was women typically learned.

'Your master taught you well.' She was still avoiding his gaze, but otherwise managed to fall into an easy stride beside him. Her long legs carried her effortlessly.

'I have no master,' he replied.

'But someone must have trained you. Your father, then?'

He stiffened. This talk of family was even more alien to him than this exotic land. 'I suppose I learned a few things from him.'

His father's brand of training had consisted of surviving one skirmish after another as they wandered endlessly through the countryside. That had changed when he joined up with Adrian's men as they fought off raiders at the borders of their homeland.

He had duties, men he could rely on and who relied on him.
But now he was alone again with nothing but his sword and,
for the moment, one very curious girl.

'Your father must be very honoured by your skill.'

Ailey's courteous flattery grated on him.

'If he were alive.'

She fell silent at the brusqueness of his reply and her expression took on that tranquil, inward quality. Probably reflecting
on ill-mannered barbarians who knew nothing about honour
or polite conversation.

'There's the town,' he said, looking into the distance.

Her mouth pressed into a thin line as she stared at the faint
outline. 'I can go on my own from here.'

Time had slipped by quickly. The rush of the morning's
battle and the all-too-brief kiss afterwards had faded away. It
was probably better for her if he did leave, but he could at least
escort her safely into town as he'd promised.

'I'll take you,' he said.

'Won't it be dangerous for you?'

'No more dangerous than the rest of the empire.'

He hadn't known how much he missed having someone to
speak to. Even if she did ask too many questions about things
he didn't want to be reminded of. But he couldn't drag his feet
any longer. It had taken over a month for him to recover enough
to make this journey and there were many obstacles to cross
between here and the frontier.

Within the hour, the road led them to the town gates. It was
decently sized for a rural city. The streets were paved with stone
and wooden buildings rose two floors high, stacked closely
together. Even in the simplest of towns, Ryam could see the
empire's wealth. Nothing like the scattered settlements of his
homeland.

The main avenue fed into a central market lined with shops.
Merchants displayed baskets of fruit and vats of crayfish, along
with a collection of handmade wares along the street. Ryam
hunched his shoulders and dragged his hood over his head,

trying to disappear into the crowd. The townsfolk stopped haggling to stare as he passed. It was impossible to disappear into a crowd when he stood head and shoulders above the average man.

'Perhaps there is a shipment here headed for Changan,' Ailey continued, oblivious to how the crowd parted in their wake.

A wooden ball bounced onto the cobbled street and rolled in front of them. A young boy scrambled forwards and crouched at Ryam's feet with his little fingers clutched around the toy. Suddenly, the boy noticed the hulking shadow over him and craned his neck upwards, mouth agape.

At that, Ryam pulled Ailey into the narrow gap between the shops. The hum of the market crowd continued around them.

'We can't just go wandering the streets,' he hissed. 'What are you planning to do?'

'Hire someone to take me home.'

Because he wouldn't. 'And if there's no one?'

'Then I go alone.'

'You can't.'

What would she do? Hire a band of mercenaries who would ignore the fact that she was worth a lot more than that bag of coins she carried?

'Your father is obviously a powerful man. There must be someone here who can help you.'

'You don't understand.' The mention of her father made her shoulders draw tight. A wisp of hair escaped from the cap to tease around the curve of one ear. She tucked it back impatiently. 'I cannot trust the city officials. Not in this province.'

What in God's name was she involved in? 'Then find a way to send a message to your father or…I don't know. Think of something better than roaming the countryside with your swords.'

'Why are you so concerned now?'

'I went through a lot of trouble to save you.' It was the best he could muster. Leaving her was the only rational decision, but he couldn't bring himself to do it. Not when she was looking at him like that.

'I need to find a stable. The journey will take too long on foot.' She nodded slowly as if to convince herself. 'It can't be too far to the capital.'

'You don't even know, do you?'

She ignored him to peer around the corner of the building.

'Tell me who you're hiding from,' he demanded.

It took an effort for her to meet his eyes. 'There are powerful men plotting against my father. Against the empire.'

With that perfectly vague explanation, she slipped past him to move down the alley, away from the marketplace. He didn't know what would be worse for her, being seen with him or being caught alone by whoever she was running from. They twisted through the city, skirting along dank lanes of grey brick while the ripe smell of rotting cabbage assailed them. Ailey continued unperturbed as a rat scurried across her path. Its long tail disappeared into a corner.

The stables were located near the outskirts of town across the canal. He was forced to wait outside while he listened to Ailey's voice through the doorway. She was talking numbers with the stableman.

Guilt gnawed a hole in his stomach as he listened to her. God's crooked nose. He knew what it was like to be alone and fending for himself, but she didn't. Ailey came from a wealthy family where she was cared for and protected. When she emerged from the stable, her look of triumph made him feel even worse.

'I purchased two horses,' she said. 'They will be ready to ride by morning.'

'Two?'

'How else will you get home?'

'You shouldn't have.'

She avoided his gaze, embarrassed. 'You have a long journey as well. Consider it payment of my debt to you for rescuing me.'

'There is no debt.'

The flush of her cheeks reminded him immediately of their

strange morning and the surprising fierceness of their match followed by her lips pressed softly to his. Bold and demure all at once.

Ailey had a generous soul at the heart of her. He, on the other hand, was the sort who could ruthlessly kiss a woman until she was melting against him and then abandon her hours later to the treacherous countryside.

'What did you tell him?' he asked.

'I told him I was a nobleman's son.'

He rolled his eyes. 'You do not look like a man.'

'He believed my story,' she insisted, chin raised. 'Now we must find a place for the night.'

She turned to the tangle of streets behind them. With a deep breath, she plunged back into the maze. He was certain she didn't feel any safer in this city than he did. At the next juncture the alleyways branched out like crooked fingers. Ailey looked from one to the other, lost. He indicated the correct direction with a flick of his hand.

'There's a good reason I can't go with you,' he said.

She kept her attention focused straight ahead. 'You've already told me.'

'I'm more likely to get us both killed than return you home safely.'

'I'm not completely helpless.' Plenty of pride in her. Her back stiffened with it. 'I'll be safe enough once I'm out of this province.'

'Just be careful.'

At the next corner, she halted so quickly he came up nearly against her heels. A crowd gathered around a group of soldiers wearing black and red uniforms. A crier dressed in embroidered state robes read from a scroll.

He could only make out bits of it. 'What are they saying?'

'It is a proclamation by Li Tao.'

'Who's Li Tao?'

'We have to go.' She shrank away from the street, but he blocked her path.

'You need to tell me what's going on. Now.'

She caught her bottom lip with her teeth, her face pale as she looked up at him. 'Li Tao is the man I was supposed to marry.'

'Marry? You're running away from your husband?'

'He is *not* my husband.'

'What was all that nonsense about a plot against the empire?' He had kissed her breathless and she belonged to another man. That stung more than it had a right to.

Ailey froze as a sharp command rang from the plaza. It echoed against the stone walls of the alleyway.

'The soldiers are searching the streets,' she whispered frantically.

He ushered her away from the square as fast as he could without breaking into a suspicious run. They wove past crates and debris that littered the alleyway. A window on an upper floor had been propped open. He stacked several crates on top of one another and offered his hand.

'Hurry. Go on up.'

She hooked her foot on to the corner of the pile and started climbing, grabbing on to the ledge. He watched, momentarily distracted, as she wriggled her slender hips through the opening.

Focus, man. After a final sweep of the alley, he hoisted himself up the rickety tower and kicked the crates over before pulling through the window.

The window led into a storeroom. An earthy, medicinal scent permeated the air and the low ceiling just allowed him to stand upright. He peered into the darkness and made out several woven baskets piled high with dried herbs and roots.

Ailey's voice came from the far end of the room. 'Behind the ginseng.'

'Which one is that?'

A pale hand waved from the corner. He picked his way through the baskets and crouched beside her against the wall.

'You need to tell me the truth, Ailey.'

She let out a breath and her fingers worked the edge of her tunic nervously. 'It was an arranged marriage.'

'So all of this is because you don't want to marry this man?'

Her gaze shot up to him. 'During the wedding procession, I discovered Li Tao betrayed our family. I hired mercenaries to attack the wedding procession so it would look as if I were abducted.'

Somehow he believed her. He already knew she couldn't tell a convincing lie.

'This Li Tao must be a powerful man if he can send soldiers to scour the countryside for you.'

'He is *jiedushi* of this province.'

Ryam let his head thud back against the wall. The military governor. These warlords had complete power over the armies and laws of their circuits. He had to admire her spirit even though no good could come of it.

'That's why you can't go to anyone for help.'

She sank her chin onto her knees in an uncharacteristically childish gesture. 'I never intended to put you in so much danger.'

'Do you know what this looks like to anyone who finds us? The governor's wife and a barbarian.'

'I told you, I am not his wife.'

He continued, undaunted. 'They'll hang me, but that is nothing compared to what they will do to you.'

'My family did not raise their daughter to live in fear.'

The rafters creaked, hushing them into tense silence as muffled voices rose from below. They crouched, listening and waiting.

'I cannot let them find me,' she whispered once the voices quieted. 'Li Tao will force me to marry him. He only wants this marriage to gain my father's trust.'

As much as she tried to hide it, he could tell she was frightened. In the empire, a woman was first her father's property and then her husband's. She was defying both of them.

'We'll stay here awhile. Wait them out,' he said. 'The soldiers will move on in a couple of hours.'

'What then?'

A sense of foreboding settled over him like a shroud. She was looking to him for answers. The last time anyone had trusted his lead, it had ended in bloodshed. His head throbbed with phantom pain as he recalled the last moments of the skirmish. Imperial soldiers had swarmed over their caravan, overpowering them. A better man could have stopped it.

'What should we do, then?' she repeated.

'We can't roam the streets all night and we can't stay here.' He needed to think. For once, he needed to make the right decision and not rush into battle.

'Perhaps we can sneak past the guards to the main gates,' Ailey suggested.

'There are soldiers at the gates and patrolling the streets. You can't leave town tonight. You'll need to hide.'

'But where?'

He knew of places, dark corners in any city that he would never send a woman to alone. 'We'll find a place at the edge of town. Tomorrow morning, we leave with the first light of dawn once the gates open.'

The scent of herbs hung heavy and bittersweet as they waited in silence. Ailey sank back against the wall. Her shoulder inadvertently brushed against him. He was becoming greedy for every touch, no matter how innocent.

Changan, the imperial capital. He'd been there before. And he could handle imperial soldiers…if there weren't too many. He had known it would come to this the moment she sank into his arms after their duel. Perhaps he had known even sooner, when he had seen her strength and her fierce determination to get home.

Maybe this was just another distraction, another reason to avoid returning to the Gansu corridor where his comrades waited. No, he was wrong about that. No one was waiting for him. They probably thought he was dead.

He had enough problems taking care of his own skin. What

made him think he could protect this woman who seemed to be in more trouble than he was? That blow to the head he'd suffered hadn't knocked any sense into him after all.

Ailey held her breath. He had said they would go together. His manners might be strange and uncultured, but there was a core of honour in him. She hadn't been wrong about that.

'Thank you,' she murmured.

His only reply was a brief shrug of his shoulders. He was helping her at great risk to himself. More than he knew. But she needed him to get home. It was the only way.

The morning came back to her as they huddled in the corner, trying not to touch and failing. His mouth had crushed against hers. She squeezed her eyes shut, but that only made the memory more overwhelming.

His hands had urged her close until she was pressed against the hard muscle of his chest. She had cast all caution aside, assuming he would leave. But he was still here. The heat of his body radiated through his tunic to find its way to her.

He shifted and she responded by inching towards the wall. His features were shadowed in the dim corner and the steady rhythm of his breathing reminded her how precariously close he was. She held herself perfectly still, afraid that if she moved she would find herself falling towards him, closing the scant space between them.

As if sensing her thoughts, he pulled away to the window, leaving her so quickly the air beside her still tingled with his presence. He braced his hands against the frame with head bent and shoulders pulled taut, a powerful silhouette against the light outside. The silence went on for so long that she began to worry he had changed his mind.

'I don't see any more of them,' he reported, peering down into the alley. 'Are you sure you want to do this?'

'What Li Tao has done is unforgivable. I would rather die than become his wife.'

Ryam nodded, and moved away from the window. 'We'll go out the back way.'

Reckless, she could hear Father proclaiming. To imagine she was safe with a barbarian she'd barely met.

Always feeling, never thinking, Mother scolded.

But she had thought very carefully and she trusted Ryam more than anyone else in this province. This was Li Tao's domain and he would kill them both if he found them.

She had vowed to her parents to be a dutiful wife, but that was one vow she could not fulfil. She prayed they would forgive her for her disobedience. She hoped they would believe her when she spoke against one of the most powerful men in the empire.

Her legs burned as she stood and the blood rushed back into them. They must have been crouched there for over an hour. Ryam led as they picked their way around the baskets towards the stairway. He scanned the room below on the first floor, and gestured towards the door at the back.

She peered over the railing before starting down, keeping her step as light as possible. Midway, a board creaked beneath her feet. Ryam muttered a curse as the voices halted down below. He gave her a small push.

'Run!'

They bolted down the stairs and through the door, abandoning any attempt at stealth. She took off around the corner and ducked into an alcove. Ryam shoved himself in beside her. They both held still, pressed against the brick. When it was clear that no one was following, she doubled over, gasping for breath.

'We'd make very bad thieves.'

She looked up to see Ryam grinning. He had a good spirit. She laughed, caught up in it. Part of her couldn't help but enjoy this adventure.

Once her breathing returned to normal, she poked her head around the enclosure. The streets had emptied in the late afternoon and the sounds of the market faded. Ryam emerged first, surveying the area before pulling her behind him. He shielded her as they ventured forwards. The protective gesture made her want to press even closer. She didn't have much experience with cities. She definitely had no knowledge of the back alleys they were navigating. Most of her life had been spent in her family home nestled in the mountains, surrounded by family and household servants.

'Where is it that you came from?' she asked.

'The other end of the world.'

'You seem to have been here for a long time.'

'Years and years.' His answers became noticeably clipped when he spoke of his past.

'We have a name for your land. We call it "Ta Chin", the Great Empire of the West.'

'I don't come from any great empire.'

She frowned.

'That empire you speak of no longer exists. Our kingdom—what was our kingdom—is a small one compared to this empire.'

The journey across the silk routes was said to be a treacherous one. If she only had the time to ask all the questions she wanted to. He must have amazing stories to tell.

'Are you part of the lost legion?' she asked. 'The wandering soldiers they speak about?'

He didn't answer immediately. 'I suppose I am.' He cast a sideways glance at her. 'Your people do love their legends.'

His smile made her pulse skip. He was different and mysterious, and curiosity made her bold. Bold enough to kiss a man she barely knew. She was suddenly out of breath. Her mind kept falling like water down the mountainside back to that moment.

'They say those swordsmen marched on Changan during the palace rebellion. Were you with them?' she continued.

This time his hesitation was obvious. 'Maybe the less we know about each other's stories, the better.'

'What do you mean?'

He halted to turn to her. 'The rest of the empire is not as tolerant as you towards unwashed barbarians.'

She stared at the coppered spots where the sun had darkened

his cheeks and the rugged growth of his beard. It was a face
unlike any she'd ever known.

'I don't think of you as an unwashed barbarian,' she said
softly.

He started to speak, but stopped. The intensity of his gaze
made her shift uncomfortably. 'We need to get you to Changan
as fast as possible,' he said. 'And then I need to disappear.'

As if to make a point, he forged ahead in long strides that
left no room for conversation. She couldn't deny what he was
saying. The empire had become fearful and suspicious. No
one trusted anyone in the capital, let alone outsiders. She hated
living with that dark cloud always over her.

At the end of the passage, Li Tao's proclamation had been
pasted on the wall. She tore down one paper. Ryam stared over
her shoulder at the black brushstrokes.

'What does all that say?'

So he couldn't read the characters. That was fortunate. She
didn't know how he would react if he discovered who she truly
was.

'Li Tao is offering a reward of a hundred taels of silver for
my return.'

He whistled. 'The man must be as rich as the Emperor.'

With a scowl, she crumpled the paper into a tight ball and
tossed it aside.

Ryam wove a path through the alleys with Ailey close
behind. He had never been this deep within the borders before,
but the change was noticeable even to a foreigner. The regional
armies were wary. Soldiers were authorised to confiscate weapons and imprison anyone they thought was a threat.

They would need to stay off the main roads from here all
the way to the capital. He had travelled for the last month in
hiding, sleeping beneath bridges and seeking refuge in remote
monasteries when they would let him. But he was responsible
for Ailey's safety now as well. Having a woman with him made
things more difficult.

He ducked through a broken section of the wall.

'How do you know where we are going?' she asked.

'These towns are all the same once you've been to enough of them.'

Vice lurked in the forgotten corners of any city of this size. Hideouts for smugglers, thieves, and citizens who wanted to escape into anonymity for the evening. He knew he had found their destination the moment they emerged in front of a dingy building tucked into a dead end. Red lanterns swayed from the eaves.

Ailey stopped short. 'Is this a brothel?'

'No. Let me see your money.'

She kept her eyes on the shadowed figure perched just inside the doorway as she handed the purse to him. He picked out several coins and then untied his cloak.

'Put this on and stay close,' he instructed.

The flash of silver was enough to get them past the guard. Once inside, the entrance hall glowed with the gritty light of oil lamps and pipe smoke. Ryam pushed through the beaded curtain and the strands clinked and slid around them. The shuttered windows of the main room cast it into perpetual nighttime. Copper coins changed hands from one huddled figure to another at the tables.

Ailey pulled his cloak tight around her and inched closer to him. Ivory and wooden dice clinked into porcelain bowls and the low hum of conversation did not rise the slightest at their arrival. The gamblers looked up with casual disinterest as Ryam and Ailey passed by. After a brief glance, the betting resumed. A man could be tattooed as a criminal and still show his face in a den like this.

An ancient-looking man with a white beard that tapered to a point sat in the far corner, surrounded by cronies. One of them blocked Ryam's path when he came forwards. The den master continued to sip his tea, staring at the bottom of the cup as if contemplating something profound.

'A room,' Ryam said, handing over the two coins.

The den master glanced once at the silver and pointed a bony finger to the stairs. With a nod of thanks, Ryam ushered

Ailey across the floor and up the steps. He pushed the first door open just as a man stumbled past with a woman in a flowery robe on his arm. Her cloyingly sweet perfume wafted into the narrow space of the hallway before the couple disappeared into the adjacent room. Ryam tugged Ailey into their chamber and, within minutes, faint moans and an unmistakable pounding came from the other side of the wall.

Ailey threw back her hood and planted her hands onto her hips. 'Are you certain it's safe here?'

'Yes.' He shut the door and dragged a chair to block it. 'A place like this doesn't care about silver if it means contact with authorities.'

Ailey stared at the bare walls in dismay. She wrapped her arms around herself, sticking them close to her sides as if not wanting to touch anything. 'I'll trust your judgement.'

'You take the bed,' he said. 'I'll take the floor.'

The bed was made of wooden slats covered with a thin, padded mattress. She made a face at the ash-coloured quilt lying rumpled upon it. The thread was worn bare in spots and marked with dark stains.

'I think I would rather take the floor.'

Chapter Four

Ailey watched from the alley as two of Li Tao's soldiers strode into the stable the next morning. She berated herself for not dropping an extra silver coin to convince the stableman to keep quiet. But what did she know about bribery and double-dealings?

'Time to think of another plan,' Ryam muttered from behind her.

She reached down to pull the butterfly swords free. The weight of the steel emboldened her as she headed in the opposite direction. 'We'll leave on foot before Li Tao's men can assemble.'

Ryam caught up to her. 'Put those away. Having your weapon drawn only invites trouble.'

She hesitated, but did as he said. He had experience surviving among strangers. That held more weight than all her hours in the practice yard. They hovered in the alleyway at the edge of the central market. Merchants had set up their stalls in the square and the morning crowd gathered. A cluster of soldiers prowled the plaza in their black-and-red uniforms. They scanned the market without particular interest. It seemed that no one had yet reported her presence.

Ryam gestured towards several workmen loading earthenware pots onto a wagon. 'That shipment is leaving town. Get in the back.'

'But Li Tao's men are everywhere.'

'Walk with purpose. You'll blend in.'

'What about you?' She looked him up and down.

His fingers tightened briefly over her shoulder. 'You go first. I'll be watching.'

Were all his people so fearless? Taking a deep breath, she stepped out from the cover of the shops. Sunlight slanted over the rooftops and blinded her, but she kept her pace steady even though her heartbeat thundered in her ears. If Li Tao's men detected her, she might be able to fend off two or three of them, but the rest would surround her. Ryam would be dragged into the struggle.

She fought the urge to glance back. She had wanted to warn him to leave if there was trouble, but he would have considered it an insult. A swordsman would never run like that. The workmen disappeared into the storehouse as she came near. She climbed onto the wagon and ducked beneath the canvas. The coarse packing straw scraped against her.

The next moments stretched out before her as she crouched in the darkness. There were wooden crates on either side of her and she tried to burrow between them. The shuffle of the market droned on outside. At any moment, the shouting would begin. The soldiers would spot Ryam and they'd circle him like wolves. She closed a hand around the hilt of her sword. If he was discovered, she'd have to help him. She was certain he'd do the same for her. He *had* done the same for her.

What was taking so long? Would he abandon her now? Just as she reached out to lift the covering, Ryam slipped under. He nudged the crates aside to shove out a spot for himself.

'Heaven and earth! How did you get past them?' she asked.

'They do call me ghost man, after all.'

She wanted to throw her arms around him, but his elbow poked into her ribs and her leg was crushed against one of the pots. They went still at the sound of voices from outside. The workmen came back to load more crates and she didn't dare move or breathe or even blink. She sighed with relief when the wagon finally lurched forwards.

The clay pots rattled around them as the wagon rumbled along the road. They attempted to rearrange themselves and Ryam bit back an oath as her knuckles struck him across his nose.

'I'll look outside,' he said after they had travelled a distance away.

He picked his way through the crates. A sliver of light cut through the darkness as he lifted the canvas.

'No one's following.' He let it fall back down.

'Do you know where we are?'

'That way is north to Changan.' He indicated with his thumb. 'We're headed south.'

Deeper into the warlord's territory. 'We need to get out of here. They'll start searching the roads soon.'

'There are woods to the right. We can jump and run for it.'

'Let me see.'

She crawled over his knees to peek out at the roadside. The area he spoke of wasn't far, just beyond a stretch of wild grass.

'Jump and run?' she asked.

He nodded. 'Jump and run. The grass will break the fall.'

The driver handled his team of horses, oblivious to them. She lifted the cover and crouched low, preparing herself. With a deep breath, she launched herself away from the wagon. Her knees buckled against the hard ground and a shock of pain streaked up her legs. Before she knew it, she was rolling in a blur of grass and sky.

She ended on her back, gasping for breath. Sharp stones dug into her spine and she tried to remain as still as possible. If she moved, she might shatter to pieces.

A moment later, Ryam's head and shoulders blocked the sky above her. 'Are you all right?'

Miserably, she shook her head no.

'Is anything broken?'

Everything felt broken. It hurt to breathe. She wriggled her fingers and made a face. 'I don't think so.'

'Good. Come on.' He hoisted her to her feet.

Her knees protested as she staggered through the wild grass, but she ignored the pain and struggled to keep up with Ryam. As soon as they cleared the tree line, she collapsed to the ground. He crouched beside her and lifted her arm gingerly, inspecting the broad scrape on her elbow. In the last two days she had suffered more bruises than in all her sparring matches. Mother would scold for days if she ever made it home.

'The grass…did not…break the fall,' she accused.

His face broke into a wide grin. 'Tough girl.'

'I have five—*four* brothers.'

His clear eyes held on to her as if he would never turn away. No man had ever looked at her like that.

'Do you need a minute?'

He stroked her cheek with his thumb and everything became brighter. His mouth was so, so close and her throat went completely dry.

'N-no. We should go.' She struggled to stand, but her knees hadn't stopped shaking.

He offered his hand to help her to her feet. His fingers combed lightly through hers, but immediately let go when she stiffened beside him. She was left standing at a loss, covered in dirt from head to toe. She swiped at a strand of loose hair, but it swung defiantly back in front of her face.

'Are you still planning to go all the way to the capital?' he asked.

'I must,' she said. 'As fast as we can. I need to warn my father.'

'Then we had better start moving. It's a long way.'

In Changan, she'd have to justify her disobedience to her family. They believed she was now wedded to Li Tao, gaining them a strong military ally against their enemies. What her father didn't realise was that Li Tao *was* the enemy.

Everything had changed since they'd left their home in the mountains to install themselves in the imperial palace. Father and Mother had become so suspicious. Their discussions now centred on politics and hidden motives. She wanted to forget the turbulence of the imperial court and the constant power struggle, but she couldn't.

The warmth of Ryam's concern stayed with her as she fell into step beside him. It didn't make sense, this giddiness that spun her around whenever he was near. When they reached Changan he would go his own way. He would be nothing but a memory and she would never be able to explain this time with him, this feeling blooming inside her, to anyone. Not when she couldn't understand it herself.

Ryam guided them northwards, in the general direction of the imperial city. Ailey asked him only once whether he knew where he was going as they climbed over twisted roots, turning and winding through the green.

The forest spread in tangled vines around them and folded them into shaded darkness. Clear line of sight extended only for several feet in any direction. Any search party would need to spend a considerable amount of energy to track them. Ryam exhaled, letting the tension drain from him momentarily in the shelter of the woods.

'We should have some cover in here,' he said.

Some of the trees grew so thick that ten men could encircle the trunks. It was another sign of the empire's wealth, the lush woodlands at their disposal, fed by several great rivers. Enough wood to build the most magnificent of cities and palaces.

They reached a stream and followed it. A canopy of cypress and ginkgo grew along the bank. The roots crawled like snakes along the earth, dipping tapered fingers into the water.

'These trees are sacred.' Ailey ran her fingers along the trunk of one as she walked by. The fan-shaped leaves flickered yellow-green with the breeze. 'They live for thousands of years. Longer than the empire. We see them in temples all the time.'

Changan wouldn't be hard to find. They only had to head north in search of the grand canal that flowed into the capital. All the major roads would lead them there as well, but they needed to stay hidden.

Ailey walked along the reeds that lined the water, arms held out for balance. God's feet, she moved with such graceful confidence. 'Grandmother always spoke of the forests of the south. She learned her technique from a southern master.'

Her hips swayed their seductive rhythm before him. He nodded absently and considered dunking his head into the cold water. All he needed to do was get her home and get out of there.

'Is there anyone in your family who doesn't wield sharp weapons?' he asked.

'Mother disapproves of my swords. She says no man would want a woman with such rough hands.'

She hopped over a tangle of roots, light-footed and sure over the uneven ground. He saw absolutely no problem with her hands or any other part of her.

'Mother was so happy when Father arranged this marriage,' she continued sombrely.

'So why did you run away?'

'Li Tao is—ruthless.' She seemed unwilling to say more.

'He's also rich and powerful,' he pressed her. 'And in command of an army of thousands. Not the sort of man who takes refusal lightly.'

The tail of her braid whipped over her shoulder as she faced him. 'It is not as if I'm refusing Li Tao because he is old or ugly or fat.'

'Well, is he?'

She stopped, caught off guard. 'I—I don't know. I mean, it doesn't matter.'

'You don't know if he's ugly?'

'I've never seen him. When he came to fetch me for the wedding procession I was wearing a red scarf over my face.'

'So he hasn't seen you either?'

'Of course not.'

'Now I understand.'

She cast him a wary glance. 'Understand what?'

'You were marrying a man you'd never met. Of course you had doubts.'

'You don't understand at all.' She turned on her heel and continued down the bank. Her stride had lost its carefree gait. 'In our custom, it would be the greatest insult for a bride to refuse a match simply because she did not like the look of her husband. It would be disrespectful to his family and a great dishonour to mine.'

'It's not important that you at least see each other before being wed?'

'Not at all. I would trust my parents would make me a good match.'

It was hard to believe someone with such unquestioning faith would run away from an arranged marriage. Even if she had been wilful or stubborn, it was unlikely a woman of her standing would risk so much to defy convention. Perhaps there was a lover. The thought alone sent a hot streak of possessiveness through him, unwarranted as it was. But why would she want to return to her family when they would certainly denounce her? Besides, her every touch spoke of innocence. He knew the signs well enough to steer clear under most circumstances.

'You wouldn't prefer someone that was strong and hand-some?' he goaded.

'That doesn't matter to me.'

'What if this Li Tao is ancient? Wrinkled, toothless…'

'He is not!' Her eyes grew wide despite her denial. She lowered her voice as if in confidence. 'Mother told me he was twice my age.'

'And what is that?'

'I was born the year of the dragon.'

'Dragons, rabbits, tigers,' he said with a laugh. 'I could never figure out your calendar.'

She regarded him through her lashes, blushing. 'I have nine-teen years. I know that is very old for marriage, but the last years have been…very unusual.'

Ailey was beyond adorable when flustered. He leapt across the stream ahead of her and stretched out his hand. She landed before him in the moss, bracing against his arms to steady herself. This time he held on. Her pulse fluttered beneath his fingers.

'You don't want someone who makes your heart beat faster?' he challenged.

She ran the tip of her tongue over her lips, too pretty and too curious for her own good. It took all of his will to hold himself back.

'I…I don't.'

Little liar. He could pull her into his arms right then and she would melt against him. Her mouth would taste just as sweet as he remembered.

He let go of her. He had to.

He swallowed forcibly, words failing him. 'So you were ready to marry him no matter how old and ugly he was. What made you change your mind?'

He held himself apart from her, unmoving while his heart threatened to punch a hole through his ribcage. The force of his reaction stunned him and for some reason, he needed to know exactly what her ties were to the man she had been promised to.

Ailey swayed in the damp earth of the riverbank, caught off balance at his abrupt departure. 'The wedding ceremony was to be completed before his family altar. On the journey, I was carried inside a palanquin, while he rode with the escort.'

'A man would be mad with lust being forced to wait so long to see his bride.'

She frowned at him. 'This is not something I do lightly. My family could disown me.'

He stopped his teasing when he saw the sudden tension in her shoulders. He was beginning to see that Ailey never did anything lightly. Every word carried weight with her.

'Go on,' he said. 'What happened?'

'You must know that there have been uprisings within the empire over the last year. My fourth brother, Ming Han, had a military command, same as all my brothers. He was sent to put down a rebellion near the border of the Jiannan province. Li Tao's domain.'

'Which is where we are now.'

'The empire is too large for the imperial army to control,' she explained. 'Control of the empire is a delicate balance between the imperial forces and the regional armies. Han joined with Li Tao's troops in the effort. We later received reports that Han had been ambushed by rebels and killed.'

She looked away, pressing her lips tightly together. For a moment, he thought she'd lose the fight. Always so strong.

'You don't have to explain,' he said.

'No, I want you to understand. A soldier who had once served under my father swore Ming Han was killed by Li Tao's soldiers. The warlord has been secretly building his army. Our marriage is merely a ploy.'

Something didn't seem right. 'One of the warlord's soldiers betrayed him to you?'

'Wu was once a member of the Dragon Guard. He's a man of honour and he risked his life for me. I trust him.'

The same way she had trusted her bodyguards. As she now trusted him.

'When Father learns what happened to Fourth Brother, he'll denounce Li Tao as the murderer he is,' she said. 'And the empire will be better off for it.'

Ailey's family was involved in the sort of politics he knew to stay far away from. The Chinese emperors ruled as descendants of heaven, but they were just as readily assassinated and replaced as any mortal.

Their lost legion had been caught at the centre of the rebellion following Emperor Li Ming's death. The Tang rulers were masters of intrigue. They had perfected the art of it over centuries of rule. What chance did a band of barbarians have against such deceit?

After order was restored, Emperor Shen had allowed them to settle in the frontier to the west, in a region that had been abandoned by the empire. They guarded one of the northern branches of the many trade routes that originated from Changan.

It had been over a month since Ryam had left the marsh-lands where they were stationed. He had brought twenty men with him into the southern province alongside a shipment of precious cargo. A routine encounter with imperial soldiers had gone badly and he was knocked unconscious in the fight. Once he recovered, there was no trace of his men.

They were soldiers, organised to fight as a unit and follow orders. They had needed someone to lead them, someone dip-lomatic enough to negotiate without starting a blood bath. But he didn't know anything about that. He was nothing more than one man with a sword.

The imperial army had tolerated their existence in the fron-tier until now. Ryam prayed the conflict hadn't changed the Emperor's mind. Without Shen's protection, they would be hunted down like dogs. He could return to find that they had all been marked for death for his mistakes.

Maybe that was why he needed to get Ailey home safely. Pay off his debt, as she liked to say. He had spent too much time within the empire and their ideas were seeping into him. For once, he needed to get something right.

They cut through the woods, following the stream over the rocks for the rest of the afternoon. Ailey could sense her spirit easing as they ventured further into the forest. The dense growth closed behind her like a barricade. If fortune favoured her, the soldiers would still be hunting for the gang of bandits who had supposedly abducted her. She could return home before Li Tao realised she knew of his cowardice and treachery.

'You've risked so much to help me.' It was so hard to start conversations with him when he didn't use any of the accepted forms of address. She didn't know whether to be formal or intimate.

'Anyone would have done the same.'

'I don't believe that,' she said.

'Maybe I just wanted the company.'

He was smiling. She definitely needed to remain formal, for her own protection.

'Those bandits could have smuggled me to a brothel in some remote corner of the empire. Or worse, they could have ransomed me back to Li Tao.'

As *jiedushi,* Li Tao had sworn to protect the empire, yet he plotted against it. They called Ryam's kind barbarians, but there was nothing barbaric about him. His manner was direct and honest. It was her own countrymen she needed to be worried about.

The water at the bend formed a pool between the rocks. He stepped over a broad stone and then his hands circled her waist to lift her. His arms flexed as he set her down.

'Be careful here, it's slippery.' He flashed another one of his easy smiles that sent her floating. His touch sent a lazy ripple up her spine and the look he gave her went on for a heartbeat too long.

She looked down at the water. 'There are fish in there,' she said absently.

'Really? Where?'

Her shoulder brushed against his as they knelt to peer into the water. The turn of a tail sent a splash to the surface. The closeness that would have been improper with anyone else seemed so natural with him. Her heart was beating so hard and she could barely breathe. A school of grey fish darted beneath the surface, but all she could stare at was his reflection. The golden hair and light eyes.

Then she caught sight of her own reflection beside his. She looked like a madwoman! Her braid had fallen apart, leaving her hair in a wild nest. Horrified, she scrubbed at the smudge of dirt across her cheek.

He turned to her, his face inches from hers. She froze with her hand against her cheek.

'Are you hungry?' There was a hint of mischief in his eyes.

She was. They had been running all morning. She needed

the rest as well, but had been reluctant to slow down their
journey.

'How are you going to catch them?'

He held up his hands and wiggled his fingers.

'You cannot,' she said.

'Watch me.'

He loosened the ties of his vest and tossed it aside. Tiny
knots formed in her stomach as one boot and then the other
landed by her side. She ducked her head to stare at the moss
beneath her knees. He had no shame at all. She peeked back
over to see that he was still wearing his shirt as he slipped waist
deep into the pool. The fish scattered in all directions, their
dark bodies gliding in frantic circles as they tried to escape.

He shot her a warning look when she giggled. With the back
of her hand pressed to her mouth, she watched as he cupped his
hands and dipped them carefully under the surface, going as
still as a mantis. The fish gradually settled and resumed their
gentle sway. She held her breath.

In a flash he scooped his arms upwards, flinging a cas-
cade of water up onto the grass. She shrieked and scrambled
away.

'You did that on purpose!'

Water dripped from his chin. He swiped at his face. 'You're
scaring the fish,' he accused.

She moved into the shade to seat herself as he crouched
again. He pounced with an even greater splash, again coming
up empty-handed. She fell back, grabbing at her sides. How
long had it been since she laughed so hard it hurt? Not since
her brothers had all been together. Not since they had left their
mountain home for the capital.

She wiped at the tears at the corners of her eyes. 'Have you
ever been able to do this?'

His mouth twisted. 'When I was hungry enough.'

'No wonder you were starving when we met.'

'*Quiet.*'

She combed out her hair with her fingers and started to braid
it again. Out of the corner of her eye, she saw Ryam crouched

for another attempt. His blond hair clung to the sides of his face as he stared into the pool with a mercenary expression.

The next moments were filled with the sounds of splashing punctuated by a string of foreign curses. For the moment, she forgot about the trouble she had got herself into. She could hide amidst the cool moss and long shadows of the forest. Li Tao would never find her.

But her ancestors would. They would call out to her in spirit and demand obedience.

When they reached Changan it would be the end of this reprieve. The hardest part of her journey would begin; the part where she'd have to explain her disloyalty to her mother and father. It would be her word against one of the most powerful men in the empire.

'Victory!'

A fish the size of her hand wriggled in the grass, silver belly shimmering.

She stood and bit her lip to keep from smiling. 'He will be a tasty bite for you.'

Ryam hoisted himself out of the pool. A river of water streamed from him, dripping onto the bank. 'Don't you dare throw him back,' he warned. 'That's all we're getting today. I'm out of practice.'

'You're not going to catch me one?'

Her words caught in her throat as he tugged the soaked tunic off. Sunlight gleamed off the broad expanse of masculine skin and muscle. The thatch of golden hair on his chest tapered over the hard planes of his stomach. A plume of heat rushed up her neck until her face burned with it.

He wrung the water from the cloth. 'Seemed like a good idea at the time,' he muttered. 'I haven't tried that in years.'

She barely heard him as she stared. Her pulse pounded hard in her ears. 'You—you are going to catch cold,' she stammered.

He looked up then and grew quiet. 'It's a warm day.'

An endless expanse of burnished skin hovered before her. When she tried to look at his face, it was even worse. Sky-blue eyes held her gaze as he tugged the damp tunic back down over his shoulders.

Deliberately, he turned away. The gesture did nothing to banish this dawning awareness that had invaded her and seized control. The sleek muscles of his back moved beneath the damp cloth as he pulled a knife from his belt and started cleaning the catch, his gaze fixed upon his task. She retreated against the trunk of a cedar tree and tried to look anywhere but at him, wishing she had something useful to do at the moment.

The gaping silence begged to be filled with anything, some sound to string one moment with the next. She hooked her arms over her knees as he sparked a pile of kindling and nursed the ember into flames.

'You should teach me how to do that.' She was babbling. 'How to start a fire, find food.'

He speared a sharpened stick through the fish and held it over the flames. 'You won't need it. You'll be home soon enough.'

She fell silent. This would all go away. This swordsman with blue eyes and the storm of emotions that came with him. She had to remember that these moments, no matter how wondrous, would die away like the fire. She needed to think, think and not feel. But how could she when he brought out so much that was hidden within her?

Ryam turned the fish over and over, the skin growing crisp and black over the flames.

'What is it like where you are from?' she asked.

'Our men are encamped in the Gansu corridor just beyond your western border.'

His wary tone took her by surprise. Were his men in hiding? Was he fearful that she would reveal their location? She pushed away that disturbing thought.

'I mean your homeland. Where you came from.'

'Very different from here,' he said, holding the skewered fish out to her.

She plucked a morsel from the bone with two fingers and

lifted it to her lips. She hadn't realised how hungry she was until that moment.

'You must have more to say than that.'

'If you keep travelling west, around the abandoned desert, you'll reach a sea. Cross that and keep on going. If you haven't been killed by hostile armies or bandits, you'll arrive in a valley bordered by two great rivers.'

She tried to imagine the world beyond the great desert. It must be a tapestry of wild and exotic tribes, where pale-skinned warriors roamed the forests.

'Grandfather would tell us stories of how his armies marched to faraway kingdoms,' she said.

He pulled off a chunk of the fish and popped it into his mouth. 'I doubt your grandfather made it anywhere near our land. The journey is not an easy one.'

'Were you a soldier over there?' she asked.

He let out a short, cutting laugh. 'Not a very good one.'

The fish was reduced to a spiny comb. He tossed the bones into the fire and lay back, resting his head on his arms to watch the trees. Sunlight filtered in pockets through the leaves, dappling his face in light and shadow. His sword was laid out beside him by the bank. Even sheathed within the leather scabbard, the weapon radiated a savage energy.

'What about your father?'

'He was no soldier either. Couldn't take orders.'

'You said he was no longer with you.'

'No.'

He spoke without emotion, but his hands curled tight before releasing. She nearly missed the gesture. Ryam didn't appear much older than her, yet he had lost his homeland and his family. She couldn't imagine any greater sorrow than that. She searched for something to say to honour his ancestor's spirit.

'He must have been a formidable swordsman. His name must have been very well respected.'

'Well respected?' Ryam sat up so abruptly she fell back. 'Why are you asking all these questions?'

'I—I'm sorry.'

He exhaled sharply before turning to look at her. 'In a week you'll be safe at home and I'll be—' Scowling, he scrubbed his knuckles over the back of his neck. 'There's no use in remembering. We'll never return. We were lucky enough to have survived the journey here.'

She knew better than to be so personal with a stranger, but his open nature made her forget her manners. 'I just wanted to know what your life was like.'

His gaze raked over her. The corded muscle of shoulders gradually lowered and he let his arms fall to his sides. 'My life is not very interesting at all,' he replied with a calmness that unnerved her.

She wasn't accustomed to this sudden shifting of mood. One moment, he would be smiling and pleasant, then, in the blink of an eye, he could replace all that warmth with a mask of detachment.

'What else do you want to know?' he asked.

Possessed by morbid curiosity, her eyes darted to the scar that cut just over his ear. She'd found it shortly after they met, while he lay unconscious in the grass.

He didn't need to ask what had caught her attention. 'I got that in a fight against imperial soldiers. Ask me why.'

She shook her head, unable to bring herself to do it. The cocoon of warmth that had enveloped the entire afternoon unwound itself in an instant.

'Are you having second thoughts about being here with me?' He planted a hand into the grass, edging closer.

'No. I trust you.'

He was giving her all the time in the world to shove him away, to rise, to flee. Her heartbeat quickened as she watched him. Moving ever so slowly, he braced an arm on either side of her, his fingers sinking into the moss.

'I asked you to come with me.' Despite her words, she dug her heels into the ground and inched backwards. 'I feel safe with you.'

'I can see that.'

He affected a lazy smile as she retreated until her back

pressed against the knotted roots that crawled along the ground. His boldness was so unexpected, so exciting. She held her breath and waited.

Her pulse jumped when he reached for her. She'd been imagining this moment ever since their first duel and wondering whether it would take another swordfight for him to come near her again. His fingers curled gently against the back of her neck, giving her one last chance to escape.

Then he lowered his mouth and kissed her.

Chapter Five

Ryam wove his fingers into Ailey's hair. Her lips parted the moment he touched his mouth to hers. Back in familiar territory.

He dragged his lips over hers until she moaned and yielded against him. No more questions from her. No more thinking at all.

It was as natural as breathing to wrap his arms around her and lower her to the ground. He settled his weight against her hips. The perfume of her skin mixed with the damp scent of the moss beneath them. At some point, her sense of propriety would win over. Until then he let his body flood with raw desire. It felt good to kiss her the way he wanted to. It felt damn good.

He slipped his tongue past her lips to where she was warm and smooth and inviting. Her hands clutched at his shirt as she returned his kiss. A muted sound escaped from her throat. He swallowed her cry, using his hands to circle her wrists: rough enough to make her breath catch, gentle enough to have her opening her knees, cradling his hips with her long legs. He stroked himself against her, already hard beyond belief. He groaned when she responded, instinctively pressing closer.

'I need to see you,' he said.

The sash around her waist fell aside in two urgent tugs while his other hand stole beneath her tunic. She gasped when his fingers brushed the swath of cloth at her breasts. The faint, helpless sound nearly lifted him out of the haze of desire.

He didn't want to think too hard about this. Not yet. He felt for the edge of the binding.

'In back.' She spoke in barely a whisper, a sigh on his soul.

She peered up at him, her face in shadow as he parted her tunic. She watched him in much the same way she had when they had first met: curious, fearless, her eyes a swirl of green and gold. He pulled at the tight cloth until Ailey's warm, feminine flesh swelled into his hands.

He soothed his palms over the cruel welts left by the bindings. She bit down against her lip as blood rushed back into the tortured flesh. With great care, he stroked her nipples, teasing them until they grew tight beneath his roughened fingertips. God's breath. Perfect. He wanted his mouth on her and still it wouldn't be enough. Her heart beat out a chaotic rhythm. His own echoed the same restless pulse.

'I knew it would be like this.' His words came out hoarse with passion.

At that moment he'd have given his soul to have her. But somewhere in his thick skull, he knew he had a beautiful, vulnerable girl who trusted him pressed against the bare earth. He sensed the hitch in her breathing and how her fingers dug nervously into his shoulders, even as her hips arched into him.

He ran his thumb gently over the reddened mark that ran just below her collarbone and felt her shiver beneath him. With Ailey's swords and determined spirit, it was easy to forget that she was innocent. He couldn't close his mind and let himself sink into the pleasure of the moment. Actions had consequences and he needed to tear himself away while he still could.

'Please.'

Her breath stroked softly against his ear and made him want to forget the consequences. He buried his face against her neck, against the softest skin in the world. His hand trailed down over the smooth plane of her stomach. She gasped as his fingertips slid past the edge of her trousers.

'Please stop.'

Startled, he released her. She sat up and backed way, fumbling for her tunic.

'We can't.'

She clutched the edges of the garment over her chest defensively. A wave of dark hair fell loose around her face. The sight of it sent another stab of lust through him. His body ached, every fibre wound tight, not yet realising that he would never have her. The taste of her lingered in his mouth.

He turned away and could hear nothing but the rustle of cloth as she dressed herself. By God's bones, he hoped she wasn't crying.

'It cannot be this way between us,' she said brokenly.

'I know.'

'Never with you.'

Her words cut to the quick and poured ice into his veins. When she faced him, her eyes were dry. Her hands tugged nervously at her clothing as if she would never be able to set herself right.

'Nothing happened, Ailey. No harm done.'

His tone held more of a bite than he intended. She shot him a hard look in reply and then bent to scoop up her knapsack. Turning on her heel, she headed down the river, her braid swinging across her back.

He supposed anger was preferable to tears. With a curse, he fastened the sword belt about his waist. This was why he didn't seduce virgins. Too many complications. And he had stopped far short of seduction, by his reckoning. She still had half her clothes on at the worst of it. He muttered a final oath before following after her, refusing to hurry to catch up.

Ailey's cheeks burned with the memory of his rough hands against her breasts and the wet, searching stroke of his tongue in her mouth. The secret place between her legs had flooded with dampness while a drugged and aching sense of yearning filled her. She had never imagined seeking a man's touch with such mindless abandon.

It was wonderful. It was terrifying.

She had barely summoned enough will to ask him to stop.

'We lost our heads for a moment, that was all,' he said.

His first words to her after almost half an hour of excruciating silence. He walked beside her, acting as if the earth had not just opened up. Perhaps it hadn't for him.

She gritted her teeth and fought to control her anger. She didn't even understand her anger. Did she want to be ruined? She was supposed to be returning home to warn her father, not kissing foreigners she barely knew.

'I suppose you've kissed hundreds of women like that.'

'More than I can remember,' he replied, his tone flat.

This was exactly what she needed to hear, but she felt as if a fist had crushed the breath from her throat. She threw him a look of black poison and fire while he kept his eyes deliberately ahead. His neck must have been stiff from staring in one direction for so long.

Everything about him confused her; his boldness, the way he looked at her, the way he listened to her every word as if she wasn't a sixth child and an insignificant female. But it was nothing but empty charm. This must be a game he played with all women.

Her voice grew deadly quiet. 'Do not try that again with me.'

He scowled. 'I can control myself.'

'Swear it.'

'God's teeth,' he growled beneath his breath. 'Fine, I swear it.'

His stride lengthened, his footsteps vibrating with anger. She had an abundance of anger to match. Anger was easier to understand than the unnameable emotions swirling through her.

'Don't kiss me back then,' he muttered.

In a flash, she had her weapon in hand. 'Draw your sword.'

'Whoa! Ailey...'

She waved the point of the blade at him. 'Do not think I will not cut you to pieces because you are unarmed.'

'I won't do anything. I won't even touch you.'

'Draw your sword!'

Everything he said only added fuel to her frustration. She was so torn with desire, embarrassment and confusion that the only choices were to cry or to exact violence. And she wasn't going to dishonour herself by crying.

She was being irrational and she knew it, but she advanced on him regardless, satisfied that the smug look on his face had disappeared. He backed away and threw his hands up in defence. The steady chop of an axe in the distance interrupted his protests.

'That could be a village,' he said quickly.

Without waiting for her response, he started towards the sound. She glared at his retreating shoulder blades and sheathed her sword. Wisely, he said nothing as they moved along the river.

The river led them to a thicket where columns of green bamboo sprouted straight up from the ground, replacing the twisted trees. In the distance, a group of woodsmen hacked at the stalks with machetes, collecting the sections into woven baskets.

'I'll speak to them,' she said, stepping forwards.

He caught her arm. The shock of his touch and the memory it invoked vibrated through her. She shook out of his grasp, once again hiding behind her anger.

The three men paused as she approached to ask about their village. They motioned past the bamboo thicket, all the while looking past her to stare at Ryam. He stationed himself securely at her side as they passed.

'I don't like how they're looking at you.'

'It was you they were staring at.'

He shot them a final, feral glance.

'No one will help us if you threaten them.'

His show of protectiveness pleased her more than it should have. She had to remind herself that he was a barbarian and a scoundrel who would never be permitted to kiss her again.

At the river bend, a huddle of wood cabins peeked through the trees, their rooftops patched with straw and reed. An elderly man hunched over a boat at the water's edge, his gnarled hands working at a length of rope. He stopped his work to regard them from beneath the wide brim of his hat as they came close.

'Greetings, Uncle.'

The fisherman's sharp gaze fixed on to Ryam and she fumbled for an explanation.

'My guard is one of the desert people.' Except the desert tribesman were dark-skinned. She cringed at her lack of guile, but continued. 'Would the honourable fisherman be kind enough to take in two strangers for the night? We can pay.'

She rifled through her knapsack, only to come up empty-handed. The purse was gone. She thought back with dismay to her tumble from the wagon. They were still a week from the capital and she was without a copper. She was prepared to beg her way home if she had to. Before she could form her plea, the boatman handed her a shallow basket and pointed to a plot between the two huts.

'Fill the basket,' he instructed. 'You may stay in the boathouse.' He went back to work untangling his nets.

They walked away from the river and found a patch where broad leaves sprouted from the ground.

'Are you sure we can trust him?' Ryam asked as soon as they moved beyond the first hut.

'He strikes me as an honourable man.'

'But you thought I was honourable,' he pointed out with a quirk of his mouth.

She shoved the basket into his hands, eyes narrowed. 'Start picking yams, ghost man. It will be dark soon.'

Kneeling, she took hold of a thick stalk and pulled at it. The leaves tore off in her hand. Ryam dropped down beside her, placing the basket between them.

He blew out a forced breath. 'Nothing happened.'

'So you've said.' She twisted the purple yam loose and tossed it into the basket.

Ryam was wrong. Something had happened. She had done things, felt things with him she needed to forget. But she couldn't when she was so aware of every movement he made. She stared at his hands as he worked his fingers into the black soil and couldn't help thinking of those broad hands moving over her.

To her surprise, he spoke next in what was almost a northern dialect. '*Ai Li, don't be angry.*'

'Your accent is pretty good,' she replied. 'Do you apologise often?'

He presented her with a half-smile, looking triumphant that he had her speaking to him. 'I'm well versed. I know how to say, *you look pretty.*'

Ignoring him, she attacked the next yam with a stick.

'I can also say, *you look pretty when angry.*'

She blushed despite her dark mood. 'I am not angry.'

'Truly? Because you are the last woman I'd want angry at me. You wield very sharp swords.'

She threw the yam at him. It bounced off his chest, leaving a smudge of dirt.

'I know you're above me.' He forged on, cutting off her protest. 'You're a very beautiful woman and I'm not a particularly good man.'

She kept her gaze to the ground. His humility wounded her. 'That was not what I meant.'

Why then had both guilt and pleasure flooded her when he held her in his arms? If she didn't marry Li Tao, she would marry another man her family chose. That was the way of things and she had never questioned it before. But in these woods far from home, her entire being reached out to Ryam, seeking the unknown emotions churning within her. She couldn't understand this new longing and she couldn't control it.

'I know the sort of people you come from,' he said. 'I may

be a barbarian, but I'm not entirely without honour. I swear to you on my father's sword, I won't touch you.' He smiled in an attempt to lighten the moment. 'I can't promise I won't think of it.'

His words left her hollow inside. He held out his hand, palm up, and she could only blink at it, not understanding.

'We shake hands. It means we understand each other. Like an agreement between swordsmen.'

'An oath?'

Uncertain, she placed her hand into his. His fingers surrounded hers, rough and warm. A tremor coursed down her arm.

'No more argument?' she asked. 'We treat each other like swordsmen from now on?'

He released her with a frown. 'Fellow swordsmen,' he echoed. 'Yes, something like that.'

The phantom of his touch lingered long after he released her. She went back to work, completely uncertain of what, if anything, had been decided between them.

Five days. That was how long he figured it would take to get Ailey home. Untouched, he reminded himself.

Throughout the day, he had found himself relaxing beside her, shaking off the weight of all that had happened and sometimes it seemed that sense of peace she gave him was all he needed. But then she'd look at him in that way that pierced right through him. In those moments, he knew he'd never have enough of her.

He'd sworn, whatever that meant. He simply would have to avoid her touch, the sight of her, the sound of her laughter.

Once their task was done, the boatman led them to the shed by the river and returned a while later with a frayed woollen blanket and a bowl filled with boiled yams. They knelt by the riverbank and Ailey folded up her sleeves to dip her hands into the swirling water. Her bare skin glowed like ivory and her arms curved with the graceful strength that marked all of her movements.

It had been too long since he'd enjoyed the soft touch of a woman. The moment he formed the excuse, he knew it wasn't true. His regard for Ailey had nothing to do with hurried couplings in brothels, with coarse seduction in patches of wild grass. Ailey was young and confused. She didn't know what she wanted—although she had made it abundantly clear she didn't want him.

Daylight was slipping away fast beneath the canopy of the forest. They settled with their backs against the worn planks of the shed to listen to the river. He plucked a yam from the basket and bit into it, making a face.

'Not bad,' he mumbled around a mouthful of paste and leathery skin.

Ailey took one and nibbled at it. As always, she took everything in her stride, never complaining. It was one of the reasons it was too easy to forget she came from nobility.

'You grew up in the capital?' he asked.

'My family home is in the northwest province, along the western frontier. We moved to Changan when my father was…' She paused as if searching for the word. 'When my father was promoted.'

The western frontier was close to where his men had stationed themselves. Perhaps that was how she developed her tolerance for foreigners, though it was unlikely she had ever seen the likes of him before.

'Life in the capital does not suit me,' she said.

'Why not?'

'Everything was different in our home in the mountains. We were free to do as we pleased, surrounded by people who were loyal and trustworthy. In Changan, no one can be trusted.'

They finished the yams in silence with the smell of the river and the earth surrounding them. She had tried to hide her upbringing from the beginning, but he was starting to form a picture of where she'd come from. Since the ascension of Emperor Shen to the throne, a renewed struggle had broken out among the *jiedushi* and their regional armies. Her father was probably one of those warlords or a close adviser to one.

The turmoil among the ruling class even reached far out into the frontier where his regiment operated. The trade routes had been disrupted and the flow of goods had become sporadic in the past year.

'We have no alliance to anyone out in the Gansu corridor other than the Emperor,' he assured her. 'You don't need to worry about me.'

She crossed her arms in front of her, as if cold. Her gaze wandered to the water and back. 'They say the corridor has become a lawless place.'

'There's no law in Yumen Guan but the sword.' He cast her a look. 'In some ways not very different from here.'

She laughed. 'You say it so strangely. It means Jade Gate.'

'I know what it means.' He made a face, which only made her laugh harder. The ease of the moment washed over him.

'You must long to return. I have only been away from my family for a week and I miss them every day.'

Ailey's home would be a glittering mansion in the imperial city, but the dusty frontier was as much a home as any he'd ever had. The pass was inhabited by outlaws and nomadic tribes. A band of displaced barbarians could almost fit in.

'I suppose when you've been to so many lands, you don't get as attached to any one place.' All that mattered to him was Adrian and the legion. After fighting alongside one another for so long, his bond with them went beyond blood. Yet he'd never truly been one of them. He had spent too much time alone, grown too used to looking after himself to entrust his well-being to anyone else, even Adrian. Still, they were the closest thing he had to a home.

'Yumen Guan is where they say the exiled princess has gone,' Ailey was saying.

'Miya? That one is a little dragon.'

Her mouth fell open. 'You refer to the imperial princess by name? In our custom, that offence is punishable by—'

'Death?' he finished with a raised eyebrow. He wondered if there was such a thing as a minor offence in the Chinese empire. 'She's no longer a princess. Miya stepped down from the throne.'

'To marry a barbarian,' she said thoughtfully.

She looked like she wanted to ask more, but she bit back her words and stared out at the river. He had to remind himself that her family's loyalties were with the current regime. No one knew who was friend or foe any more.

He had avoided returning for too long. It wasn't punishment that he feared. He'd convinced himself that the men were better off with him gone. But Adrian had trusted him with a command. He deserved to know what had gone so terribly wrong.

So he had been making his way back slowly, dreading the outcome. He'd never expected to meet someone like Ailey. The only peace he'd known was when she was near…there was no way to describe it. She trusted him without question and he had no choice but to try to live up to her expectations. He didn't realise how long he had been staring at her until she averted her eyes.

'Earlier when I said…' She hesitated, twisting her braid around a finger. 'When I said that it could never be that way between us…'

He sat up in alarm. 'I thought that was settled. Swordsmen, remember?'

'I did not mean that I considered you inferior in any way… that you weren't good enough.'

He rubbed at the back of his head, struck with the insane urge to take her in his arms and hush her with his mouth over hers. It was so much easier to seduce a woman than talk to her.

'It's getting late. You must be tired.' He stopped her before she could go on with her apology and thrust the blanket into her hands. 'Go on inside and get some rest.'

The blanket dangled from her hands. 'Will you sleep out here?'

'I'll stay right outside by the door.' He rapped the doorframe with his knuckles and leaned back to concentrate on the orange sliver of daylight lingering on the horizon. Anything not to conjure up the smooth skin he knew she kept hidden beneath the grey tunic.

Ailey stood, but paused at the entrance. 'I must ask this one thing. Why were you attacked by imperial soldiers?'

Better that she knew the truth about him. Maybe then she'd stay just far enough away.

'We were hired to guard a shipment into the empire,' he said. 'This was the first time I was put in command. Imperial soldiers stopped us on the road and discovered that we were transporting weapons. Swords from Parthia, what you call *Anxi*.'

Her breath caught. 'Did you know what you were carrying?'

'I should have known. I was in command. But we checked the cargo beforehand and saw nothing. We travelled south through several districts without any challenge at all. When the imperial soldiers stopped us on the road, I still thought there was nothing wrong.'

He had checked the goods when they were handed over by the Parthian traders. He should have checked again once they were loaded onto the wagons. Or again, before they crossed into the empire. He should have slept alongside those rugs and crates.

'There must have been a traitor among you,' she said. 'Someone who was paid to do it.'

'I don't know. To this day, I'm not certain of how it happened.'

He rubbed a hand over his temples. His head throbbed as he recalled the battle, or at least the first few minutes of it. He had tried to negotiate, but his knowledge of the language was worthless. The tribesmen travelling with them tried to explain, but before he knew it, swords were drawn.

'I drew my sword and fought for my life. We were foreign devils caught with illegal cargo. We could go peacefully and be hanged, or fight tooth and nail for our lives.'

'And the men you were with?'

'All dead.'

The words left him cold inside. It was the first time he had admitted it to himself. He had tried to refuse, knowing from the start he wasn't the right person to take responsibility for the task.

'I'm sorry. It was a mistake, as you said.'

Her sympathy didn't make it any easier. He shut his eyes and let his head fall back against the doorframe. The silence went on for a long time.

'I was afraid you had done something unforgivable,' she said faintly.

He'd lost his entire command and endangered the very survival of their outfit. It made him wonder what in God's name she considered unforgivable.

'Then what would you have done?' he asked.

'I would have asked for your death.'

He had no doubt of it, with her sense of duty. Ailey was a warrior, heart and soul, and it had nothing to do with the swords she carried. She believed in the empire and its preservation above all else. He had never believed in anything so deeply, not even the oath of protection he had sworn years ago, in a place a thousand leagues from here.

'You're not good enough to beat me, Ailey.'

'Honour is not about winning,' she replied before retreating into the shed.

Chapter Six

When morning came, Ailey woke alone in the shed to the gentle lap of the water against the bank and the low rumble of Ryam's breathing. He'd fallen asleep outside and had slumped across the doorway in a heap. She stifled a laugh when she saw him. He was going to be so sore.

A sound from outside caught her attention. The fisherman was gesturing to her from the river bend. The venerable old man had been so kind to them, that she went to him without a thought. She gathered her swords and stepped carefully over Ryam.

The huts were quiet and still around them. She had never known of these tiny settlements along the rivers.

'Come help with these nets,' the fisherman said.

The nets lay in a tangle by the water. She knelt beside the old man and reached for one edge to start working at the knots.

'This girl must humbly thank you, Uncle. She will find a way to repay you for your kindness.'

He turned to her. He was close enough that she could trace the deep lines etched into his face. 'I know who you are.'

Her pulse quickened. 'Uncle, what do you mean?'

'Princess Ai Li.'

He lowered his head. His hands clasped on to the rope, but she caught the tremor in them. The sword in her boot rested inches away. When he looked up, his eyes were wide with fear.

'Go now!' he hissed.

She grabbed her swords and twisted to her feet. Two men dressed in black broke from the line of the bamboo thicket and rushed at her. The red dragon insignia of Li Tao's battalion showed clearly on their uniforms.

Instinct guided her feet forwards. She met their advance and caught the lead man before his sword was completely drawn. The butterfly sword bit into his elbow, slicing tendon and muscle. He staggered back, cursing.

Two arms wrapped around her. The second man had manoeuvred behind her. She wheezed as he tightened his grip. Her cry for help came out as a gasp.

A roar cut through the morning air. Ryam was upon them in a blur of motion. With one swing, he knocked the sword from the first soldier's grasp and kicked him into the river. Water splashed onto the bank as the man thrashed about.

More soldiers sprang from the forest like wild boars. Three this time. Ryam turned to face them while Ailey struggled against her captor. Her arms were trapped and she couldn't get any leverage to kick at him.

She dug in her heels as the soldier dragged her away. 'Ryam!'

But he was unable to help. The other three were circling him. Ryam's arms flexed as he raised his sword. His opponent tried to meet him strength for strength and failed. The broadsword cut through and sent the soldier to the ground.

The arms around her hoisted her up. Ailey threw her head back, hoping to connect with something. The arms squeezed tighter and shook her violently. She hated being so weak. All the training meant nothing as soon as some brute overpowered her.

Ryam had defeated another of the attackers. The darkly

clad bodies collected on the ground at his feet. But it was the fisherman who came to her aid.

The old man came at her captor and struck at his head and shoulders with the bamboo fishing pole. The soldier swatted at the scrawny fisherman and Ailey tore free as his hold loosened on her.

'She-demon!'

A hand grabbed at her arm and she stumbled. Then a shadow fell over her. Ryam. He wrapped an arm around her waist to pull her behind him, shielding her with his body. Without a word, Ryam advanced on the final soldier. The man didn't have time to draw his weapon before the broadsword cut his legs out from under him. The soldier sprawled onto the ground, rolling in pain. There was a brutal efficiency in the western style.

Ryam whirled around. 'Where were you? You can't run off alone like that.'

She stared at him. His chest was heaving and his eyes blazed with anger. Only now did the fear hit her. Her heart was pounding and her hands started shaking so badly she had to sheathe the swords or else she'd drop them.

Li Tao had found her.

'More will come.' She stared at the mass of bamboo stalks as if the entire forest would come alive any moment.

'Take the boat!' The fisherman hurried to the shed.

Ryam ran beside her. He helped her in before stepping into the boat behind her. The vessel swayed beneath their weight as he grabbed the steering pole.

'There is a great lady who lives down the river. She can help you.' The old man's shoulders strained as he stooped to push them away from shore. 'Go safely.'

Ryam stabbed the pole into the water to steer them away. 'I can hear them.'

She could as well. The bamboo stalks rustled with movement. There was no telling how many there were. Li Tao commanded an army of thousands. He could scour every inch of these woods. Ryam frowned with concentration. The muscles in his arms tensed as he pushed hard against the river bottom. They began to pick up speed.

The fisherman stood by the bank to watch their departure. She was reminded of Old Wu standing beside the abandoned palanquin, and prayed that she hadn't brought Li Tao's wrath into this simple fishing village.

'Get down,' Ryam commanded.

She ducked low. Shouting broke out back at the river bend, but the huts had grown small in the distance, swallowed by the surrounding forest as the boat glided towards open water. Ryam found his balance and pushed off steadily into the swift current. A sheen of sweat covered his brow.

He hadn't said more than two words to her. Had he worked out who she was? Would he stay with her if he knew she had lied to him?

'I woke up and you were gone.' His hands gripped the wooden pole until his knuckles grew white. 'What were you thinking?'

The sun overhead cast his face in shadow, hiding his expression, but she could see how his jaw set into a hard line as he stood over her.

'You were still sleeping. The old boatman asked for my help.' Her explanation sounded weak to her own ears.

'You can't be so careless.'

Heat rose up the back of her neck. He had no right to reprimand her. 'I didn't see any danger.'

'You asked for my protection.' He stabbed the pole into the water again. 'As if I need someone else to look after.'

They fell silent after that. The buzz of the dragonflies droned in the emptiness while she listened to the lap of the river against the wooden hull. The boat caught the current and sliced through the water. She said nothing while Ryam lowered himself to sitting position, casting the pole aside in agitation. It landed with a thud.

He stared into the river, too angry to look at her. 'Not everyone lives by the same code of honour you do.'

Tension knotted his shoulders. Still she said nothing. Anger upon anger would not resolve anything. It was then that she noticed the scrapes over his knuckles. A bruise ran along his cheek and his blond hair was tossed haplessly. The sun caught the golden threads in it.

'You were truly concerned for me,' she murmured.

She had never seen him show any fear at all, yet he had been afraid for her. He had rushed into danger without a thought for himself. Perhaps it was not only for honour—she didn't dare to hope. Could he actually care for her as something more than a burden?

'That head wound you suffered nearly killed you, didn't it?'

He shifted his gaze away from her, but there was nowhere to hide. They were in the middle of open water, the current carrying them fast downstream as the river widened. She inched closer and touched her fingertips to the back of his hand.

'What happened?'

Finally he met her eyes. His look sent an odd heat through her.

'I don't remember anything after I was struck,' he muttered.

'You're fortunate to be alive.'

'The men under my command were not so fortunate.'

Boldly, she took hold of his hands. They were so much larger than hers. Broad and scored by a field of scars. Marks of living by the sword. He dropped his hands against his knees, his back stiff and straight as he regarded her.

He was not so very different from Father or her brothers, though he had journeyed from his faraway land across the silk roads. Grandfather had travelled the same desert routes before his service to the August Emperor. Her family still guarded the border near the western frontier.

'I come from a line of swordsmen,' she said. 'From soldiers and generals. I know what happens when a warrior loses a battle for the first time.'

'This wasn't a battle, Ailey. It was a senseless brawl. And stop looking at me like that.'

She frowned, confused. 'I don't understand.'

'I don't need you to understand. I need—I just need to get you home.'

His eyes deepened to a clouded grey as they reflected the churn of the river. For a moment she could barely breathe, enthralled by his nearness and the sway of the boat beneath them.

She struggled to find the right words. 'When a man learns that he is not invincible for the first time, it shakes the ground on which he stands.'

'How many battles have you fought?' he asked with a snort.

'This is something my father tells me.'

'Well, I've lost plenty of fights in my lifetime.'

'None that truly mattered until this one.'

He laughed at that, as if she were joking. Maybe it was absurd, giving advice to a seasoned warrior when her experience extended no further than the practice yard.

'You cannot doubt yourself because of one mistake,' she went on stubbornly. 'I would trust you to the ends of the earth.'

His laughter died and he let out a sigh that seemed to shake his entire being. He reached up and brushed his thumb over the corner of her mouth, his touch as light as a leaf on water.

'No wonder Li Tao is willing to move mountains to get you back.'

The sound of the name made her flinch. Li Tao knew nothing about her, cared nothing for her. Their marriage had been arranged to reinforce an alliance. The warlord would never listen to her as Ryam did. No one had ever paid such careful attention to her.

Closing her eyes, she broke away. Whatever was forming between them, it could not endure. Her father had promised her to the traitor Li Tao. If she wasn't considered ruined for marriage, her father would promise her to someone else.

Her father was Emperor. Their lives were not their own.

What one wanted and what one needed to do were seldom the same. That was duty. That was sacrifice.

When she opened her eyes, Ryam had shifted further from her. His elbow rested against the edge of the boat and his hand dangled near the water. He looked to the shore, watchful of any movement.

'We won't be able to stay on the river long,' he said after another stretch. 'They'll follow it and find us.'

A thought came to her. 'The weapons shipment you were guarding—where was it destined?'

Ryam frowned. 'Chengdu. Why?'

'The shipment could have been going to Li Tao,' she said, rising excitedly.

'Get down. You're going to fall over.'

The connection was so clear. A clandestine weapons shipment amidst rumours that Li Tao was building an army in secret. It was exactly as Wu had warned her. She had been right to escape when she did.

'The Emperor has taken control of the forges and armouries in order to control the *jiedushi*,' she explained. 'If Li Tao needed weapons, he would need to smuggle them from outside the empire.'

'All the way from Parthia through Yumen Guan?'

'He needed to keep it secret,' she insisted. 'And he may have had help from someone at the fortress.'

'It's possible.' He frowned, considering it. 'Between us and the tribesmen, we try to stay away from the affairs of the empire.'

'But Princess Miya is there. They still speak of her in Chang-an. When she was in the palace, she could get anyone to do her bidding.'

'How do you know so much about her anyway?'

'Everyone knows of her.' She fell silent then, praying she hadn't revealed too much.

'You're wrong about the princess,' he said. 'We risked our lives to rescue her from the palace. It was her choice to abdicate the throne. She doesn't want to be involved with the empire. Not with something like this.'

In the previous reign, the Emperor had been considered god-like, the Son of Heaven. The people seemed content to accept his rule. The borders were protected by powerful warlords and the merchants grew fat and decadent.

Her father's succession had been brought about through war and rebellion. His detractors claimed that a barbarian had taken the throne, a man of common birth and mixed blood. Heaven had turned its back on the Middle Kingdom in disgust, and responded with famine and disorder.

Perhaps it was true that Emperors had to be born. Father had never dreamed of ruling. He had only accepted the duty out of honour. Secretly, Ailey wished there was a way that all of this could be undone and their family could return to what they once were. Fourth Brother wouldn't be dead. Father and Mother wouldn't be desperate to negotiate alliances with powerful warlords.

Ryam stood to steer them around an outcropping of rock. His sleeves were rolled up past his elbows and the muscles in his arms pulled taut against the drag of the water. Once again, he had saved her life.

She had to remember that he was still a stranger, inextricably linked to the power struggles that were tearing apart the empire she loved. She could never completely trust him. It seemed she couldn't trust anyone, any more.

He had warned her that not everyone lived by the same code of honour she did. She knew it too well. When it came to power and the people who wielded it, loyalties became twisted and honour washed away like sand.

By the middle of the next day, they abandoned the boat and pushed it down the river. They continued on foot along the opposite bank to put a barrier between them and their pursuers. Ailey jumped every time the breeze stirred through the trees or a twig snapped in the distance.

'Stay calm,' Ryam said.

He steadied a hand against her back and his touch nearly made her jump again. Ever since she'd made him swear, he'd kept a noticeable distance between them. She almost hated how careful he was with her now.

'We need to get closer to Changan, into lands under imperial jurisdiction,' she said. Everything they spoke to each other was in lowered tones, as if Li Tao's men were hiding behind every tree.

'Once we reach the city, I need to figure out a way to get you to your family and then get out of there.'

She reached for her braid, twisting it in her fingers. 'I could take you to my father. He can help you.'

'You know we can't. Your father will either kill me with his own hands or hand me over to the soldiers he obviously commands.'

His tone grew harsh and she fell silent. They both knew there was no way to explain her being alone with him. It was unthinkable that Ryam could rescue her so valiantly, yet still be chased down as an outlaw.

'I don't know what to tell him myself,' she said. 'To break a wedding arrangement like this is unspeakable.'

'And the sight of a white demon like me would only make matters worse.'

'You're not a demon,' she denied fiercely.

He regarded her with surprise and her skin grew hot under his scrutiny. She looked away, but the sight of his blue eyes stayed with her. It was impossible. Even if he weren't a foreigner. Even if he were a swordsman of Han descent, her father wouldn't allow it.

They were in danger with every breath, yet part of her never wanted to reach the capital. She would have to face her family in Changan. She would have to tell them what she'd learned about her brother's death and open old wounds all over again.

She glanced over at Ryam and wished he would look at her again the way he had by the pond—as if she was the most enchanting thing he'd seen in all his journeys. For a moment

in his arms, her worries had vanished. The palace and all of
its lies didn't exist.

'What is that?' Ryam asked.

A patch of red broke through the endless green of the forest.
He slowed his step and Ailey crowded closer to him as she
peered through the trees.

'A house,' she said.

Not at all like the thatched huts of the fishing village. The
winged rooftop of a mansion rose over the trees, breaking the
natural landscape. The wooden columns along the bay were
painted bright red for good fortune. A peach orchard grew
behind the building, the blossoms clinging like snow among
the branches. This magnificent residence, complete with intricate latticework and gilded rafters, belonged in Changan or
Luoyang, not in the middle of the woods by the muddy banks
of the river.

A gardener saw them first. He left the flowering trees to
hurry inside. The lady of the house emerged in an embroidered
robe that, like the mansion, reflected opulence worthy of the
imperial court.

The boatman had spoken of a great lady. Ailey's breath
caught as she recognised the mysterious woman. It was Ling
Suyin, former consort to the August Emperor. A legendary
beauty. The woman breezed into the garden, surrounded on
either side by her servants, and stood waiting by the orchard,
draped in silk and elegance.

The legends were true.

'We should move on,' she urged.

But Ryam didn't appear to have heard her. His gaze was fixed
upon the vision among the peach blossoms. 'Lady Ling?'

Ailey could only stare in surprise. Before she could stop
him, Ryam headed towards the house. It would have been pointless to warn him about the tales of men being seduced by the
mere sight of Lady Ling. He was already caught. Ailey wanted
to hit him. Hard.

The lady followed the path to the river's edge; her dress
floated with her as she walked, shimmering like pearl. She

appeared youthful, her skin flawless. They said the August Emperor had been twenty years older than her when he was enthralled by her.

For a moment, Ailey was stricken with a sense of fleeting glory. Who would ever see such beauty in these woods? Yet the imperial consort still dressed as if the deceased Emperor would come to her.

Ryam didn't look back once as he climbed the path to the house. Ailey had to run to catch up with his long stride.

'Lady Ling, I would know you anywhere,' he greeted.

Her perfectly painted lips curved into a smile. 'Ryam, is it? The wayward swordsman. You are far from Yumen Guan.'

A wonder she could even move in all that silk. Ailey blew at the strands of hair that strayed over her face, feeling like a street urchin in her drab clothing. She set her feet on the bank and refused to go any further. Ryam must have said something amusing because the courtesan's laughter rang out like a bell. The dainty sound made Ailey's skin crawl.

He had been to the imperial court and knew people in the highest ranks of power. She had to rethink her initial thoughts of him as a harmless outlander.

It was Ling who finally took notice of her by the shore.

'Who is your companion?' she asked.

'This is Ailey.'

So he hadn't forgotten her name. She gave a short bow out of politeness. 'This humble girl is honoured to meet such an exalted lady.'

Ryam raised an eyebrow at the crispness of her voice. 'We are headed to Changan to return Ailey to her family,' he explained.

'Changan?'

Ailey wanted to jab him for his carelessness. Ling's eyes flashed with catlike interest as they surveyed her from head to toe. She tried to assure herself that the courtesan wouldn't recognise her. She had lived far away from the imperial city during the reign of the August Emperor. Still, the association was too close for her to let down her guard.

Lady Ling spoke in the most formal of dialects. 'You must accept my offer of hospitality.'

'We would not dare to trouble the lady,' Ailey responded in kind.

'There is no need for such politeness. Are we not friends here?'

No, they were not friends in the least. Ailey's instincts told her to decline immediately and return to the forest. Ling Suyin had ruled over the inner palace during the most treacherous years of the court. This woman was no delicate orchid.

Lady Ling extended a hand onto Ryam's arm and Ailey glared at her manicured nails as if they were talons. She measured the seconds until the woman took her hand away.

'How could I refuse such a gracious offer?' Ryam said with an uncustomary show of manners.

He moved away from the dock, walking beside Lady Ling as they ascended the path to the orchard. Ailey dug her nails into her palms and had no choice but to follow them. The smile on his face was too wide and the way Ling tilted her head towards him made Ailey itch for her butterfly swords.

'We cannot stay long,' she cut in. Had he forgotten they were being tracked?

They glanced back, moving as one. She wanted to tell Ryam he looked like a fool standing beside such a refined lady, but it wasn't true. He appeared tall and rugged and gallant as if Lady Ling had bestowed her grace on to everything around her. The corner of his mouth tugged upwards, bemused by her ire. She scowled at him, eyes narrowed, not caring what the lady read into it.

Ling's pleasant smile never wavered. 'For the night at least,' she said. 'It has been so long since I've heard news from beyond this river.'

She stepped aside to let Ailey join them. Ling's gaze again flickered over her as she passed.

Ryam continued to stare at the imperial consort as if he

were seeing the moon for the first time. He could defeat a gang of bandits easier than blinking, but put a beautiful woman in front of him and he was helpless.

Chapter Seven

Ailey settled into a private room overlooking the orchard. Within minutes, the servants rolled a wooden tub into the outer chamber and poured buckets of heated water into it until thick steam rose to dampen the air. It seemed that Ling still lived as if she was a favoured concubine in the palace, but Ailey couldn't complain with the promise of a hot bath before her.

Once she was alone, she stripped off her tunic and leggings, folding them carefully. A surge of heat rushed to her breasts as she loosened the bindings. The memory of Ryam's hands tugging at the cloth assailed her. His palms had been rough, but his touch gentle.

She'd made him swear not to touch her, but now she could think of nothing but the hundred secret things he made her feel with his mouth and his hands, all in a few brief moments.

She curved her hands around her breasts to relieve the ache as she slipped into the tub. The bathwater flowed around her, the warmth seeping into her skin. She laid her head back against the wooden edge and willed her limbs to relax. Even with her eyes closed, all she could see was Ryam standing next to Lady Ling, his face bright with laughter. She had been so easy to overlook, as she had always been. Little Ai Li, sixth child, a daughter among precious sons.

She grabbed the cake of crushed soapbean and scrubbed it over her skin, washing away the dust and grime from the days on the road. A faint jasmine perfume rose from the water, but did nothing to calm her.

No man had ever looked at her the way Ryam had, but would he feel the same about any pretty face? Was that the way of men? She wanted to sink beneath the water. All the women Ryam must have known. Across the span of the Silk Road. Worldly, beautiful women like Lady Ling. Women who wouldn't shrink away from his kisses.

She stood from the bath, ignoring the slosh of water over the side. Cool air tingled across her skin and she dried herself with a linen cloth. On the bed the servants had laid out several garments. The first was a sheer, long-sleeved robe the colour of rose petals, as fine as the garments she wore in the palace. With a swipe of her arm, she pushed the silk aside and chose the tunic and trousers, slate grey and unadorned. She folded the formless tunic across her front and tied the sash about her waist. Her hair went back into its simple braid.

When she opened the door Ryam was already there, hand raised to knock. For a moment she could do nothing but stare. Her gaze skimmed over the clean, strong lines of his face, no longer covered by the rough stubble of a beard.

She let out a breath. 'You look so strange.'

He laughed at that. 'Less like a lion?'

She wanted to run her hands over the smooth skin in disbelief. He appeared so much younger. His mouth took on a teasing, sensuous quality. How would it feel if he were to kiss her now? She found herself wishing that she hadn't demanded such honour from him.

'You look charming as always,' he said through the rushing sound in her ears.

It was like looking at a stranger. Like meeting him once again. She had been holding her breath and she let it out in a rush, fiddling with the neck of her tunic. Her thoughts strayed to the delicate, feminine robe the servants had laid out for her and she berated herself for making such a poor choice. Ryam's blue eyes sparked as he watched her.

'Suyin has invited us to have dinner with her,' he said.

So now it was Suyin instead of Lady Ling.

'I don't trust her.'

He paused, choosing his words carefully. 'Our paths have crossed before. She's a friend.'

'How does a barbarian befriend an imperial concubine? They are locked away in the inner palace. No man is allowed to speak to them unless he is a eunuch.'

She glanced down, then back up. Ryam's lips pressed together, forcing back a smile.

'An interesting story, but a long one,' he deflected. 'Lady Ling may be able to help us.'

'We have no need of her help.'

She didn't like this woman with her knowing looks and her elegant air of superiority. And Ryam seemed to think so highly of her.

'Changan is several days' journey from here and she may still have influence there.'

Her dislike increased tenfold. 'You're different around her.'

'Different? How?' He leaned against the doorframe, his broad shoulders filling the entire passage.

'You puff your chest out like a—' She struggled to find something suitably insulting. 'Like a rooster.'

He only seemed to enjoy it more. 'A rooster,' he echoed, grinning wide.

She would have hit him if it didn't seem so childish. 'You go on without me. I'm very tired.'

He stopped the door as she moved to close it. 'Come on. I'm hungry and so are you.'

He ushered her out of the room with a hand at her back. She dragged her feet in protest as he nudged her forwards. He could be just as insufferable as her brothers.

A set of wooden steps led into the main atrium of the house.

The servants led them through a side door on to a veranda facing the river. A low table had been set in the open air. Orb lanterns swung from the rafters, the muted candlelight glowing through the waxed paper. Lady Ling stood at the far side, her back to them as she gazed upon the river. If Ailey wasn't in hiding, she might have appreciated the hospitality.

Ailey grabbed Ryam's arm before he stepped forwards. 'Don't tell her about Li Tao. He could have informants everywhere.'

He nodded without argument, and she was reassured that he still had some sense about him. The lady continued to face the water as they approached. Dusk transformed the swirling water to inky blackness. The breeze caught the edge of her robe and whipped the layers about her. She resembled the brush paintings of immortal beauties that hung from bamboo scrolls.

Their footsteps on the boards must have signalled their approach. Lady Ling started speaking without turning to face them. 'The August Emperor had this mansion built before his death. I have no need of such splendour, but it pleased the Emperor to do so.' Placing her hands on the wooden rail, she leaned forwards, and inhaled as if breathing in the fading sunlight and the breeze. 'I grew up along this river.'

Ailey detected a hint of longing in the lady's voice.

She turned to them. 'I thought we would enjoy the evening outdoors. And I can become acquainted with your lovely companion.'

'She is not—'

'We are not—'

They both started to protest. Lady Ling cast them a pointed look before beckoning them to sit.

The servants flowed around them as they moved to take their places at the low table. Ling knelt on the pillows, arranging her robe around her while Ryam took much longer trying to fold his long legs beside the table. Uncertain of where to go, Ailey took her place at the corner beside him. Social etiquette had no provision for dining with a man who wasn't your husband and a former concubine while hiding your true status.

Ling turned her attention to Ailey. 'So your family lives in Changan?'

'Yes, my father is a tea merchant.' She glanced over at Ryam, who stayed silent.

'I was not aware there were tea plantations in that area.'

The consort's tone remained pleasant, but Ailey had the impression she was being prodded for the lady's amusement. An object of curiosity. Ailey kept silent, using decorum to her advantage, as the servants poured the wine and brought out the first dishes of the evening meal. Out of the corner of her eye, she noticed Ryam slide the cup of wine away with a finger.

'Our business is nothing to boast about. There is nothing to interest the lady,' Ailey said.

'Oh, nonsense. Every little detail interests me.' Ling folded her hands in front of her expectantly.

The gap of silence that followed was nothing if not purposeful. Father had warned of the slippery ways of the court long before they moved to the capital. Every word has two meanings, he would say. Other than Mother, their family had no way with words. They were people of action. Navigating the political landscape left them flat-footed on lower ground.

'This insignificant girl is curious as to how the Emperor's consort befriended a foreigner,' Ailey replied.

Ryam cut in. 'I visited the palace once.'

'He was quite the diplomat.'

'Lady Ling—'

His warning tone was unmistakable, but the lady continued, amused by his discomfort.

'So humble. Your swordsman is a hero,' Ling said. 'I am surprised you do not know of it.'

Ailey didn't understand why, but the woman was taunting her. She found herself inching closer to Ryam for reassurance.

'After the death of the August Emperor, there was a palace rebellion.'

'I've heard of this story,' Ailey replied coolly. 'But my family was not in Changan at the time.'

Ryam cleared his throat and grabbed a set of ivory chopsticks, positioning them between his fingers. 'See? I know how to use these now.'

'The barbarian legion marched on Changan to rescue our princess,' Ling continued.

'Shen An Lu was the one that rescued the princess.'

The words were out of her mouth before she could stop them.

Lady Ling smiled at her. '*Emperor* Shen,' she corrected.

Ailey could feel her face growing hot. No one spoke the Emperor's given name out loud.

'Of course, not everyone considers saving the princess an act of heroism,' Ling said to Ryam. 'In Changan they call her "the Pretender", while many in the empire consider her the rightful heir.'

Ailey tapped her chopsticks gently against the tabletop to straighten them, using the gesture to gain some pause for reflection. She wanted to simply demand of Lady Ling where her loyalties lay. It was too confusing, this twisted knot of allies and enemies.

'This looks good,' Ryam interrupted, poking at a plate of pickled radishes and quail eggs. 'Eat before it gets cold.'

'It's already cold,' Ailey replied.

Ling hid her laughter behind her wine cup. Ryam squeezed Ailey's hand in warning beneath the table, but she shook free of his hold. The gesture was too personal and she was certain Ling caught a hint of it.

'I no longer follow the politics of Changan,' Ling said dismissively. 'Instead, I spend my days here, free from the cares of the world.'

The courtesan knew intimate details about the imperial capital. Ailey couldn't risk slipping and revealing something dangerous. And she certainly couldn't risk Lady Ling detaining them until Li Tao arrived.

She set her chopsticks down. 'This girl must apologise. She is too tired from her travels to be good company.'

'I will send a tray to your room then. You must keep up your strength, for it is a long way from home.'

Lady Ling looked at her so intently that she feared the woman did recognise her. But it was impossible. The consort could not have had more than a glimpse of her in the imperial palace, perhaps on one of her father's visits to the August Emperor. She would have been an insignificant child at the time.

She bowed. 'The lady is very kind.'

When she stood to go, Ryam rose to accompany her, only to be summoned.

'Let her rest,' Ling chided. 'We have much to talk about. I have not seen a familiar face in a long time.'

He gave the lady a brief excuse and rose to walk part of the way with her into the house.

'Ailey, what's wrong?'

The brush of his fingers against her wrist sent a shiver up her arm. He had a way of angling himself towards her, shielding her with his broad frame whenever he stood close, as if he would never let anything touch her. Even his use of her name, spoken with that odd accent of his, beckoned to some corner deep within her heart.

She wanted to demand that they leave this place and this woman with all of her questions. They should return to the river where there was no one but the two of them, but Ailey had no claim to him.

'Stay,' she said, backing away. 'You two seem to have much to talk about.'

'I won't be long.'

It wasn't the answer she was hoping for. He left her without another word. When she looked back, he was seated beside Lady Ling, one elbow propped on the table. They were absorbed in conversation. The sound of their laughter echoed in her ears as she retreated into the house.

'She is very beautiful.' Ling watched him through her lashes as she sipped her wine. 'I can see that you are in trouble.'

In lieu of answering, he plucked a dumpling from a plate and stuffed it into his mouth. The servants brought out more plates to set in front of them, roasted duck and sesame greens and more delicacies he didn't have words for.

'How long have you known her?'

He concentrated on handling the chopsticks. 'If you keep on asking questions, I'll think you're jealous.'

She laughed. 'Anyone can see you're already taken with her.'

He remembered how the consort would take hold of a conversation and twist it off centre to keep the advantage. It was just her way.

'I'm taken with all women.'

'She is quite spirited. I would have guessed a woman like that would catch your interest.'

Either the former courtesan was probing for information because it might be useful to her, or she was simply starved for intrigue out here in the woods.

'You sound like an old matchmaker, my lady,' he said around a mouthful of rice. 'All I want is to get her home.'

'Very noble of you.'

He laid his chopsticks across the bowl. 'What is it you're prying at?'

'She is no merchant's daughter—you must know that already. It is apparent in her manners, how she speaks, how high she holds her head.'

He exhaled slowly. Despite all of Ling's plays for power, he trusted her judgement. She had a talent for gauging people and he was going to have to confide in her for what he wanted to do. 'Her father is an official in Changan.'

She nodded as if expecting it. 'There are a number of minor officials by the name of Chang.'

'Lady Ling, swear to me you are not involved with anything. Any schemes against the throne.'

'Of course not.' She tapped her fingers against the table in agitation. 'I spoke truthfully when I said I no longer cared for politics.'

'I know little about her family, but I know they're loyal to Emperor Shen,' he said.

'And so am I,' she insisted.

He looked over at his cup of wine. Picking it up, he tossed it down, relishing the familiar burn as the alcohol slid down his throat. He was going to need much more to relax the tension twisting his stomach.

'With all the talk of unrest and rebellion, Changan has become a dangerous place for barbarians like me,' he explained.

'Dangerous for everyone.'

She leaned forwards, her perpetually serene expression replaced with a shrewd look. He decided not to tell her of the smuggled weapons and his confrontation in the southern province. It was best to keep Ailey and Lady Ling as far away from that as possible.

'I need to ask for your help. Ailey needs to get home to her father, but I can't take her.'

'You want me to go with her to Changan?'

He passed a hand over his temples. Occasionally his head would ache, the tension centred above the scar from his head wound. He wondered if it was a phantom reminder or was he not yet healed.

The plan had come to him only hours earlier. Ling could escort Ailey without having to hide in muddy river banks and forest groves. Her escort wouldn't be accosted by imperial soldiers the moment they reached the capital. She could use whatever contacts she had to get Ailey home.

And, most importantly, Ailey wouldn't be shunned when she was seen returning with Lady Ling. He had weighed the strength of his sword against the rest and the answer was easy.

'She will not be happy,' Ling said quietly.

'I know, but this is the only way.' His fingers curled into a fist as he said it.

'Where will you go then? Back to Yumen Guan?'

He nodded.

Ling folded her hands in front of her, fingers entwined. 'You surprise me.'

'How so?'

'I did not think you would sacrifice something you wanted so easily.'

There was an unfamiliar tightening in his chest. 'It's not a sacrifice.'

He had planned to leave Ailey with her family once they reached Changan anyway. What difference did it make if they parted several days earlier? He'd have to tell her when they were alone and make her see that this was the best decision. The only decision.

Ling's almond eyes slid over him, urging his secrets to the surface. It was said she could captivate a man with a single look, but the face he kept seeing was Ailey's.

'There is another reason you are so eager to part with her. You're afraid.'

He leaned back, willing to let the lady have her fun.

'Certainly. She has four brothers with swords who would not be too happy to find their youngest sister travelling alone with a barbarian.'

'You were never afraid of men with swords.' She tapped a nail against the table thoughtfully. 'She looks at you with such adoration, completely infatuated. What a powerful temptation that must be.'

'Nothing has happened.'

So he had kissed her twice and nearly lost control both times. Nothing worth dwelling upon.

Her lips curved. 'I believe you that nothing has happened. Otherwise, you would not burn for her so. Unrequited love.' She sighed.

The thought of having Ailey sent a flood of heat between his legs, but it wouldn't be enough to fill the even deeper ache within him. And it simply wasn't going to happen.

'She is a pretty girl,' he said casually. 'One of many pretty girls.'

'Yes, I remember. You wreaked havoc among the palace girls.'

'I don't remember it quite like that.'

Ling leaned forwards, a tigress on the prowl. She was enjoying herself. 'You feel guilty being here with me while she's not here, yet you have not so much as touched my hand. Tell me, do you remember every single time you've touched her? Are you thinking of her right now?'

It was useless to try not to think of Ailey. He conjured up the softness of her skin, her arms wrapped around his neck, even the stubborn tilt of her chin whenever she faced a situation she didn't like. He was going to see that bit of wilfulness again very soon.

'Why are you so concerned?'

'I was worried you would let a pretty face cloud your judgement, but clearly you have the situation under control.'

Completely under control. He grabbed his wine and swallowed it down. The servants had been diligent about keeping the cups filled.

'We two are so very similar,' she said softly. 'You want women to fall at your feet, but you cannot stand to be at anyone's mercy.'

He traced a fingertip over the edge of the table. 'But I'm completely at your mercy right now.'

'You are not.' Her eyes sparkled. 'I would know. You've always kept yourself apart, beholden to no one.'

Maybe everything she said was true. All the more reason to let Ailey go, untouched. 'Can I trust you to get her home safely?'

A shadow of sadness crossed her face. It was the only sincere emotion she'd allowed to escape the entire evening. 'I do owe you a debt. This may be my one chance to repay it.'

'Thank you.'

It was done. This was a woman who had survived assassination and rebellion. She would be able to protect Ailey much better than he could. When he'd been given command of that shipment, he had known he wasn't the right man for the task. He'd gone through with it blindly and lost everything. He'd be damned if he let the same thing happen again. The hollowness he felt inside must have meant he was making the right decision.

He finished the last of the wine and stood, the emptiness threatening to swallow him. Now he had to go and tell her.

Chapter Eight

The sound of movement brought Ryàm out to the side of the house. A shadow wove through the peach trees, wielding butterfly swords. Only Ailey would be working through fighting forms late into the night. She broke the pattern as he reached the railing and then continued without glancing his way. Moonlight flashed off the blades as they whirled through the darkness.

He couldn't hold back his smile. 'Were you waiting for me?'

She stopped and kept her gaze focused ahead, breathing hard from the exercise. 'I'm training.'

He braced a hand against the rail and leapt over it, his feet landing solidly on the bare ground.

'It's late,' he said.

'Yes. It is.'

With a flick of her wrists, she lowered the swords and turned to him. Experience told him he wouldn't be able to leave until Ailey got the confrontation she wanted.

'Did you have a pleasant dinner?' she asked.

'Yes, I did.' He folded his arms over his chest to brace himself for battle. 'You left rather quickly.'

'Is Lady Ling the type of woman you prefer?'

He'd been thinking quite a bit about what sort of woman it was that he preferred. Ailey argued the same way she fought—with clean, precise cuts. Her skin glistened from the exertion and her hair hung in loose strands that framed her face.

'Lady Ling could tear a man to pieces and he would beg for more.'

Her mouth drew tight. 'You like her.'

'When I'm not afraid of her.'

She swung away to start another drill, her braid whipping over her shoulder. Her movements lacked their usual fluid grace. The flow of energy was disrupted, the Chinese would say. He watched her with perverse pleasure. She wouldn't have him, but there was hell to pay if any other woman came near. He should have been too jaded to be aroused by jealousy, but from Ailey he loved it.

'Is there something you want to say to me?' he asked.

'Nothing at all.'

Her swords cut through empty space. She was probably imagining him in front of them. Now was definitely not the time to tell her what he and Ling had decided.

'Your swordplay is quite aggressive,' he said. 'Surprising, for someone your size.'

She lifted her eyes to him. 'It's the best way against a larger adversary.'

'Interesting.'

The drill came to a stop as she turned to him, her stance guarded and tense with challenge. He would miss that quiet fire. The journey out of the empire seemed to stretch out an eternity now that he knew he would travel the rest of the way alone.

He ventured forwards, keeping his attention on the butterfly swords. Ailey had an even temper, but she did have an impulsive streak.

'Show me,' he said.

She hesitated, but lowered her weapons. It was good thinking on his part to distract the both of them.

'A large fighter would want to hold his opponent back where he has the advantage. When I move within arm's reach...'

She demonstrated by stepping close and the scent of her hair drifted to him, mysterious and feminine. His heartbeat quickened.

Fellow swordsmen, he'd sworn. Ridiculous. He only had to look at Ailey to want her. Every movement sang of strength and hinted at her passionate spirit.

'It becomes difficult for you to strike,' she finished absently. When she tilted her chin upwards they were nearly face to face. She was standing closer to him than she needed for this demonstration.

Not as close as he wanted.

The corner of his mouth lifted. 'I could just grab you.'

'That's why I have these.' Her blade shot up between them.

He laughed and she joined in, the sound of it washing warm over him. Between the lanterns and the moonlight, her face radiated confidence and sensuality with a touch of innocence, the same combination that had caught his attention from the first moment at the roadside tavern.

'Here, let me show you,' she said suddenly.

She reached down to pull the sash loose from her waist. The sane part of his mind knew she wasn't undressing for him under the night sky, but the hint of it was enough to make him stiffen.

She stood on her toes. 'Lower your head. You're too tall.'

He bent down and closed his eyes as she placed the sash over them, tying it securely around the back of his head. Her jasmine scent caressed over him and her fingertips brushed lightly against his ear as she straightened. His skin prickled with awareness, sensitised to her every movement as he was engulfed in darkness.

'You train blindfolded?' he asked.

She laughed, sounding so close. 'This is how you train your touch reflexes. It's called *chi sao*.'

'You are a constant surprise,' he murmured.

He strained to listen for her through the whisper of the breeze, his vision blocked. She took hold of his hands and he let himself be led. Her skin was flushed from training. He found it incredibly sensual, waiting in the dark as she positioned his arms into a guard.

'Stay relaxed. Try to maintain the contact when I move.'

Her voice was intimate, soothing. He could feel the line of her wrist, the tension in her arm as she pushed against him.

'Ready?'

'Yes.'

'Slowly first.'

She moved and he followed her, turning his body to keep her in front of him. When the pressure withdrew, he sought her out, shifting his feet to maintain contact.

'Keep with me.'

She guided him with her touch, testing him forwards and back. They stepped side to side; each time he used the contact against her arm to gauge how she moved. Gradually she quickened the pace, using different patterns, breaking the rhythm so he would have to adjust.

'How does this help you fight?' he asked.

'Touch allows me to read an opponent faster than seeing him. Every time I deflect a strike, I can read your movements. If you push too hard, you will over-commit. If your touch is too light, I can sense an opening.'

It had been a long time since anyone had tried to teach him anything about the art of the sword, not since his father's death. But he couldn't fully concentrate on the technique. Her voice flowed over him like water, his awareness heightened by the blindfold.

'Let me try it,' he said devilishly.

His movements became more aggressive. He pushed forwards. Attack and retreat. She responded, her movements complementing his, the ebb and flow of her breathing increasing with the rhythm. He could hear the soft pad of her footsteps against the ground. A dance in the darkness.

It would be that way if they made love. Completely attuned

to each other's bodies through simple touch and tension. He sensed it in his soul as heat and energy pumped through his veins.

He stopped abruptly and let go of her, reaching up to remove the blindfold. Ailey came back into view.

She blinked at him. 'Why are you stopping?'

He sucked in a breath. 'Do you even know what you do to me?'

She could entice him to madness without even trying. With a combat exercise, of all things. Sooner or later, he wouldn't be able to keep his hands off of her. And when he gave in to his need, he wouldn't know how to let go.

'You're not for me, Ailey.'

She shook her head. 'I don't understand.'

He needed to get this done. Ailey respected directness and honesty and he didn't have any time to squander. By morning, he would be gone.

'I spoke with Lady Ling. She can escort you the rest of the way to Changan.'

The light drained from her as she looked at him, silent and stricken. The urge to put his arms around her was overwhelming, but he forced himself back. That would be the easy thing to do. Hold her close and take away the sudden chill that had set in between them.

'So this is what the two of you have decided?' she asked.

'You should be accompanied by someone like her. Someone respectable.'

Not by a barbarian who would drag her into ruin. Ailey had her own honour and her family's reputation to uphold. Even he knew these things.

'You promised.' She was grasping and they both knew it.

'I told you I would get you home safely. That's all.'

His voice sounded too loud among the peach trees. She was the one who'd made him swear not to touch her, and he'd kept his word despite being an irresponsible bastard.

'In a few days you'll be home,' he went on. 'We were always planning to go our own ways in Changan.'

Her lip trembled, but she fought hard to control it. Methodically, she bent and returned one sword after the other into the sheaths.

'You are right. You have no obligation to me. But I don't trust Lady Ling and I won't go with her.'

He was ready for this. '*I* trust her. Ling Suyin is a friend. She owes me a debt.'

Her pained expression told him he had pierced her armour. Ailey lived by honour. It ran thick in every drop of her blood.

'She won't let any harm come to you. I swear it.'

'You'll go tomorrow, then?' she asked tightly.

'Yes.'

He had to leave while he still could.

She held his gaze for a long time, unflinching. He could see himself reflected as tiny spots of light in her irises. He would never know what it was she saw in him. Then, with a nod, she walked past him. Her shoulder brushed stiffly against his arm as she retreated from the orchard.

Warrior pride.

She slipped into her room, the door creaking shut. He had known she wouldn't plead or throw a tantrum. In a way, she'd made his announcement dreadfully easy on him.

He stayed in the orchard until the servants came to extinguish the lanterns, blowing out the candles one by one.

Ailey closed her bedroom door behind her and leaned against it. Before she could compose herself, a tear slid down her cheek, followed by another. She swiped at them angrily with the back of one hand.

She couldn't grasp her own emotions, didn't understand the feeling of loss as if something had been ripped from inside her. Ryam was right. They were going to separate in Changan. It shouldn't make any difference for them to part now. But she had thought she would have a little more time. Time for what, she didn't know.

She moved to the bed and lay down, twisting her hands into

the coverlet. Ever since they'd kissed by the river she'd lost all ability to centre herself. Even their sparring exercise had become an excuse for her to touch him.

In the empty spaces between their conversations, she would imagine Ryam staying by her side. They would never reach the capital. But it was nothing but a childish fantasy. She had a duty to her family and to the empire.

She could have argued with Ryam and convinced him not to go just yet. She could have reached up and kissed him as she had been fantasising about the entire day. He might have just laughed at her if she had. Or he might have kissed her back, as he had done in the woods.

She took a deep breath and let it out. He was a wandering swordsman. She was a princess. What did she think they'd do? Cross swords and wander through the forest for ever? If he was determined to go, she wasn't going to stop him. This was best. She would never have to tell Ryam who she was.

But part of her wished she'd dared to tell him the truth. She wished that she didn't have to hold anything back. That they would never have to swear to anything, except what they truly wanted.

Chapter Nine

Ryam stood by as the servants loaded a trunk onto the litter in the grey of the morning. He winced at the imperial insignia carved on the front. Lady Ling was a symbol of the old regime. It was impossible nowadays to tell if the affiliation would help or hurt on the road to Changan.

Ailey held herself a distance away and watched the preparations impassively. He had worried she would attempt to flee again. Despite her talk of honour and duty, she harboured a defiant streak. But this morning, she had emerged from her rooms without complaint. She actually wasn't speaking to him at all.

The stableman hitched a single horse into the harness as Lady Ling emerged from the house wrapped in an opulent robe, every hair in place and her face painted to perfection. He went to speak to her and immediately caught his mistake when Ailey angled herself away from them, the stiff point of her shoulder speaking louder than any words.

The lady bestowed an almost sympathetic look on him. 'There is one trail that leads to the main road.'

'I'll stay with you until then.'

'It has been a long time since I've been in the city, but I still remember how things are done,' Lady Ling assured him.

The lady had survived the most treacherous period of the imperial court. She would have hidden contacts throughout the empire. She'd know who to bribe and coerce. Ailey would be fine. Yet he couldn't bring himself to go. Once he left, there was no way to find out what happened to her. He'd never know.

Lady Ling glanced towards the litter. In profile, her features were striking, a balance of perfect curves. As a man, he couldn't deny her beauty tapped into something primal. His response to her was immediate, devoid of any conscious thought. But it was only a ghost of what he felt whenever he thought of Ailey.

'Go and say farewell to her.' The courtesan read his thoughts perfectly. 'I remember what it was to be young.'

Ryam nodded, letting out a slow breath as he went to Ailey. She stood alone and silent, her back turned towards him. He knew she could hear the pad of his boots on the dirt trail. Her shoulders raised a fraction and her fingers curled almost imperceptibly by her side as he approached.

'Take care on your long journey,' she said in a brittle voice.

'Ailey, look at me.'

She turned to him. Her face and the clouded jade of her eyes filled his vision, and he decided then and there that Ailey in a faded tunic could outshine all the imperial consorts of the world.

'You know this is the right thing to do,' he said.

'No.' Her gaze would not waver. 'I don't know.'

One of the servants came running from the woods. He found Lady Ling and began firing off a rapid stream of Han Chinese. Ailey strained to listen, tensing.

The lady swung around. 'Governor Li Tao has sent an armed regiment through the forest. They will be here soon.'

'Son of a dog,' Ryam muttered.

'You are familiar with the name, then?' The lady looked

coolly from him to Ailey. She held up a hand when he started to explain.

'There is no time. Take the horse.'

'Take Ailey and go ahead,' he said. 'I can hold him back.'

'Nonsense.'

Her tone allowed no further argument. She commanded the servants to unhitch the steed. 'This humble woman is going to be away, devoting prayers at the local temple this morning. Hopefully, Governor Li's soldiers will not tear down the house when they search it.'

The courtesan turned in a flutter of silk, setting her servants in motion with a series of short commands. Beside him, Ailey had reached for her swords. Her jaw was set with grim determination.

'You should know,' Ling addressed him from the threshold. 'Next to Emperor Shen, Li Tao commands the most powerful army in the empire.' She cast a pointed look towards Ailey. 'And he is not known to be merciful.'

They rode together in the saddle with Ailey in front. Ryam held the reins. He veered them away from the river and into the thick of the forest, urging the horse into as much of a gallop as possible in the cluttered terrain. The impact of hooves sent her jostling against Ryam's chest, and she could feel the force of his heartbeat against her shoulder blades.

They said nothing. Conversation was a distraction and they needed every sense on alert.

She hugged her knees against the horse's sides and sank her weight down to stay seated. The dense brush whipped past. She searched through it for dark shapes that would indicate their pursuers had caught up with them.

'We need to stop,' she said finally.

The animal had borne their weight on his back for over half an hour and she noticed the slight droop of his head. Flecks of foam gathered at the bit in his mouth.

She didn't know if Ryam had heard her. He continued on without a word, but soon he slowed them down to a walk and directed them towards a grove of trees. Ailey dismounted first.

Ryam drew his sword the moment he planted his feet against the ground. 'Can't see a thing here. Maybe that means they can't see us,' he said beneath his breath. Sword in hand, he made a brief scan of the perimeter.

'Do you know where we are?'

He whipped around brusquely. 'In the middle of nowhere, Ailey.'

She was taken aback by the fierceness of his response. 'You're angry that we're still together.'

'I'm angry because I can't defeat them all if we're found.'

They only dared to speak in whispers. He stood before her, shoulders squared and feet wide. His chest rose and fell steadily and she could nearly smell the fever of battle churning within his blood.

'The soldiers will fan out to search this area,' she said. 'They wouldn't attack at once.'

His eyes widened with surprise at her declaration. He shouldn't have been so shocked. She was the daughter, the granddaughter and the sister of generals. The vastness of the forest was to their advantage, but it was their only advantage.

'We'll keep going north,' Ryam said. 'Towards Changan until we find the main road. We can't rest here long.'

She looked to their mount doubtfully. The horse bent his long neck to drink from a pool of water. This was no war horse. He would need to rest. She went to sit while Ryam remained standing, his muscles coiled and ready as he watched the trees. Neither one of them spoke.

Then it happened. The snap of a branch cut through the natural hum of the forest and they froze. The leaves rustled as something large shoved through the brush. Suddenly they were face to face with two of Li Tao's soldiers.

Ryam sprang into action. He cut the lead man down before the soldier could draw his sword. The second one shouted out and crashed back through the forest in retreat.

'Stay back.' Ryam started off in pursuit.

'No.'

She slid the butterfly swords from her boots, one in each hand. The steel nestled into her palms as her heart hammered out a frantic rhythm. She followed Ryam's massive form as he chased after the scout. There could be more of them. He could be outnumbered.

There were more. Five men scattered among the trees. They glanced from her to Ryam, then separated, two coming after her.

She forced her breathing steady to prepare herself for battle. Breath, mind, body. This was not the practice yard.

She faced the first attack with her swords centred. It wasn't a man she faced, but a series of targets: weak points, striking points. She found an opening and aimed for it, slashing up into the arm, cutting at the elbow to render it useless. She followed with a slash across the chest with the other blade. That target fell back and she sought out the next man coming at her from the side.

Among these branches, in the close space, her blades gave her an advantage over the long swords the men wielded. She sidestepped behind the cover of a tree trunk and let the attacker get close before slipping through his guard to bring her knee up into his groin, channelling her entire weight into the point of impact. He folded under the force. Upward stroke with the right blade, downward stroke with the left. Both swords always alive.

To her left Ryam disarmed his man, then sent him to the ground with his fist. He turned to the next one and swung his sword. The soldier blocked in time, but the force of the attack flung him against a tree with a thud.

'Stop them from alerting the others,' she cried.

She started after the remaining soldier. He was young, barely more than a boy. His hand shook as he groped for something in his belt. Before she could reach him he lifted the small object to his mouth and blew.

A shrill whistle pierced the air.

'We need to get out of here.' Ryam grabbed on to her arm and tugged her back.

The boy stared at Ryam, eyes wide in shock, before staggering off.

They ran back to the pool where the horse waited for them, ears perked straight. At any moment, Ailey expected a stampede of footsteps behind them. Li Tao could easily spare a hundred men to send after her if he wanted.

She gripped the hard leather of the saddle horn and hoisted herself up. Ryam climbed onto the mount behind her. His arm circled to grab hold of the reins and he dug his heels into the horse's side.

They tore away from the thicket in a full gallop. A low branch snapped across her arm. She ignored the sting and fisted her hands into the coarse mane as Ryam urged the horse faster, swerving through the trees. Ryam's hard body ground into her. The laboured pull of his breath dragged against her ear as she hung on for her life.

Their horse stumbled. With a grunt, the animal dug his hooves into the ground and struggled to right himself. The lurching motion nearly threw her from the saddle. Ryam grabbed on to her to keep her upright.

'God's teeth.'

He pulled them to a full stop and ushered her to dismount. Her boot jarred against the ground as she landed and pain spiked through her ankle. She ignored it.

'He's done,' Ryam said.

He swung from the saddle. She protested when he slapped the horse's flank and sent it off by itself.

'We need to keep moving,' he said. 'They're still too close.'

His fingers clamped over her arm like steel as he took them in the opposite direction. She'd never seen Ryam like this. His jaw tensed into a rigid line, rendering his face hard and expressionless. He stared ahead with single-minded focus.

She struggled to keep up with his long-legged stride, scrambling over moss-covered rock and uneven ground. Her ankle was beginning to throb, but Ryam forged on relentlessly. Gritting her teeth, she swallowed the pain and pushed herself until her body refused to go any further.

With a gasp, she fell back.

'I'm sorry.'

'What is it?' Ryam demanded.

She shook her head and clutched at her ankle with one hand. She hated this weakness.

'You're hurt.'

His expression remained hard as he moved to throw her arm over his shoulders to lift her. Without knowing why, she shoved him away, angry and exhausted.

'Go.'

With a low growl, Ryam pushed her hands aside and scooped her up anyway. He searched out a nearby ravine and started down the incline with her lifted in his arms. All the while, she wanted to rail at him that he was being stupid, that he was going to fall and break his neck. A swordsman couldn't let sentiment cloud his judgement.

'I can walk,' she choked out.

He wouldn't answer. His knee bumped against her as he walked down the loose bank of the ravine. His tunic was damp, soaked through with sweat as he tightened his hold. Her head pounded and she couldn't hear above the beat of her own heart. Nothing could be worse than this feeling of helplessness.

At the foot of the incline, he carried her towards an outcropping of rock and set her down in the enclosure. Straightening, he scanned the surroundings.

'This will have to do,' he said gruffly as he knelt down before her.

Her vision blurred as she blinked back hot tears. When she could see again, Ryam towered over her, staring at her with a mix of concern and anger.

'Why didn't you tell me?' he demanded.

She bit her lip, shaking her head. She reached for her boot, but his hands got there first. He pulled her foot free and she inhaled sharply, biting hard into her bottom lip.

'God's feet,' he muttered under his breath.

Her ankle was swollen to twice its size, the flesh tender and red. His blond hair fell over his eyes, hiding his face from her as he massaged his thumbs over her ankle. The gentle pressure of his hands stroked a warm, tingling sensation from her toes all the way up her spine.

They were in danger and all she could do was stare at his hands, marvelling at the rough texture, the careful gentleness.

'*Don't.*' She pulled away, wincing as pain snaked through the joint.

Startled by her withdrawal, Ryam let his hands drop to his sides.

Her words came out in a rush before she could stop them.

'I wasn't thinking.' A stinging, pinching sensation hovered at the bridge of her nose. 'I never think.'

'You think too much sometimes.'

She didn't even know what she was saying. All of her doubts poured from her at once. 'I didn't want you think I was weak and worthless. You never wanted to go to Changan.'

They were lost and outnumbered. All because he was too noble to leave her when he first found her. All because she had begged a stranger for help when she had no one else to turn to.

'Ailey, I'm not angry at you.'

'I'm a child,' she lamented. 'And spoiled. My brothers always say so. I made you come here.'

He let out a harsh breath. 'You are not a child. You fought off armed soldiers. You were—' the words caught in his throat '—you were magnificent.'

Everything that happened that day crashed over her in a wave: the fear that morning that she would never see him again, the fight with the soldiers, even her stupid jealousy over Lady Ling. Before she knew what was happening, she was leaning towards him.

Ryam stiffened as she pressed her lips to his. His mouth was warm and inviting. She only tasted him for a second before his hands jerked to her shoulders to hold her away. Undaunted, she grasped at the neck of his tunic while she kissed him, brushing over his lips again, searching, pleading. Slowly, his grip loosened. He yielded with a groan, sliding his tongue past her lips to feed on her desire.

She wrapped her arms around him, barely able to circle the broadness of his shoulders. A soft, aching sound rose from her throat as his fingers dug into the nape of her neck, tilting her to him, fitting their mouths together even more intimately. She clung to him, guided by nothing but the desperate beating of her heart and a sharp, sweet yearning deep within her.

His hands moved restlessly to grasp her hips, but then he tore himself away from her so abruptly she made a startled sound.

He gritted his teeth and turned away, his hands clenched into fists. His pulse skipped along his neck as he gulped in breath after ragged breath.

'You can't kiss me like that,' he growled. 'You can't look at me like that.'

Ailey was staring at him. Her fingers lifted to press against lips swollen with want and sensation.

Naked desire. He could see it in her eyes, smell it on her skin. She was flushed with it, overflowing. God, the silken taste of her. She didn't know how to hide her feelings and they clawed at him until the ache between his legs reached an acute peak.

'What do you want from me?' he demanded.

One moment she made him swear not to touch her and the next she was kissing him into madness. If she made a single move towards him, made a single sweet sound he'd take hold of her, lower her to the ground and make her his right now with the fierce throb of combat and their wild escape still in his veins.

Some part of her must have known it. That was why she stayed petrified, her only movement the rise and fall of her breasts as she struggled to breathe.

'Tell me what it is you want from me and it's yours,' he promised dangerously.

It was an unfair demand, almost cruel. She had no way to answer him, no experience to empower her. Not that his own experience gave him any more control. He wanted her so much his body strained towards her, hard, ready.

He straightened. His knees dug into the ground. She had driven him to the brink, stripped him bare. He wanted her not even for the pleasure of it, but for the raw and simple need of possessing her for the moment. For ever, if he could.

'So what is it to be?'

Her lips parted, flushed and full, unable to form words. 'I just want to get home,' she whispered after an interminable silence.

She looked into his eyes as she spoke. Her chin tilted to expose her neck, so vulnerable while she tried to appear so strong.

He swallowed slowly, nodding, each movement measured. 'I'll take you home, but you need to remember...' He moved close, as close as he dared. His voice lowered to a low rumble. 'Every man has his limits.'

He rocked back on his heels to settle on the ground. Across from him, Ailey sank against the ravine and pulled her injured ankle close, hugging her leg to her as she watched him with wide eyes. Even through her confusion, she still wasn't afraid of him. Was she so open with everyone, so quick to trust?

With a scowl, he laid his sword across his knees. Without any barriers between them, it was too easy to forget. That was why he'd tried to leave. Every time she was next to him, fearless and open-hearted and beautiful, he was reminded how much of a scoundrel he was. He was careless by nature, careless and unthinking. He couldn't allow himself to be careless with Ailey.

Chapter Ten

Ryam was sitting in the same position when she woke in the morning, sword across his knees, eyes open.

'Did you sleep at all?'

He shook his head and looked over his shoulder towards the edge of the ravine. The dark hollows beneath his eyes tore at her heart.

'Can you walk?' he asked.

She rotated her ankle, testing it. 'I think so.'

'We should keep moving.'

He helped her up and offered his arm for support. She refused. He offered to carry her and she most certainly refused. After several steps, she risked setting her weight onto her foot. The swelling had gone down and she could hobble along steadily.

They walked that way for hours, losing track of time in the shade. They would not, under any circumstances, say a thing about what had happened yesterday.

The longing for any small contact consumed her and she couldn't even look at him.

There was no sign of the soldiers, but she couldn't believe

Li Tao would give up so easily. They could be anywhere. Every flicker of movement in the green had her jumping.

If Li Tao found them, he would have Ryam executed. He could be rid of her as well. With circumstances as they were, he was within his rights. The moment she left her house in the wedding procession, she belonged to the warlord.

Ryam stared at the drag of her feet with exaggerated interest. 'If they find us, I'll hold them off while you run,' he taunted.

She rolled her eyes. 'Clever.'

He moved in casual strides alongside her, as if they were on a morning stroll through a garden. But she caught the way his hand drifted near the hilt of his sword. A true warrior could not tense up before a battle. Relaxed muscles moved quicker.

'Do you know any one-legged fighting styles?'

So much like her brothers, ever protective.

'I know what you're doing,' she said. 'But if they find us, you have to run.'

He didn't even dignify her suggestion with a response.

'Li Tao is not a forgiving man,' she insisted.

Ryam shrugged. 'And I am not an apologetic one.'

His worn, haggard appearance made him appear more dangerous. Unpredictable.

'According to Lady Ling, your intended is a powerful man. A man who can challenge the Emperor.'

'He's a traitor, worth no more than a dog.'

'What if he forces his claim? Your father won't be able to rescind his promise. Wouldn't that be some matter of honour?'

Her heart sank. Could Li Tao use his influence to bend the will of an Emperor?

Distracted, her foot slid against a rock. Immediately, Ryam was at her elbow to steady her and their eyes met. She should have spent the night in his arms, lying with him beneath the sky. It was her only chance to be with him, her one taste of freedom.

Ryam moved away first. 'We need to find the road,' he said, his expression hooded.

'We should be in imperial territory soon,' she said. 'We'll be safe once we reach the plain.'

She would be safe, but he would be in just as much danger. Ryam was risking his life to stay with her. It was easy to forget when he appeared so fearless all the time.

'When we reach Changan, you should go and see my father,' she insisted.

Ryam swiped a clump of vines aside with his blade. 'Your father will have my stones cut off.'

She blushed at his crude remark. 'I will speak to him on your behalf. He can resolve the misunderstanding over the smuggled weapons.'

Father had fought alongside the lost legion during the palace insurrection a year earlier. He would recognise Ryam as the honourable swordsman he was. She wanted to believe it so much, it hurt inside. She considered telling him who her father was, who she was.

'I only wish to repay my debt to you,' she said instead.

'Maybe I like having you in my debt.' He smiled at her, sending a tiny quiver to her stomach. 'It means we'll meet again.'

'Do you believe that? About debt and meeting again?' It was such a Han way of thinking.

'I don't.' He stopped and scanned the area before deciding to change direction. 'Some things are simply left undone.'

Undone? His words left her with a sudden loneliness. If they evaded Li Tao's men and escaped the forest, Changan would be within reach. She would return to her family. A week earlier she couldn't think of doing anything else, but now she was torn. Ryam had become so much more to her than the stranger she'd met at a dusty tavern.

If things could be different. If not for duty and responsibility. But without honour, she wouldn't be Shen Ai Li. She'd be nothing more than smoke and air.

They did find the road. A well-travelled one, judging from the stamp of footprints and the grooves cut deep from numerous wagon wheels. An hour passed before a wagon rolled into view, headed north. Ailey waved it down and hurried to speak to the driver while he held back. Once again, Ryam was forced into hiding.

To his surprise, she beckoned him over several minutes later.

'They will take us to the city,' she said.

The wagon master and his assistant looked him over sceptically. Before they could mount a protest, she spoke to them again, her tone sharp. The old man made a grunting noise and ushered them to the back with a wave of his gnarled hand.

'Did you use that tea-merchant story again?' he asked.

She made a face at him. 'I told him we'd help protect the wagon. Come.'

He circled his hands around her waist to lift her onto the wagon and then climbed up beside her. They pushed aside the sacks to make room as the wagon rumbled forwards. Raw wool, judging from the musky smell. At least it was going to be a cushioned ride.

'What exactly did you say to them?' He couldn't believe a couple of merchants would welcome strangers so easily, especially in these times.

'I have my ways,' she said with a mysterious tilt of her chin.

He frowned at her. In their travels everyone they met was exceedingly helpful until they tried to seize her and drag her away.

'We're safe now. Li Tao has no authority here.'

The wagon rolled steadily onwards as they made themselves comfortable among the sacks of wool. Ailey lay back, pulling an overstuffed sack beneath her head as a pillow. He sank down beside her. For the first time that day, he gave in to the exhaustion weighing down his limbs. He'd gone nearly two days without rest.

The trees thinned out and the ground flattened as they continued. He allowed his eyes to close. The shipment of wool was the most comfortable bed under heaven. Occasionally, the wagon jolted and he would wake briefly before falling back asleep. He thought he felt cool fingers brushing over his forehead, smoothing back his hair.

Ailey shifted beside him some time later and he finally opened his eyes. She was lying on her side, facing him. Twilight had descended upon them, casting her face in shadow. The wagon was still rolling along. Another day gone and Ailey was still safe. His oath not to touch her was still intact.

'Not much longer now,' she said softly.

'How is your family going to react when they learn you've run away?'

'Father will believe me. I have never lied to him.'

He detected the faint uncertainty in her tone. 'I've heard stories about what happens to daughters who defy their families.'

'Father is not like that.'

'As long as he never sees you with me.'

She fell silent. Women could be beaten for disobedience. An act that brought shame to her family could be punished by disowning or by death. He had witnessed hints of this honour culture reaching far out into the frontier.

What if it wasn't as simple as returning her home? 'If your family won't accept you—'

'They will.'

He eased off at the note of desperation in her voice. Perhaps he was only looking for excuses to keep from leaving. As much trouble as they'd encountered, she had a way of filling the days, making them seem like more than random moments strung together.

'Some say my father's sense of mercy is his weakness,' she said. 'As if ruthlessness was the only way to command respect.'

He studied her while she spoke, tracing the curve of her lips with his eyes. 'No matter how merciful he is, you never saw me. We never met.'

A look of pain crossed her face. 'I know.'

'This is for your own safety.'

'I know.' She sighed, and squeezed her eyes shut. 'Do you know that not two generations ago, my family was also considered of low class? Grandmother lived in a little town no one has ever heard of. My grandfather was a wandering swordsman, much like you, with barbarian blood.'

Anyone could see the world of difference between them, but Ailey would never admit it. She was endlessly kind.

'The merchant says we will arrive in two days,' she said.

'And you'll be safely home.'

She picked up her braid and toyed with the end of it, looking into the distance. 'I have never been away for so long. My family will be worried.'

'Why do you look sad, then?'

She shook her head slowly, then looked up at him with those captivating eyes, muted jade with flecks of copper. He knew exactly why she seemed so sullen. He let it feed his male ego for the moment, but he couldn't delude himself into believing this was anything more than infatuation.

'I wish that you were not going—' She stopped herself, chewing her lip fretfully. What he wouldn't give to press his mouth over hers.

'I wish that I wasn't leaving you alone after this,' she amended.

'I'm used to being on my own.'

He couldn't imagine how it would be in a couple of days when he couldn't look for her the moment he awoke.

'If you won't speak to Father, you should at least visit our home in Longyou,' she said wistfully.

The tail of her braid fell over her shoulder, the tip of it resting where the swell of her breasts would be if she didn't insist on keeping them wrapped. A shame to keep such beauty hidden.

God's nose. He had been able to keep thoughts of Ailey away for only five minutes.

'Where did you say you were from?' he asked.

'Our home was outside of Longyou, west of the Liupan Mountains.'

A prickly, nagging sensation hovered at the back of his mind. Those names sounded familiar.

'Longyou is near the western frontier.'

She seemed pleased he knew of it. 'My father was assigned the defence command at the border. Fifth Brother took over that post when the family moved to the capital.'

'By God, we were practically neighbours.'

It wasn't entirely true. A sizeable stretch of land separated the border defences and the mountain corridor of Gansu. But it explained her openness towards him. The people of the western regions were exposed to foreigners through trade.

'You must pass through on your way back to Yumen Guan,' she said, her face bright. 'Fifth Brother would be hospitable to you. He enjoys news of the inner empire. He had wanted so much to go with us to court, but duty demanded that he stay.'

'Your family must be quite influential in the court, then.'

She glanced away. It mattered little whether Ailey's father was a lowly soldier or the highest of generals. The gap between them was wider than the great desert.

'Our old home is beautiful,' she went on. 'Surrounded by the mountains. Enough open land to ride out for hours. I can write a letter to Fifth Brother.'

'Perhaps. I've stayed away for too long as it is,' he said, already knowing he was going to disappoint her on this. He didn't want any reminders of her once they went their separate ways.

Stretching out his hand, he took a strand of her hair and ran it through his fingers, stroking gently. He'd seen her hair unbound once. It had taken his breath away, dark and rich as it draped over her shoulders, framing her face.

'What was your life like before you came to the empire?' she asked. She turned onto her side so they were facing each other. 'I still don't know.'

He laughed at her persistence. 'Same thing I've always done. I wandered the countryside and tried to stay alive.'

A little wrinkle creased the bridge of her nose. 'You are being difficult,' she complained. 'You never told me what your father did. He must have been a master, like you.'

Ryam shook his head in denial. He was no master. Just a man lucky enough to have stayed alive. 'My father was a swordsman. He trained soldiers, helped men build armies.' When he wasn't drunk. When he wasn't picking fights and he still remembered who he was. 'When he died he left me this sword, the only thing he owned.'

He preferred not to think of the past since it was done and gone, but he felt the urge to indulge Ailey's curiosity for however long he still had her.

'I would fight in duels and wagers to earn coin and ale. I went wherever people didn't chase me away. I hired out my sword when I could. Then I met up with a man rumoured to be the bastard son of the king.'

'The man who married the Pretender.'

'You have to stop saying that. I am going to slip one day and address Princess Miya like that and she'll have me flogged.'

She smiled. 'You're afraid of her. Afraid of a woman.'

'Women are the only thing I fear.'

His answer amused her. Her hips wriggled as she settled in more comfortably, destroying his concentration.

'What happened when you met the prince?'

'Adrian. I was drinking, I don't remember why. And I challenged him to a fight, I don't remember why either.'

'And you defeated him.'

'Of course not. He somehow talked me into hand-to-hand combat.' He held out his hands in front of him. 'He wrestled me to the ground and beat me to a pulp. In my head, I put up a fierce battle, but I don't remember.'

Her lips parted in surprise. 'Someone bested you?'

He didn't like that look of admiration on her face when it was for another man. 'Adrian wasn't drinking and I didn't have my sword,' he protested.

She rolled onto her back, sinking into the wool as she laughed. There was no denying it, there was going to be a hole in his chest when she was gone. Had anything changed when he'd joined up with Adrian? He had others fighting alongside him for the first time in his life. They were a brotherhood bent on keeping each other alive. But nothing had chased away the sense of isolation until he'd found Ailey. Nothing had ever made him feel a sense of regret for what he didn't have.

'You're a good storyteller,' she said. 'Like Grandmother.'

'Your sword-wielding grandmother?'

She nodded, looking up at the sky. It was growing dark. The creaking of the wagon wheels measured out their distance on the road. He wanted to touch her, just to capture how she looked at that moment.

'What about your mother?' she asked.

He rolled onto his back, startled by the question as if someone had given him a blow to the gut. 'She had golden hair, blue eyes.' Did he actually remember, or was he making this up for Ailey?

'Was she pretty?' Ailey's voice sounded far away.

'Of course.'

'Was it an arranged marriage?'

Strange question. 'No, they fell in love.'

'You can fall in love in an arranged marriage, just the same,' she said stiffly.

Ailey must have gone off on some path of feminine logic to start asking these questions. He wasn't sure what to make of it, until she spoke again quietly.

'I never thought of it. Of love separate from duty until now.'

He exhaled slowly. Male pride, he reminded himself, nothing more. Except that that didn't explain the knots in his stomach.

She laid her forearm over her eyes. It was a good thing he was leaving before her heart started playing tricks on her.

His father had never recovered after the death of his mother. He'd wasted away searching for oblivion until he had finally found the sword fight that killed him. Ryam believed in love.

The all-encompassing kind that hooked into your soul and sucked it dry.

'You are going to be fine, Ailey.'

She nodded, eyes still hidden.

She was going back to her family where she'd be cared for and he would return to the lawless frontier of Yumen Guan where he belonged. Fortunately, it would happen before she made the mistake of falling for a scoundrel like him. The only thing he'd ever done that was worth a damn was leaving her alone.

A halo of warmth enveloped him and his eyelids dropped. Even if he could never bed her—though, by God, he wanted to—he wouldn't complain about having one or two or a hundred more days with Ailey.

They could just trade stories, if that's what she liked. And she could teach him how to fight with his eyes closed.

Chapter Eleven

The great gong in the central square of Changan sounded ten times. Hour of the Rooster, Ailey told him. The hour closest to the autumn dusk.

The wagon entered the city through the west gate, past a line of archers stationed high on the earthen walls. He sank behind the mountain of wool and pulled Ailey down beside him as they rolled by the first garrison of the Eagle Guard. The capital city was laid out in lanes with a guard station at each major intersection. He touched a hand to his sword, even though he knew it would do no good if they were caught.

The sprawl of the city assailed him once again, unlike anything else he'd encountered in all of his travels. Thousands upon thousands of people crowded on to the criss-cross of streets, a living sea of black hair and honey-toned skin. The myriad rumble of a hundred conversations clattered in his head.

The name meant perpetual peace. But peace was hard to come by in what must have been the largest city in the world. Not even the greatest stone fortresses of the West touched on the breadth and scale of the imperial capital. The buildings were packed tight together. Laughter rang from the upper floors of the taverns and restaurants.

Their progress slowed to a crawl. He could hear Ailey's soft breathing beside them as the wagon stalled at a bustling intersection. Even late in the afternoon, the lanes were clogged with pedestrians and pushcarts making their final rounds through the market. The hawking cries of the vendors rang out to announce final bargains before they packed up for the day. Fish, rice cakes, candles, medicines.

The last time he'd been here, Adrian had led them through the streets in a fury. The imperial palace at the north end was under siege and Adrian had been hell-bent on reaching Miya. The city seemed to have returned to its natural state of controlled chaos under Emperor Shen, though Ryam did notice a marked increase in the city guards on patrol. Shen had been one of the *jiedushi*, the only one with enough military power to maintain control of the empire after the death of the August Emperor.

The wagon bore a twisted path into the textile ward. With dusk upon them, the evening sentries began lighting lanterns at the main intersections. Activity in Changan continued late into the night.

The merchant Yin pulled the wagon to a stop before a storehouse just as another gong sounded. He started speaking rapidly to his assistant as they scrambled down onto the street.

'Close of market,' Ailey explained. 'They must get their goods inside the warehouse or they will be fined.'

Ryam transferred the sacks of wool down to the assistant. As he hefted the last one, he glanced up to search for Ailey. She had circled around and stood beside the team of horses. Yin was bowing to her, his long beard dipping low. The movement caught Ryam off guard. Before he had time to make anything of it, a line of imperial soldiers came marching from the other end of the square.

He called to her. 'Time to go.'

He jumped from the wagon and started for the nearest alley. It took him a moment to realise she wasn't following. Ailey remained out in the square, in plain sight. She glanced over her shoulder at the approaching troops.

'Third Elder Brother,' she murmured.

A man in full imperial armour led the line. The dragon insignia displayed on his breastplate differentiated him from the city patrols. He had the same lean build as Ailey and the same proud demeanour.

Ryam stopped at the edge of the shadows while Ailey stared at him, looking lost.

So this was it. She had returned to the safety of her family.

An invisible fist closed around his throat. 'You go on,' he urged.

The guards were close. Ailey's brother had sighted her and she stood caught between the two of them, her feet rooted to the ground. Ryam raised a hand in farewell. A pit of ice settled in his stomach.

She passed the tip of her tongue over her lips. 'Will you meet me here tomorrow morning?' she asked in a rush. 'Fifth hour.'

This was a bad idea. She needed to leave it like this. His presence was too difficult to explain.

He heard himself answering without thinking. 'Yes, of course.'

She backed away from him step by step, still watching him until her brother called out her name. Ryam took the opportunity to slip away.

Third Brother was surprised to see her. Her family had sent her off in her wedding sedan only weeks earlier. The first half of the marriage ceremony had been completed. She learned from Third Brother that Li Tao had not reported her disappearance to the capital. He probably planned to capture her and force her into silence as if nothing had happened.

'I need to speak to Father,' she insisted when her brother tried to demand why she had returned.

'Are you hurt? Why are you alone?'

'I am not harmed. Where is Father?'

He gave a frustrated sigh, falling into old habit. Someone

else would have to handle little Ai Li. Third Brother had always left the discipline to the older brothers and the tormenting to the younger ones.

He led her to the north end of the city and through the triple gates that led to the Daming palace. The great entrance hall stood before them, a palace within its own right. A sense of foreboding fell over Ailey as she went up the steps. No matter how long they lived there, she'd never feel as if she belonged. She was the true pretender, a false princess trying desperately to act the part and failing.

Mother stood waiting in the centre of the chamber. The hall had been cleared of its usual retinue of ministers as they waited for an audience with the Emperor. The dark brocade of Mother's robe stood out against the painting of the heavens on the wall, making her appear even more imposing. Ailey caught the familiar crease between Mother's shaped eyebrows.

'Heaven and earth!' The sharp line deepened. 'Where is your husband?'

She flinched. Mother's sharp tone always made her want to hide behind something. As she stumbled over a reply, the seriousness of what she had done started to sink in.

'Li Tao is not my husband…' she began.

With a gasp, Mother took hold of her arm and pulled her out to the stone courtyard and past the administrative halls towards the inner palace. The entourage of servants parted in their wake, bowing perfunctorily as they passed. Back in Longyou, Father commanded the military outpost while Mother managed the household. Wen Yi knew how to rule long before she became Empress.

'What has happened, Daughter? Did Governor Li send you away?'

'I need to speak to Father immediately.'

She tried to pull away, but her mother held on fast, surprisingly strong for a woman who barely reached Ailey's chin.

'He will return tomorrow. Come along.'

The attendants were tiptoeing behind them, trying not to look rabidly curious. She would never get used to the army of servants that hovered around them like a swarm of evening gnats.

She followed Mother through the central garden, past the lake to the private apartments tucked away at the far end of the palace. When they had moved from Longyou to the palace of the Tang Emperors, the opulence had failed to touch her. She felt trapped within its sections and compartments. The lavish gardens that so impressed outsiders, to her seemed like a life-less recreation of the wide world outside. It was filled with tiny trees cut into patterned shapes and ponds that had been dug up by hand.

But at least she was finally safe. She couldn't say she felt relieved being here. She longed for the openness of the mountains and wished that Mother wouldn't stare at her with such fire in her eyes.

In the Empress's residence, Mother banished the servants to unseen corners with several waves of her hand. She pulled the doors closed herself and then faced Ailey.

'Why would you leave your husband?'

Ailey took a breath. 'I had to.'

'Was he cruel?'

Mother's expression softened. She came to Ailey and cradled her face as if she were still a child. Her frown lines etched deeper than ever, but Ailey was grateful to see that her mother wasn't angry. Yet.

'Tell Mother what he did.' She dropped to the same hushed tone she had used when trying to explain the expectations of the wedding night to Ailey. 'Was he too rough?'

Ailey brushed her mother's hands away nervously. 'Nothing like that.'

Mother so rarely fussed over any of them and it made what she needed to say even harder.

'We never completed the marriage ceremony. There was no wedding night.'

Mother's eyes flashed black fire. 'How can that be? Did you run away with someone? Another man?'

'Your daughter would never do that!'

Even though Ailey spoke the truth, the blood drained from her face. Immediately, her thoughts flew to Ryam and the thrill of having him to herself for so long. She was certain Mother could read every torrid memory that played across her face.

'Daughter, what demon has possessed you? Governor Li will be affronted,' Mother was aghast. 'You have brought shame to our family.'

She couldn't bear it any more. 'I've never done anything to dishonour our name. I learned something about Ming Han's death.'

Mother's hand flew to her throat. 'I don't wish to speak of your brother.'

'One of Li Tao's servants came forward. Wu Jiang, who served under Father—'

Mother cut her off with a raised hand and Ailey had no choice but to bite her tongue. Wen Yi never shouted over anyone. She made sure she didn't have to.

'Li Tao is *jiedushi*,' Mother declared. 'He served the August Emperor faithfully. His armies protect the southern border and he is a war hero.'

Ailey felt herself shrinking as she was browbeaten by the litany of Li Tao's accomplishments. For a moment, a worm of doubt crept into her. Wu could have been out to cause trouble, playing on her innocence. The old loyalties seemed to shift back and forth in these times. She had no understanding of politics. She only had instinct to guide her.

Her voice trembled. 'I know that I'm right.'

Her mother drew herself upright, shoulders back and looking every bit the Empress she'd become. The Shen family was comprised of warriors. They rarely fought among themselves. When an impasse was reached, both sides knew it and it was time to reassess, to find another approach. But Mother was aristocracy. She expected to be obeyed without question.

'You are a princess now,' Mother said coldly. 'Change out of that shameful peasant clothing and put those swords away. What does a woman need with swords?'

'But Father needs to know.'

'You will indeed speak to your father when he returns tomorrow. And you will be ready to apologise to him on your knees for what you have done.'

There was no sleep that night. Over the last week, she had slept on grass and rocks and sacks of musty wool, all more comfortable than her gilded bed. She thought of Ryam, lost in the cluttered wards of the city. The last time she had seen him, he had stood so far away from her, hiding in the shadows. Very much the way he had appeared when they first met. His face showed no emotion, but there had been an unspoken longing in his eyes. She knew him well enough to see what lay beneath the stoic mask. In their short time together, she'd gathered all the tiny details she could about him and locked them away.

Her thoughts of him carried into her dreams. He would be waiting for her come morning. They could leave Chang-an together. Her words mattered when she was with him. He believed her when she spoke.

But then she would be disowned by her family. Her ancestors would turn their backs on her ghost when it was her time to join them.

She rose from bed before sunrise and waited patiently as her dressing attendants floated around her, tugging and draping and powdering. All fashionable ladies of court started each day with the same long process. Usually she tolerated it, having become familiar with the routine after a year in the palace, but today she was actually grateful at the effort her attendants put into her appearance.

They combed her hair and twisted it into an intricate knot, tucking in pins one after another to secure it. One of the girls held up a tray of hair ornaments and Ailey absently selected several ivory combs and a golden pin with a butterfly design inlaid with jade.

The other girl dabbed jasmine perfume onto her shoulders and down at the low neckline of the embroidered bodice of her undergarment. The swath of silk was designed to pull the

silhouette of her waist and bosom into one smooth, uninter-
rupted line, accentuating her figure while causing her curves
to flow together. It wasn't nearly as uncomfortable as the
binding she'd worn around her breasts for the last two weeks.
Maybe that was why she'd always seemed out of breath around
Ryam.

'A good day today, Princess?' the older girl asked, seeing
her smile.

They were sly. The palace girls thrived on gossip and no
doubt they had all heard of her bold escape from Li Tao. She
wouldn't be surprised if they were making wagers on whether
she'd be beaten or cast into exile. The thought dampened her
excitement over seeing Ryam again, but only for a moment.

The girl wrapped a turquoise-coloured top about her shoulders. The sleeves draped like a waterfall over her arms. She
turned this way and that, watching silk swish around her ankles.
She wanted Ryam to see her like this for their final meeting.
One of the elegant ladies that floated through the palace like
spring flowers in the breeze.

She left her chambers and made her way out of the palace
into the public area of the city, opening a parasol to shield her
from the morning sun. The oiled paper stretched over bamboo
spines gave her the illusion that she had some privacy when the
truth was she was never alone in Changan. Two palace guards
followed her the entire way. Coming and going as she pleased
was one of the freedoms she relinquished when Father became
Emperor.

Fifth hour, the hour of the Dragon, she'd told Ryam. But
she was early. The wide lanes of the West Market lay barren.
It was long before the market hour and the city hoarded its last
moments of sleep before the stamp of a million feet crowded
the shops.

She stood at the corner of the square, twisting the bamboo
handle of her parasol, the palms of her hands damp. Her brothers would tease her mercilessly if they could see her, dressing
this way for a man. Especially one that she would never see
again.

A tiny ache pierced her heart, the same ache that crept in every time she'd thought of Ryam during the night. She ran her tongue over her lips and then stopped herself, remembering that they'd been painted that morning.

He wouldn't forget, would he? They had parted so abruptly the night before. Perhaps the night guard had snatched him up or he'd fled the city. She scanned the square again for the third time in what must have been less than five minutes.

Still empty.

She waited for the clang of the morning gong.

Ryam hung back in the alley, one shoulder propped against the wall to watch for a moment longer. That was Ailey for sure, her owl-grey linen traded for a swirl of blue and pink. He would know the confident sway of her hips anywhere.

He had considered not coming that morning. The consequences of them being discovered would be worse for Ailey than for him. Then he decided he would go, but not show himself. Now that he was here, he knew he had to see her, if only to say a proper farewell.

Ailey hurried to him the moment he stepped out of hiding. He'd found her desirable enough to fill his fantasies for a lifetime in her formless tunic, but she appeared before him that morning with a full arsenal of feminine guile. He didn't know if he could withstand the onslaught.

As much as he wanted to pull away every layer of silk from her exquisite body, it was the way her face brightened when she saw him that shook him the most.

'You can't wield a sword in that dress,' he teased.

She blushed, the colour rising to the crest of her cheeks. God's breath, he liked that.

'Where did you get this?' She stood on her toes to tug at the brim of his wide conical hat. 'You look like a native.'

She smelled like heaven and the way she looked at him had his blood pumping hard, every inch of him alive. She didn't even have to touch him.

He clamped down on his rising desire. Ailey was back where

she belonged, a nobleman's daughter. This was the only way it could be.

She took a breath and held it. The moment hung in the air between them.

'This is for you,' she said finally, thrusting a purse heavy with coins at him.

'No, I can't.'

'There is a horse in the east market stable for you,' she said, ignoring his protest. 'The stableman won't ask any questions.'

The city was waking up around them, but he wouldn't have known if the entire imperial army swarmed into the market then. When she looked back he saw the proud tilt of her chin, the warrior strength he admired so much. It wasn't only with her when she fought alongside him. It was in her skin and in every breath she took.

'Be careful,' she said.

He nodded. 'I will.'

There was nothing left to say. All they could do was look, and not for long. She twirled her parasol one complete turn in her hands and glanced furtively to the guards in the corner. They stood their ground, but kept their attention focused on her. She turned back to him, her jaw set with decision.

She took a step closer. 'Thank you.'

With the parasol shielding her, she raised herself onto her toes. Ryam dug his nails into his palms, willing himself to remain still. She kissed him once, only touching him briefly with her lips. And then she was gone.

Chapter Twelve

Ryam was gone.

By now, he would have ridden beyond the gates and well on to the westward road. Ailey was left to pace an imaginary line between the painted columns outside Hanyuan Hall. The doors remained shut before her, the dragon carvings on them twisting in a serpentine dance. It would take two strong men to open them. Soon, she would have to face her father, the ruler of the Tang Empire.

He had been detained inside the audience hall for hours, ambushed by court ministers the moment he returned to the palace. It was too much to hope she would reach him before anyone else. As the Son of Heaven, he always had men fighting for an audience as they counselled and flattered.

With a creak of hinges, the iron doors finally opened. She stood aside as the ministers filed out, conferring in twos and threes. The colour of their robes denoted rank, but regardless of status, every man lowered his head respectfully as they passed her.

'Princess,' they greeted her, bowing.

She was not yet accustomed to men, especially elder statesmen, bowing to her. Today, she detected more than the perfunctory sign of deference. Conversations halted when the ministers passed by.

She forced herself to breathe as she walked past the guard sentry. Father stood by the throne at the far end of the hall as the last functionary departed. All her life, her family had served the empire under the dragon banner. Now Father wore the insignia as its ruler. His broad shoulders appeared as if they longed to escape from the confines of the imperial robe.

She bowed her head. 'Father, there is something your daughter must tell you.'

She wasn't even supposed to call him that any more. She had been coached a year ago on the special imperial forms of address to use for her parents, but they sounded too alien on her tongue.

'Governor Li is well respected,' he said sharply. 'He has many supporters in the empire.'

Father moved past her towards the annex and swept the beaded curtain aside with an impatient wave, ignoring the attendants who rushed to perform the menial task for him. She rushed after him. As he stepped up the dais to the writing desk, instinct told her it was not time to speak. She remained at the foot of the steps, her fingers twined nervously as he sat and picked up a stack of notices.

Streaks of grey threaded his beard and silver marked his hair. She wasn't certain of his age. Her own father. As a sixth child and a daughter no less, Father was a distant, towering figure of authority. She would stand by as he spoke to Mother or sometimes her brothers. It was rare that he would speak directly to her. Those times had grown ever scarcer since he had been named Emperor.

'Li Tao was honoured I considered him worthy of my daughter. Now I must explain why she thinks she is too good to be his wife.'

She doubted that honour had any part in it, but Father glared at her and she went numb with fear.

'Be careful of what you are about to say,' he warned.

Mother must have spoken to him. Ailey bent her head to

stare at the rug. Her parents were intimidating enough even before they became Emperor and Empress. When she glanced up he had picked up a brush and was writing in short, harsh strokes.

'Li Tao was responsible for Fourth Brother's death.'

The brush stopped. He held it suspended over the paper, knuckles tense. Father had never shed a tear for her brother. He had remained silent through the funeral rites, the unassailable Son of Heaven.

'That is a serious accusation,' he said. 'One you cannot make lightly.'

She felt like an ant staring up at a mountain in its path. She had made no plan of what to say other than to speak in earnest. Father was known for his keen instinct when it came to judging people. It was impossible that he could be blind to Li Tao's ambition.

'Wu Jiang told me. He served in the Dragon Guard—'

'I know who Wu Jiang is.' His expression remained hard.

Desperately, she tried to recall what Ryam had told her. 'And there was an illegal weapons shipment. A hidden shipment of swords to Chengdu sent through Yumen Guan.'

'How do you know about this?'

A ray of hope drew her forwards, but then she remembered this was the same shipment that had incriminated Ryam and his men. 'The weapons were hidden so they could be smuggled in. The envoys knew nothing about the cargo.'

Father set the calligraphy brush down slowly. 'I knew my daughter would not be so disobedient without reason.'

He beckoned her to him, a remarkably generous invitation. She stood at the corner of his desk. A fan of notices and proclamations lay before him, awaiting his attention.

'This last year has not been easy, Daughter.'

She sensed a restlessness in him as he sat confined behind the desk. The same restlessness had broiled within her since they had come to Changan. She yearned to be back in the mountains, where they weren't trapped by the rules of the imperial court.

'Li Tao is a practical man,' Father said. 'He knows the instability of our rule creates a dangerous climate. He is only acting out of caution by arming his troops.'

'You already knew.' She gripped the edge of the table to keep from shaking. Father was defending Li Tao despite his schemes.

'The stability of the empire is most important for everyone,' he said. 'Your wedding will assure Li Tao that we can work together for peace.'

'But what about Han? What about your son?'

'I know you and Ming Han were always close. His death caused us great sadness.'

Father wasn't listening. How could he speak so calmly after what she'd told him?

'But Li Tao was responsible for Han's death! He owes us a debt of blood.'

'You have never been in battle, Ai Li.' Father stood and took hold of her shoulders. The rare display of affection only made the pain in her chest sharper. 'Lives are lost. As men of war, we grieve, but ultimately no one person is to blame.'

Once she had fallen when playing with her brothers. The breath had been knocked from her, leaving her gasping and unable to move. She felt the same way now.

'Would you rather I send one of your brothers to meet him on the battlefield?' he asked, seeing her stricken expression. 'Should I weaken the empire further with civil war?'

'Father always told us, honour is everything.'

Her words echoed in the empty chamber. They were answered with deadening silence.

'How can your daughter marry a man that even Father doesn't trust?'

Deep lines showed around her father's mouth. 'It is a complicated matter, ruling an empire.'

Then maybe they were not meant to rule. Her father knew about Li Tao's treachery and would do nothing. She was being bartered away for the warlord's compliance. She heard Ming Han's spirit calling to her. Honour had been everything to him.

He had wanted so desperately to join their older brothers in service to the empire.

Ailey could barely form the words. 'One cannot buy loyalty.'

His eyes were flat and unyielding. 'I have sent word to Li Tao. Your mother and I will journey to the southern defence command to personally take you to your husband. The Shen family honours its commitments.'

A cry rang through her apartments, announcing the arrival of the Empress. Ailey ignored it and continued searching through her closets and drawers. She even rifled through the embroidered pillows in the sitting room, tossing them aside impatiently.

'Where are my swords?' Ailey demanded, mistaking her mother for a servant when she appeared at the door.

Mother looked on with measured patience. 'I had them placed in the armoury with the other weapons.'

'Those swords were forged specifically for the length of my arms. No one else would use them.'

'You sound like a child looking for a lost toy.'

Ailey scowled and dropped herself down onto the chaise. Mother sat down beside her.

'You smuggled your swords into the wedding sedan,' Mother said evenly. 'You intended to run away from your marriage from the beginning.'

Nothing could be further from the truth. Father's ascension to the throne had uprooted their family from Longyou and thrust them into the crowded imperial city. Then, before she could settle into this new home, she was betrothed to a stranger. The marriage traditions centred on her family giving her up, losing all claim to her as daughter. She had been sent away with trunks packed with newly made clothing. From that point forwards, she would have nothing but what her husband provided for her. She had needed something that belonged to her, some reminder of home.

'Your daughter would never bring shame upon our family,'

Ailey insisted, but she thought of Ryam. She wanted him so much it hurt inside.

She hadn't been thinking of her family honour when she was with him, but she had hidden that desire away. She had done what was expected of her.

Mother continued, not truly listening. 'Perhaps I did not do enough as a mother. After raising five sons, I overlooked what a daughter needed. You looked so scared on the day you left.'

'I was not scared.'

'You were pale. A bride is always nervous.'

Of course Ailey had been nervous. She was marrying a man known for being cold and merciless. Mother had sent her off with carefully worded, yet frustratingly vague instructions on what to expect in the marriage bed. Ailey shifted in her seat. This conversation was beginning to feel just as uncomfortable.

'A woman can never be assured until she meets her husband,' Mother counselled. 'I knew from the moment I saw your father that we would have a happy life together.'

'That was Mother's wedding night?'

'Of course.'

Ailey frowned. 'What if I look at my husband for the first time and know that he's wrong for me?'

Mother touched her hand gently. 'Your father and I would never make such a poor choice. You have always been a dutiful daughter.'

Ailey had believed that once. She had trusted her parents completely, no matter what they did. Now when she pictured bedrooms and wedding nights, all she could imagine was Ryam and the feel of his arms around her. Not this faceless man her parents wanted to give her to.

'Father knows I am right about Li Tao. I cannot marry his enemy.'

The familiar worry line appeared across her mother's forehead again. 'Li Tao and your father have always been rivals. That does not mean they are enemies.' Mother reached out to tuck a strand of Ailey's hair behind her ear. 'You went out to the city this morning,' she said, switching subjects. 'There was a man.'

Ailey looked away, unable to meet Mother's eyes. She had known the guards would report her.

'I have not told your father. Was it one of his soldiers? They are always stealing glances at you.'

Mother was being uncommonly gentle about this. It made the truth harder to deal with. Ryam's words echoed hollowly in her mind. *You never saw me. We never met.*

'He was a swordsman who rescued me. He brought me home safely.'

The hand on her shoulder tightened. 'You were alone with this stranger?'

Heat rose up Ailey's neck. Her mother could only be thinking one thing.

'He was an honourable man.'

Ryam had done everything in his power to protect her virtue. They only lost their heads those few times. Those heated, precious moments.

Mother grew pale. 'Have you dishonoured all of us? Did you give yourself to him?'

Only in her heart. She had come close, closer with every moment she had spent with him. Ailey bit into her lip to chase away the memory of Ryam's kiss. Burdened by shame, she hesitated too long before shaking her head.

'You never think, Daughter,' Mother wailed. 'You never think of consequences.'

'He saved my life. He was courageous and honest.'

And beautiful and kind. She couldn't find words to describe even the beginnings of what she felt. Ryam was gone and every moment took him further away.

Mother's voice shook. 'This will ruin you.'

Ruin her for who? For the traitor Li Tao? Some dark, reckless part of her wished she had given herself to Ryam to have the memory of it with her. Li Tao did not care a thing about her virtue. His only concern was power.

If Mother had known the moment she saw Father, then a week was enough for Ailey to understand what was in her heart. But it was all pointless now.

She took hold of Mother's hands and squeezed them tight. 'This stranger has nothing to do with what is happening here. I'll never see him again. I did not—give myself to him in the way you mean.' Her voice hitched and she forced herself to continue. 'Father knows Li Tao is building an army to wrest power away from the throne. How can I be his wife when he is plotting against our family?'

Mother twisted the rings on her fingers around, one after another. 'We all must make sacrifices for the sake of the empire. Your father needs Li Tao's support.'

Her mother would not look at her. Her lips trembled as she spoke and her hands shook so hard, she had to clasp them together. Ailey had never seen her shaken by anything.

'Mother, what do you mean by sacrifice?'

'Emperor, Empress. These titles do not change who we are. Loyalty is a trait of our bloodline. Without it we are nothing.'

'Tell me what is wrong.'

With a deep breath, Mother gathered her spirit around her like a shield. As her chin lifted with aristocratic grace, Ailey suddenly wondered whether her own strength came from the warrior side of the family after all.

'To solidify his claim on the throne, your father plans to summon Princess Miya and make her his Empress.'

Ailey shot to her feet. 'He can't do that.'

'This is politics, Daughter. He has a responsibility to stabilise the empire before it falls to ruin.'

This was senseless. She wouldn't listen to it. 'Mother has given him five sons. You have been his wife for more than thirty years.' Her voice rose and she didn't care who heard.

Mother tried to reach for her, tried to calm her down. 'He spoke with me this morning to explain. I will be known as Second Wife, but only in name. These titles do not matter.'

'Everything matters! You can't let this happen. If he does this, he is not my father.'

Ailey didn't expect the slap that came stinging across her cheek. She pressed her hand to her face. Mother stood before her without apology.

'If I can do this, you can do this. I am demanding your loyalty as a daughter.'

With that, her mother swept out of the room with her head held high, carrying herself with the grace of her title of Empress. For long moments, Ailey didn't know what to do. Her parents never struck her. She fought to hold back tears of anger: anger for her mother, anger at her mother. Eventually the burning in her face was replaced by shame. Not for what she had done, but for what her family was becoming.

She changed out of her silk dress, the last outfit Ryam had seen her in. Her vision blurred as she stormed to the practice yard and pulled the butterfly swords from the cabinet. She ran through training drills for hours until her arms were numb and her body weak, but exhaustion could not beat back the frustration.

Returning to her quarters, she tore through the maze of hallways, slamming one set of doors after another behind her, until she was finally locked away in her bedroom. A murmur of alarm rose from the servants outside, but she ignored them to sink to the floor.

She cried then, letting hot tears run unchecked down her face until her chest hurt and there was nothing left.

Never in her life had she thrown a tantrum. Perhaps she was not the same either. She was changing inside, like the rest of her family and the empire around them.

In their old home, Grandmother's room had been next to hers in the main house. In the palace, Ailey had to cross an expanse of gardens and courtyards to reach the mansion where her grandmother stayed with her own set of servants.

Sleep had not banished the gnawing, empty feeling inside her. Lifting the hem of her skirt from the morning dew, she quickened her pace through the grass. Grandmother's servants bowed as she came through the gates.

'The Empress Mother is in her garden.'

Grandmother knelt in the central courtyard, wearing a simple brown robe. Her wispy shoulders jutted sharply from beneath the dark cloth. Her high cheekbones were accentuated as she thinned with age. Her hair was knotted into a bun that had gone completely grey. She refused to dye it black or adorn herself with jewels and ornaments.

The plot of earth in front of Grandmother was divided into rows of leafy herbs and vines that climbed over the wooden trellises.

'The caterpillars are eating the pumpkin vines.' Grandmother picked at the broad leaves, clucking regretfully.

Ailey knelt beside her on the stone tile, folding her hands in her lap as if waiting for lessons. The last time she had seen Grandmother was at the start of the wedding processional. Grandmother led her to the sedan and Ailey had held on tight until the last moment.

'You have been crying, little Ai Li.'

Though her cheeks were dry, no amount of powder could hide the swollen circles under her eyes. She plucked wanly at a withered leaf. 'Do you know what has happened, *nǎinai*?'

'Yes, indeed. I hear there is a boy.'

Ailey looked up in surprise. 'Mother spoke to you?'

Her grandmother's eyes were bright with mischief. 'We are getting along much better since we have been trapped in this palace together.'

'I am not crying over this…boy.'

It was strange to think of Ryam as a boy. He was the only man she had been alone with aside from her family. As much as she ached for Ryam, what troubled her was something far more appalling.

'You have always spoken to me about loyalty.'

'Your grandfather sacrificed his life for loyalty. Loyalty is in your blood. It makes you Shen as much as your hands, your eyes and your face.'

'And loyalty means obedience.' Ailey's fingers curled tight in her lap.

Grandmother hesitated before answering. 'Yes, to a certain point.'

What she was about to say was so defiant, even Grandmother would disapprove, but she needed to say it out loud.

'Father should brand Li Tao as a traitor and march an army against him. He should avenge my brother.'

Grandmother said nothing. She merely waited. Patience, she would say when Ailey would attack too soon.

'I won't do it. I won't marry Li Tao and bear his children. Let me be disowned.'

Her voice broke as an unbearable tightness clamped around her chest. Disobedience to her family was the ultimate sin and a crime punishable by death. If she was allowed to live, she'd be untouchable. Even as a ghost, she'd be left to wander. The spirits of her ancestors would be blind to her.

'So dramatic.' Grandmother sighed. 'Just like her parents.'

'Father wants to marry the exiled princess for the sake of the throne,' she whispered. 'How can Mother allow that?'

At that moment, when the future looked as black as smoke, Grandmother smiled gently. There was sadness behind it. 'Honour is everything. Your father will remember, given time… or if he's given a push.'

She could tell Grandmother had a plan, but she wouldn't lay it out just yet. That wasn't her way.

'When I was young, a rich man wanted to make me his wife. Not first or second, but *third* wife.'

When Grandmother told a story, her face lit up and became so animated that everyone listened and knew exactly when to laugh or be sad. Ryam had the same ability. The tiniest of cracks splintered her heart.

'He had arms this big and had a belly out to here. I declared that I would only marry a man whose sword skill was greater than mine. Well, the rich man decided he didn't need a third wife after all and shunned me as a madwoman. Who wants to be publicly humiliated in a contest with his bride-to-be?'

She knew this story, but with each telling Grandmother nudged it in a different direction. For the first time since she and Ryam parted, Ailey found herself smiling.

'Other men insisted on trying. I was pretty then, a long time ago. Like you.' Grandmother stroked each one of Ailey's cheeks, her black eyes shining. 'But I defeated them all. When your grandfather came to town, he was so tall and serious. I liked how he looked at my face when he bowed to me before the duel. And so I let him win.' She chuckled and stood with much effort, unfolding her limbs carefully. 'I never told him. To his last breath, he thought he had beaten me.'

Ailey held on to Grandmother's arm and she noticed for the first time how much taller she stood than her *nǎinai*. Grandmother had fallen in love with a good man. They would have defied heaven and earth to be together, whereas Ailey had been betrothed to a murderer.

She fought back tears. 'Father wants to take me back to Li Tao tomorrow, but I can't stop thinking of Han.'

'Your father grieves for your brother in his own way.'

'He seems to have forgotten everything.'

Grandmother bowed her head for so long Ailey thought she was finally growing forgetful in her old age. Then she looked up, revealing a mischievous glint in her eye.

'How long has it been,' Grandmother began, 'since you visited your brother Huang in Longyou?'

'But they won't allow me to leave the palace after what I've done.'

Grandmother patted her hand and smiled. 'Little Ai Li, they call me Empress Mother here now.'

Unforgivably reckless. She had got that part from Grandmother for certain. They walked through the garden in slow, brittle steps.

'So, this boy of yours. One day you bring him to meet me. You tell him he has to defeat your grandmother if he wants a chance with you. If I like him, I will let him win.'

Chapter Thirteen

Ryam sat on the second floor of the tavern and poured rice wine from the ewer into a bowl. The young noblemen next to him were practically his best friends by now. They had been sitting for as long as he had, drinking, trading insults and occasionally singing. He lifted his wine in a toast and then downed it in one long swallow amidst a chorus of cheers.

The heated liquor spread through him, seeping into his blood. Rice wine didn't have the punch of the grain alcohol of the frontier, but it did the job. Let it come.

He'd made it one day away from Changan. One day of riding and thinking of Ailey, of her dark hair and long legs and how unattainable she had looked the last time he'd seen her. During the day, he found himself thinking of the serious expression she would adopt when they spoke. At night by the roadside, he dreamt about holding her soft breasts in his hands and instead of pulling away and begging for him to stop, she would beg him to continue.

The next morning, he decided the only cure was to get into a drunken stupor worse than what the memory of Ailey did to him. It was the best idea he'd ever had.

Tired of skulking around in alleys and back roads, he'd gone straight to the tavern after getting into town. The coloured banners flying from the second floor indicated there was a lot of alcohol being poured there and he was ready for any sort of trouble they could provide. He made sure his sword was visible as he strode in and threw the purse Ailey had given him onto a table. But there was no fight at all. The proprietor of the drinking house had no problems accepting his money. The man gladly poured him bowl after bowl of rice wine and slid savoury dishes in front of him.

When the last coin had been wiled away, maybe Ryam would be ready to take the next step that would drag him away from her. He grabbed the handle of the ewer and tipped it over, shaking it. Empty. His companions at the next table groaned sympathetically at his plight.

He motioned to the server. *'Jiŭ, lǎo jiā!'*

That usually got him more. His Han Chinese was improving by the hour. Blinking, he glanced over the balcony as he waited for his next drink. Was it morning already?

A lone woman dressed in blue led a horse down the street. Something in her walk made him think of Ailey. He followed her with his gaze until she disappeared at the end of the road.

Ailey and again, Ailey. He scrubbed his knuckles over his eyes. Was he cursed to see her in every woman he encountered?

Yesterday, two ladies of the evening had approached him after several hours of drinking. He was drunk enough that it was time to get into a fight or take pleasure in a woman. He had gone so far as to pay for a room downstairs, but the girl had reminded him too much of Ailey with the inky blackness of her hair set against smooth ivory skin. He had paid the girl without availing himself of her services and then dragged himself back upstairs to drink more.

Being around Ailey had calmed him, given him purpose. She had needed him. He would have thought that being needed was the last thing he wanted, but it had meant something. The moment she left, a restlessness had filled the void. It had always been there, whether he was in the western lands of his birth or the desert frontier. The only time he'd felt at home was when he was lost, exploring the lakes and rivers of the empire with Ailey beside him.

The clap of the ewer on the table awakened him from his reverie. The server bowed once before retreating. Ryam poured and drank.

The slide of alcohol down his throat no longer burned. The storm of it was abating and soon he would be left with a few moments of calm. He knew the pattern of the drink, had practised it as diligently as Ailey practised her sword forms.

Ailey always spoke of family traditions. This was how his father had done it, he thought ironically. They had wandered from the moment his father had lost the love of his life. Ryam couldn't even remember what his mother looked like. His only memory was that his father had worshipped her and blamed himself when she had died. Without her, his father had searched for one aimless fight after another until he found the one that killed him.

An honourable death, it wasn't.

When he drank again, the wine coated his tongue bitterly, like camphor and ash. He washed it down with more.

What was this? He was acting like a youth of fifteen, obsessed with a girl he had put on a pedestal because he'd decided to be noble enough not to bed her. As if keeping his manhood in his breeches deserved commendation. That was the pearl of wisdom this moment of irrational, drunken logic bestowed upon him.

He'd wanted Ailey more than he'd allowed himself to want anyone, or anything. And she had told him within days of meeting him that she wasn't for him, speaking of honour and loyalty in a way that he could never understand.

Two days without a woman he barely knew and here he was. Wine or women, it was always that way with him. Old habit, that was all. Ailey meant nothing. He laughed at himself, the sound biting into the lull of silence.

Heads turned in alarm at the table next to him.

'A woman,' he explained.

His cronies nodded their heads solemnly and went back to their cups.

Ailey accompanied her grandmother to the Imperial Park outside the north gates. Grandmother smoothed back her hair before handing her a parcel with money and the names of men who would help her on the journey to Longyou.

'I will tell them you are sulking in my palace,' she assured her.

Ailey was going home, her true home. Not the imperial palace in Changan where her family struggled to fill an empty space left by the Tang rulers before them. She would convince Fifth Brother to help her. Out of all of her brothers, he had always loved her most. He would at least try to understand why she couldn't go to Li Tao.

Grandmother was convinced she could make Father see reason. He was her son after all. If that didn't work, Ailey didn't know what she would do, but she couldn't stay and watch her family dissolve into something she no longer recognised. Ailey rode through the night, taking no one with her. No one should sacrifice themselves for her impulsiveness. When her father realised she was no longer in Grandmother's mansion, he would send soldiers to hunt her down. No matter what the punishment, it could be no worse than the betrayal Mother had spoken of.

By the time she reached the first town, her joints ached from riding and her muscles were spent. The only sleep she'd had was a stolen hour of rest by the roadside.

The town had no wall around it. Its function was primarily to support travellers to and from the capital. Several establishments lined a cluster of dusty lanes. In the mistiness of early morning, the streets stood empty and the buildings silent. Better for her. She could leave without being seen by too many people. She led her horse to the stable yard where a groomsman looked over her court dress briefly before bowing his head.

'My horse needs water and rest.' She slipped him several coins. 'Your immediate consideration will be appreciated.'

She couldn't afford to stay long. A couple of hours at most. Time enough to find less conspicuous clothing and collect supplies for the journey.

The groomsman ran an appreciative hand down the horse's neck. 'A fine animal, mistress. Long ears, strong legs.'

The steed was from the herd bred by her family for battle. He had been crossed with the sturdy nomadic breeds of the northern grasslands and was handling the gruelling journey better than she was.

'There was another horse like this one brought in a few days ago,' he said as he led the animal into the stable.

Her heart seized as she followed him inside to peer into the stalls. The onyx stallion she had given Ryam was stabled at the far end. The animal recognised her and lowered his head to nuzzle her hand.

'That one was brought in by the Turk.'

'The Turk?'

She had given the horse to Ryam as a gift and he had sold him already.

'Peculiar-looking man. Light-skinned, yellow-haired. He's been drinking in town for days.'

Ailey bit back a cry and left the stable yard to hurry to the main avenue. The drinking house stood at the centre of town marked by colourful banners hanging from the second floor. Raucous laughter came from above. The night-time crowd had not yet surrendered the battle.

She hesitated as she pushed through the red curtain over the doorway. Ryam would not go to such a place. It was an expensive establishment for distinguished customers. A night of food and drink there would cost a fortune. She was only getting her hopes up.

Pipe smoke and incense enveloped her the moment she swept the curtain aside. Through the haze, she could see the wooden stairway that wound up to the tavern floor. Male voices sounded from above, drunken and taunting.

Women did not enter a place like this unless they were courtesans or entertainers—or prostitutes. She thought of the swords she had strapped beneath her skirt. No need for them yet. Ryam had told her not to draw her weapon unless a fight was inevitable. There was probably nothing more than a couple of harmless drunks upstairs.

She had just started up the steps when he appeared from above, pausing at the corner of the stairwell. Her feet locked in place, rooted to the floor. If she moved at all, she would collapse. Ryam stood before her looking rough and tawny and perfect. He braced a hand against the wall as he stared at her.

The knot at his throat rose and fell. 'Ailey?'

That was all she needed to send her bounding up to him. The soreness in her limbs fled all at once and she threw herself into his arms. He held her, confusion obscuring his expression.

'They wanted me to marry Li Tao anyway.' A tear escaped down her cheek. 'I couldn't do it. I couldn't let him touch me.'

She was rambling and she hadn't even greeted him. He was so wonderfully solid and *there* that she had to lay her head against his chest and breathe in the comforting scent of leather and masculine skin. An edge of doubt crept into her mind when he said nothing. She raised her eyes and saw how his jaw had clenched. His breathing came in unsteady bursts.

'I thought we'd never see each other again,' she said faintly.

A shudder travelled down his body before his arms tightened around her. He kissed her then, his mouth hard and his hands pressing into her back. She let out a startled sound that transformed into a moan as his lips teased against the soft edges of her mouth. Rice wine and the tang of cloves seeped over her tongue and her vision blurred, every sense overwhelmed as she let him past her guard.

This was recklessness and she knew it. It was exactly what she wanted. It was better than the anger that had fed her through the night. Ryam held her and she wasn't alone any more.

His fingers laced through hers as they moved down the stairs. A few steps and she was back in his arms, melting into him as he kissed her until she was dizzy with pleasure. Her hands roamed over the ridges of his back, over his shoulders, into his hair, needing to touch every part of him all at once. He lifted his head and his eyes met hers in a shock still moment that penetrated deep, seizing her heart.

She didn't know how they made it down the steps. She could barely feel the floor beneath her feet as Ryam directed her through the corridor with its flickering lanterns. With an arm secured around her waist, he pushed open a door. As soon as she was inside, he pulled it shut.

'You're here,' he said, his voice thick and heavy in his throat.

He kissed her again as she hooked her arms around his neck. The press of his body anchored her against the door and she felt like she would never fall.

'You're here,' she echoed.

She traced the planes of his face, his throat. Each touch made him more real before her. His lips parted to kiss her fingertips as she explored him.

He slipped his hands into her hair. 'I don't want to say anything to you that I've ever said to another woman.'

His gaze held on to her as if she would disappear the moment he looked away. One by one, he tugged at her combs and pins, dropping them to the floor until the entire knot came loose.

'You don't need to say anything,' she whispered against his neck where the skin was hot and smooth and his musky scent surrounded her.

With the next kiss, he parted her lips and eased his tongue inside to savour her. He angled his hips to hers and the hard friction against the juncture of her thighs made her ache for more. He held her tight as her knees buckled and then lifted her to carry her to the bed.

Ryam reached for his sword belt. At the same time, she pulled at the ties of his vest. The only sound in the room was the ragged draw of his breath and a wild pounding in her head.

He worked the belt loose and dropped it to the floor. Then he was easing her back onto the mattress, one hand beneath her skirt.

'You still have these.' His laugh was low and thick as honey.

He freed her butterfly swords from the strap around her leg and let them slip to the floor. His hand wrapped around her bare thigh and she could feel the calloused ridges of his palm and the imprint of his fingers against her sensitive skin. Her breath caught as he inched higher, stroking a trail of heat. Her body went liquid and damp in welcome.

With exquisite care, he parted her legs and brushed his hand over her delicate sex, teasing her before easing his touch into her. She gasped, her entire body arching tight as his fingers stroked in a long, slow glide. Her hands twisted into his tunic and she dragged him to her, kissing him blindly. He returned the kiss, but his focus remained on the secret place where he touched her and touched her.

'Is this what you want?' His voice came out hoarse, roughened with desire. He found the tiny pearl of sensation, sending pleasure arching through her until she struggled for breath.

Her answer came out as a plea. 'Yes.'

She clutched at his arms, pulling him closer still. Heaven and earth, he was beautiful. Everything else she knew had become so twisted, she couldn't recognise them any more: her father, her mother, the gilded palace she'd never call her home.

This was what she wanted. This man and this moment. She'd never been more certain of anything in her life.

Ryam slipped his fingers into her silken, heated flesh, loving the look of anguish on Ailey's face as she shuddered against him. He could touch her like this for ever just to watch her response.

He lowered his mouth to her ear and couldn't resist scraping his teeth over the lobe. 'You know what is going to happen between us?'

Her lashes lifted, and he saw in her passion-clouded eyes the full realisation of where this would lead.

'Yes.'

He already had his answer in the way her hips strained towards him and the soft moan that escaped her lips, but he wanted the words to make it all the sweeter.

Parting her with his fingers, he stroked deep in slow circles. Ailey's nails bit into his arm as she cried out his name, her voice smoky with desire. There was nothing complicated about it. He finally had Ailey in his arms, vulnerable and open and willing. Soon she was going to be his and his alone. Very soon.

The thought of the hot, exquisite slide of his body into her made him unbearably hard. He ground himself against her to soothe the dull throb between his legs. Too many layers of clothing separated them.

With his face at the curve of her throat, he drank in the perfume of her skin. But then a different scent assailed him. Another woman had lain in this bed. Nothing had happened, but the trace of her lingered to spoil this moment. It was a dash of cold water, clearing his lust-riddled mind.

He lifted himself from her. 'I can't.'

'What's wrong?' she asked in alarm.

She tried to sit up, but found herself pinned by his weight. He removed his hand from her and lowered her skirt over her legs.

'We can't do this. Not here.'

'But…but I want you to.'

He knew he wasn't making sense to her. He was hardly making sense to himself. He let his forehead sink against hers and forced himself to remain as still as possible. She was liquid silver in his arms. Only an imbecile or a monk would not continue.

'I've been drinking,' he ground out, squeezing his eyes shut. If he looked at her, he'd come apart.

Desperately aroused, he took a deep breath and tried to regain some measure of control. She was a virgin and he was about to take her while he was drunk and in a bed tainted with another woman's perfume. Even he wasn't that much of an animal.

'I won't. Not now. Not in this place.'

Confused and hurt, she started to wriggle out from under him. His arms shot out to recapture her. She gasped and tumbled against him.

'Where are you going?' he asked slyly. He rolled her onto her back, pinning her snugly beneath his hips.

'I thought you said…'

Her voice trailed off as he pushed her skirt up to rest his hand once again against her thigh. Watching her reaction, he ran his fingers down to hook around the back of her knee.

'Stay there,' he said huskily.

He kissed her mouth briefly before lowering himself. Gently, he pulled the layers of silk away until there was nothing before him but warm feminine flesh. A tremor ran through her legs as he parted them. They were beautifully formed, strong and supple. He made a mental note to spend more time appreciating them when the situation was less urgent.

When he glanced up, Ailey's head was thrown back onto the pillow, eyes closed. Her lips fell open as she tensed with both fear and eagerness. Beautiful, vulnerable, completely his.

He bent and slid his tongue in a slow path over her slick folds.

'Heaven,' she gasped.

Her legs jerked in his grasp and he held them still, tightening his grip before caressing her again. He used his mouth to make her moan, to make her cry. Arousal rendered her shameless. Ailey arched her hips against his mouth while her fingers twisted in his hair, silently demanding.

The force of her need stunned him. She had never known this pleasure before and he wanted more than anything to be the one to give it to her.

Carefully, he ran the tip of one finger over her to part her. She made a startled little sound that sent anticipation rushing hot through him. Holding her open, he licked over the hard pearl of her sex, circling and torturing and loving.

Her entire body seized and the taste of her honey filled his mouth.

She cried out when she climaxed. He smiled at the intimate knowledge and held on to her, absorbing every shudder of surrender. When she finally sank into the mattress, he teased her sated flesh in one final, lazy stroke of his tongue before crawling back up to her. She blinked at him drowsily. Without a word, she circled her arms around him and fell asleep with her head tucked against his shoulder, holding him tight.

Ailey awoke to the gentle nudging of lips against her throat. Her weight pressed into the mattress, her body heavy and drugged with sleep. With a moan, she turned her face away and felt a sprinkling of kisses against her neck while a low chuckle vibrated against her ear.

That sound brought it all back in an instant. Ryam's mouth on her and the sweet, searing pleasure-pain that had taken hold of her body and lifted it high for an endless second before plunging her down. Desire heated her skin once again, but it was tainted with guilt. She'd been in the palace with her family the day before. This morning, she was waking up in a strange bed.

When she opened her eyes, Ryam was smiling down at her. Flecks of auburn and gold hid in the stubble that covered his chin. His hair was tousled and she remembered raking her fingers through it. She pushed her doubts aside.

His fingers combed absently through the dark spill around her shoulders, his touch soothing. 'I love your hair.'

What was she supposed to say? Were they lovers now? 'I—I didn't expect to find you here.'

His eyes sparked playfully. 'I must have been waiting for you.'

He kissed a trail down her cheek, then along the line of her jaw with exquisite tenderness. His stubble grazed against her skin, the rasp of it exciting her. She was floating in a warm bath, her skin tingling with a drowsy hum that filled the hollows of her spirit.

She blinked up at the ceiling as his lips found her ear. 'Ryam?'

He murmured something incoherent as his teeth scraped against her earlobe, sending a ripple down her spine.

It took a long moment to recover. 'Earlier, why did you not… why did we not…?'

Gradually, his smile faded. 'God's breath,' he muttered. He pushed himself up to sitting position, turning his back to her as he moved to the edge of the bed.

'What's wrong?'

He stared at the floor, the bed, then the walls, before mumbling an oath that might have been in her language. He ran his hand over his face. 'Ailey, what are you doing here?'

She was confused. Hadn't she told him already?

'My father insisted that I marry Li Tao, so I ran—'

He cut her off, his tone ragged. 'I need to get you out of this place. I was drunk…I was careless.'

The way he had touched her felt anything but careless. He was acting as if she hadn't just woken up in his arms.

'Are you still drunk now?'

He turned his head to look at her. His gaze dropped to the line of her silk bodice and his eyes sparked with desire. Her breasts swelled with the memory of his touch. An echoing ache of desire awakened within her.

His breathing quickened and she knew exactly what he was thinking. She remembered the wicked skill of his tongue and her insides went liquid and restless. The walls of the room shrank and her world narrowed down to the space between them and the wild beating of her heart. She'd moved into a forbidden, unknown place and she couldn't bring herself to feel any regret.

Ryam looked away from her and stood. For a moment she was lost, but he reached out to take her hand, reassuring her with the solid clasp of his fingers over hers. 'Come. You shouldn't be in a place like this.'

A slant of sunlight pierced through the tiny window and sent a new wave of panic through her.

'How long was I asleep?'

'A few hours.'

'We have to go. It's nearly midday and I wasn't supposed to stay here long.'

A dimple appeared on his chin as he frowned. How odd she had never noticed it before or how boyish it made him look. She forced herself to move, wriggling over to the side of the bed to reach for her swords. When she stood, Ryam was right beside her. He seemed to be trying to resist, but his hand brushed a lazy path down her back and came to rest on the curve of her hip. Possessive was the only word for it.

'Where are you going?' He still looked surprised that she was there.

Ailey didn't care. It was so good to be with Ryam again. She couldn't believe how good. Nothing could harm her while he was near. He had always been true to her. He would never betray her trust.

'I'm going home,' she said. 'To Longyou, in the mountains.'

'Then we'll go together.'

Once again, she needed him and, once again, Ryam was there. She wanted to throw herself into his arms again and squeeze tight to make sure she wasn't dreaming and he wouldn't slip away. But she didn't have time. Father would be sending his troops after her. Whatever had begun between them would have to wait.

Ailey was here. Somehow she was here with him and he wasn't going to ask any more questions. It felt right to be talking about the two of them together. He could conquer the world. He could slay dragons with his bare hands. First he had to get them out of this seedy place.

'Father will have found out that I am gone by now.' Ailey tried to pin her hair, gathering it up and shoving the combs into it. 'He wants to force me to marry. I won't do it even if he sends the entire imperial army against me.'

She fastened her hair into an uneven coil. Errant strands fell to tease against her neck and shoulders, making her look flustered and tempting.

Ryam paused in the midst of brushing back a wisp of black hair from her face. 'Your father can send the imperial army after you?'

There was something strange about how she'd spoken. Ailey didn't tend towards exaggeration.

She blinked at him, then pressed her lips together nervously. 'Our family name is not Chang,' she confessed. 'Our name is Shen. My father is Shen An Lu.'

'Shen An Lu is the Emperor of China,' he said, his tone flat.

'Yes, he is now.'

'A warrior family with five sons,' he muttered under his breath. 'I didn't know the Emperor had a daughter.'

'He does.'

He scrubbed his knuckles over his chin, back and forth, waiting for good sense to kick in. Maybe it was the rice liquor swimming in his blood, but he would have fought an entire army to keep her at that moment. So Ailey was the imperial princess of China. Her father would stop at nothing to get her back. If Ryam wasn't marked for death before, he certainly was now. Beheading would be considered too kind a punishment.

But the threat of death wasn't enough to get rid of him. Not when he'd found her again. He'd risked his life for much less.

'We need to go,' he agreed. 'Now.'

Chapter Fourteen

West of the central cities the land opened up to arching blue sky and untamed grassland as far as the eye could see. The road disintegrated into a trail of wheel ruts and tracks overtaken by weeds. The last time Ryam had been this way, he'd been riding alongside the cache of weapons, heading unknowingly into disaster.

Ailey stopped and dismounted to watch a herd of wild horses thundering across the plain. She had traded her court dress for riding clothes, but kept the turquoise robe as if unwilling to hide herself any longer. It draped down her back, the edge of it catching the breeze. She had pinned her hair up and the sunlight played over her face.

For days he'd ridden beside her. Their stolen morning remained fresh in his mind, never more than a meaningful glance away. Her body had been awakened, eager and hungry, and it called out to him. He could conjure the feel of her hips arching into him and a sweat would break out on the back of his neck. Desire was nothing new to him, but this feeling was.

He could see the question in her eyes when the day faded into night. She would crawl into his arms and they would fall asleep like that, day after day, curled together in exhaustion. That was enough for now.

'Our home lies in the valley before that ridge.' Her finger followed the sloping grey line at the horizon. 'Two, maybe three days from here.'

He lowered himself from the saddle onto the packed dirt of the road. Ailey gripped her reins loosely with one hand, dwarfed beside the chestnut steed. Her gaze set fiercely on to the point in the distance. She led the horse along with her hand on the bridle,

'Fifth Brother heads the defence command at Longyou. We were always close. He will understand why I had to leave.'

'Your father will eventually find you there.'

'Then I'll keep on going.'

He was the one who always went along, never asking the how or why of things. It was how his party had been attacked and caught unaware by imperial patrols. He didn't know if he liked that attitude on Ailey. Everything with her held weight and purpose. It wasn't like her to be so careless, especially with something as precious as her honour.

There was something different about her. A restless energy simmered beneath her calm demeanour. It was anger, he realised. The slow, quiet kind. She had lost her sheen of innocence to replace it with defiant purpose.

'You're the imperial princess,' he said. 'They will never stop looking for you.'

'I will not be used as a bribe. And I'm not really a princess. My father was a different man before he was made Emperor.'

She narrowed her eyes as she looked towards the horizon. He didn't know how to deal with this side of her. Ailey seemed suddenly willing to turn her back on everything she held dear. Something had happened in Changan between Ailey and her family. Whatever her reasons, it couldn't be purely for him.

At the first sight of home, Ailey breathed in the crispness of mountain air and her heart opened and lifted. The orange light of dusk filtered through the peaks to fall across the grey-slate tile of the rooftops. Their family banner flew from the mast, dragon-green edged with yellow. She had always thought her home a humbling place. The height of the mountains stretching above reminded her that she was in the smallest corner of the world. But it was her corner.

'We are here,' she said simply.

Ryam pulled his mount in front of her, looking tall and confident in the saddle. 'Look at you. You're glowing.'

The imperial palace would never welcome her the same way, with the curve of the mountains taking her in their embrace.

She pointed her horse towards the mansion across the valley. 'I'll race you to it.'

Ryam's mouth lifted slyly. 'What do I get if I win?'

A smile lit his eyes that sent ribbons of delight through her. She dug in her heels and the horse surged forwards. Head lowered, Ailey leaned into the rush of air and the rhythm of hooves pounding into the grass. Ryam appeared beside her, his blond hair whipped back by the wind, the dark head of his stallion nudging ahead of hers by inches. She dug her heels in harder, gripping the saddle with her thighs, and lost herself in the freedom and thunder of the run, each beat bringing her closer to home.

Ryam reached the grounds moments before her and dismounted, swinging one leg over the saddle and landing with confidence. He took the reins from her to help her down. She ended up in his arms as her feet touched earth.

It had been like this for the last several days, light touches against her shoulder, holding her arm, taking her hand when he didn't need to. Each touch pulled her awareness back to him, but there had been nothing to match the delicious passion he had shown her in the tiny room of the drinking house.

There were times when she wondered if Ryam remembered what had happened between them. He had confessed that he was drunk that morning, after all. But then he would catch her eye, his gaze smouldering and dangerous, and she knew without a doubt he remembered every detail.

'What would your family think?' He pulled her closer inch by inch. 'Finding you out here in the arms of a barbarian?'

His voice slid over her, low and sensual, almost a challenge. They would think she'd gone mad. She raised herself onto her toes and he slid his arm across her back. Her heart thudded as she pressed close, feeling every angle and contour of his body.

'I meant everything I said to you in the drinking house,' she replied.

Her arms wound around his neck. His skin was heated and damp. The bronze skin at the hollow of his throat glistened with a sheen of sweat.

'I know.'

'I mean it still.'

His eyes turned turbulent as he held her securely against him. He lifted one hand to the nape of her neck, his fingertips twining gently into her hair. She loved how he always looked at her so intensely before he kissed her. He would hold her, seeing her and tasting her all at once. It was the height of boldness, letting him embrace her out in the open. His presence beside her felt more real now that they were in Longyou, in this place that was so much a part of her.

He had just fitted his mouth to hers when a crowd of footsteps marched towards them. She released him immediately, but Ryam let his hands linger, curving unhurriedly down her back before letting her go. His rueful smile sent her heart racing, as if the only thing worrying him was that they had been interrupted.

They were shielded by the horses from the approaching guard patrol. 'Shen Ai Li is here,' she called out in answer to the warning shout.

She stepped out into view of ten armoured soldiers who were all reaching for their swords.

'Lady Shen.' The captain stared at her in surprise. He signalled to the others to stand down.

'Where is my brother?' she asked.

The captain's gaze darted from Ryam back to her. 'The commander is out on patrol at the border.'

'Then I will wait for his return.'

The captain bowed formally and gestured for his men to lead the horses to the stables. He glanced once more at Ryam, but said nothing. Her father's soldiers made a point of treating her with a detached air of deference, probably under orders. These men would not dare to question why she was here. She was the youngest daughter of the household and fell under the rule of Grandmother and Mother.

Ryam watched the men go. If he felt any apprehension, he hid it well. His thumb was hooked casually into his belt near his sword. He scanned the training fields and the cluster of barracks beyond the main house.

'How many men are garrisoned here?'

'A hundred. There are nearly a thousand more stationed along to the western border. Come, I'll show you the house.'

He shook his head as he followed her. 'I don't have a shred of good sense, do I?'

At the front entrance, a pair of servants dressed in dark wool jackets came out to light the lanterns for the evening. They greeted her with muted surprise and then continued with their duties. She led Ryam up the steps into the main room while the servants kept their backs conspicuously turned.

The house looked the same as when she had left. The hall lay vacant and solemn now that most of the household had deserted it for Changan. Only Fifth Brother stayed in Longyou with the border command.

Their ageing housekeeper came out to greet her, shuffling in her slippers. 'Little Ai Li has come to visit us. So kind of her to remember Amah now that she is a married woman.'

She had known Amah all her life. The dear woman was older than Grandmother, too old to make the journey to Changan. With Amah's failing eyesight, Ailey was convinced she navigated the rooms by memory and by touch since she had taken care of the household for so long.

Amah reached out with thinning fingers to pat Ailey's hand and then squinted up at Ryam. 'Your husband is very tall.'

'Amah.' Ryam greeted her with a polite bow, his inflection nearly perfect.

The old woman craned her neck at him, like a bird sensing a disturbance in the air. She leaned close to Ailey, but didn't whisper as quietly as she thought. 'He has a strange look about him. He might be mistaken for a Mongolian.'

Ailey laughed and hooked her arm around Amah's shoulders affectionately. 'Amah, can you prepare my room for me? And put our honoured guest in Third Elder Brother's room.'

Amah doddered away to do her duties, calling out in a shrill voice to the servants at the other end of the house. At her age, the others were expected to come to her.

Ryam was grinning at her. Her chest welled with happiness and relief to be back at home, no longer running.

'She thinks you look Mongolian.'

'I know.'

'How much of the Han language do you understand?' she asked.

'A little here and there. We barbarians have been out here for over six years. We're not completely unteachable.' He turned to look about the chamber. 'So this is where you grew up.'

'Here, come to the map room.'

His fingers closed securely around hers as she took his hand. Finally, she was able to let go of her weariness and her anxiety over her father. Li Tao and the hundred other things that didn't make any sense were swept away as she led Ryam down the familiar corridors. She would work them out later. For the moment, she was home and she was safe.

The mansion at Longyou was as still as a mausoleum, the servants scarce and the rooms empty. Ailey led him from room to room as she chattered about how Fifth Brother made her paper cranes and the older brothers tormented her.

'Ming Han was the worst.' Her brightness flickered for a

second. 'He would pick me up and spin me around until I felt sick.'

'No wonder you had to learn how to fight back,' he said lightly, taking her hand to urge her to continue with the grand tour. He hated the look of sadness on her face. It took her to a place he couldn't reach.

'Well, everyone, no matter how fierce of a warrior, was deathly afraid of Mother,' she went on. 'Except for Grandmother, of course.'

'Of course.'

Ailey blossomed as she breezed through the house. One moment, he would be content to listen to her. Then, without warning, the need to hold her would overpower him. As if touching her would allow him to absorb the energy that vibrated through her.

She pulled him along. 'The map room is where Father would meet with his captains.'

In this corner of the house, the rooms were separated by silk screens framed with lacquered wood. She lit the lanterns in the chamber, revealing a rectangular hall with several chairs and tables laid out in the centre. A map of the empire spanned one entire wall.

He stood beside her, looking up at the black and red lines marked with spidery characters. The Chinese empire stretched through the continent, reaching from the ocean into the desert.

'This is Changan. These lines mark the different defence commands. The flags show where our soldiers are stationed.'

Ailey stretched out her arms to point out the different areas to him. He began to see where she had come from, raised in a guarded mansion as the descendant of exalted generals and warriors.

'The command at Longyou has long been a target of barbarian raids and attacks from foreign kingdoms since we are so close to the western frontier,' she explained. 'One of the most important defence points.'

'That was one of the reasons the Emperor allowed us to stay at the Jade Gate. Barbarians fighting barbarians.'

His mismatched legion had been stationed in the corridor by the Emperor's grace. The empire had pulled back its military outposts from Gansu, but imperial rule continued to cast a shadow over the region. His ill-fated mission had likely strained the tenuous truce to the breaking point. And then he'd stolen the Emperor's daughter. Although Ailey had run away on her own, a father would never see it that way.

'Where is Yumen Guan?' she asked.

He tapped a spot at the far left of the map. 'This is the Gansu corridor. The fortress is situated in this pass.'

She looked at the spot for a long time. 'That is where you will go from here?'

'Eventually.'

What else could he tell her? He needed to return to the corridor. He owed Adrian that much.

'It looks far.'

'Less than a week, if you know the way through the mountains.'

Just like that, she grew quiet, the light in her eyes extinguished. She stiffened when he rested his hand against the small of her back. Taking a breath, she tried to continue, speaking rapidly into the gap of silence between them.

'The last year has been an uncertain time for my family. The August Emperor passed away and there were questions about who would rule next. He had no sons to carry on the line.'

'I remember.'

The August Emperor had sought an unlikely alliance with their barbarian army, mistaking them for a more powerful force than they were. Adrian had been summoned to the capital just as those events began to unfold.

'Before the insurrection, my father was denounced as a traitor by the palace. He sent us into hiding, while he refused to abandon this post. Li Tao could have vouched for my father's honour, but he said nothing.' Her eyes sparked with anger.

'He must have been already plotting then, searching for his opportunity.'

'Li Tao was your father's rival?'

'They were both *jiedushi* until my father was made Emperor.'

A dull ache snaked through his chest. 'Your father chose someone for you who was his equal.'

'Li Tao is nothing like my father. He knows nothing about loyalty.' Her hands clenched as she looked from one edge of the map to the other. 'My father has always loved the empire. He would sacrifice anything for it.'

Ailey had grown up in this magnificent home surrounded by wealth and power and deserved someone who could provide the same. If he had any decency, he would leave her now.

But the look of trust in her eyes turned him into a needful creature. He'd suffer a lifetime in hell for whatever moments he could steal with her. He wasn't a strong enough man to refuse what she offered. The only way he could go was if she turned him away. And she would, when she realised he could give her nothing but heartache in return for all that he took.

Ryam concentrated on balancing the pair of sticks between his thumb and third finger. He could get through a meal without starving, but he'd never feel comfortable using these things.

'I swear you can only do this because of your years of sword training,' he remarked.

Ailey's eyes twinkled from across the dining table. 'This is the first time we've sat down to eat together.'

'There was that time at Lady Ling's when you ran off and left me in the clutches of that woman.'

She ran her fingers along the edge of her collar. He wanted to be doing the same, following the silk edge down to the neckline that stopped just shy of her breasts.

'I was so jealous of her,' she laughed.

'You're ten times prettier than Lady Ling.'

She glanced at him in surprise and there was nothing for him to do but snatch up a morsel from the nearest dish and stuff it into his mouth. Ailey scooped up rice daintily from her bowl. An irresistible little smile tugged at her lips.

What would it be like to end each day this way, sitting beside someone and sharing food and idle talk? Not with just anyone, but with Ailey. He clamped down on the feeling that swelled in his chest at that thought.

'Try this.'

Ailey darted through the dishes with her chopsticks and selected choice morsels into his bowl. 'Whatever you think, just tell Amah everything was delicious,' she instructed.

'It's good. Everything is very good.'

They ate in comfortable silence, enjoying the roof over their heads and a hot meal.

'What does Yumen Guan look like?' she asked when the dishes were nearly empty. 'Does it gleam with jade?'

He laughed. 'It's a great hunk of rock on the edge of the desert. Occasionally, caravans will cross through that part of the corridor on the northern trade route.'

She looked disappointed that the description wasn't as grand as the name. 'Who lives in the fortress?'

'Other than us, there's a tribe of mountain people, desert nomads. All wanderers without a home.'

'And the princess lives among them?'

Ailey's continued interest in Miya brought his defences up. Her military family might have a great interest in the Jade Gate pass.

'Miya and Adrian have been married for nearly a year,' he answered cautiously.

'I find it strange.'

'That a princess would marry a barbarian?'

'That she would willingly go into exile,' she countered. The thought of exile obviously saddened her.

He'd been away from the fortress for months. It was the return that plagued him. He would have to stand before Adrian and account for his failure. He buried the sobering thought as deep as he could. Much harder to do now that Yumen Guan loomed just beyond the mountains. He folded his hands together and tried to absorb the peace of the surroundings. Harmony, the Chinese called it. It eluded him.

This dining room and the feast they'd shared was more civilisation than he'd ever known. He had vague memories of his parents living in a cottage held together with mud and straw on the other side of the world. The tiny hovel had been cold most nights. He remembered running outside in the dirt during the day. The memories were a lifetime away.

'I want to show you one more thing,' she said after the servants came to clear the dishes.

They went outside to the central courtyard, a square of earth surrounded by sleeping quarters. A knotted tree stood in the corner, gnarled branches fanning out haplessly. She pulled him into a nook between the branches. Her fingers curved around his and her hair gleamed like black water in the dim light.

'Here.' She pressed his fingertips to the characters carved into the wood. 'This is how we keep score, one mark for every win.' Her face relaxed into happiness as she traced the characters.

'Which one is Ailey?'

She circled the trunk, knowing immediately where to go.

'This is me.' She tapped her spot triumphantly. 'Ai Li.'

He traced the two characters that represented her name and the wins marked beneath it. 'You have quite a few here.'

'If you were bigger and stronger, you had to fight two against one or with one arm tied behind your back. And sometimes I would fight—how would you say?—dirty.'

'That wasn't considered dishonourable?' he asked with a laugh.

'I was a girl.'

She smiled sweetly and he remembered the pain of getting kicked where it mattered. A wave of emptiness hit him as he brushed the scarred wood. This was what was important to Ailey. Her family and its memories. He had no such memories, no traditions in his past. Ailey belonged here, in her home. He belonged nowhere.

'Give me your dagger.' She found a blank spot on the wood.

She spoke his name in two distinct sounds to herself. 'The first sound is difficult,' she murmured, scratching the point of the blade back and forth in tiny strokes. She added one mark beneath the two new characters.

His fingers dug into the wood as he watched her. When she straightened, her head was right by his shoulder and he caught the scent of her hair. Soap and sandalwood. And that was all it took for his entire body to tense, growing hard with desire. He needed to touch her so much it burned away every other thought in his head.

Ailey looked up and the dagger nearly slipped from her fingers. Ryam had gone still, one hand braced against a branch, arm flexed. His pupils dilated as he took the weapon from her, returning it to his belt without breaking eye contact.

'Which one of these is your room?' His gaze circled the courtyard.

She drew in a shallow breath and pointed to her door.

'Show it to me.'

He beckoned to it with an irresistible tilt of his head. His easy smile belied the glint in his eyes.

Her heartbeat skipped like the wings of a hummingbird as they crossed the courtyard. As they neared the threshold of her room, he reached over her shoulder to push the door open. The commanding gesture took hold of her senses and her body no longer felt like her own. She floated outside of it.

Inside, she lit the oil lamp and glanced about her room as if seeing it for the first time. Most of her possessions had been moved to the imperial palace, but the room had never been lavishly adorned. She had set her butterfly swords on the stand on the wardrobe. Ryam let the door fall shut behind him and stepped past her to inspect the only decoration, a paper scroll brushed with four characters that hung from the far wall. The black strokes stood out boldly in the bare surroundings.

'Did you do this?'

She came to stand beside him, feeling lightheaded as if in a trance.

'A long time ago. My calligraphy was never any good. I'm too impatient. It shows in the strokes.'

He lifted his eyebrow sceptically and then turned his attention back to the scroll with a half-smile. She waited, afraid to look at him as she measured out the time with each breath she took. The span of his shoulders seemed to take up all of the space in her tiny room and she couldn't stop from babbling.

'We believe that a person's character shows in everything they do, every little action like the motion of your hand on a brush.'

'I've always liked that about you. The way you move.' His voice was deep, sliding along every meridian in her spine. 'Every little movement is uniquely yours.'

When she dared to turn, his eyes were so blue they seemed to shine with their own inner light. A blush rose from her neck until her face burned. She lifted her hand to her throat absently.

His gaze shifted to the door before returning to her face. 'Ask me to leave.'

Her throat went dry and the air grew heavy between them, vibrating with energy. She shook her head once. Still, he waited before reaching for her, cradling his palm against her cheek in a feverish caress.

She clutched at the front of his tunic and sank against him, closing her eyes when his mouth captured hers. It was always like this. Possessive, devastating. He knew how to make her melt into him, how to steal her breath and fold himself around her until she couldn't think of anything but him.

He didn't ask her. Not with words. He stroked her face with fingertips rough with callouses. With his other hand he pulled her hair free from its pins. As it fell, her entire being unravelled and opened to him.

He was backing her towards the bed, his tongue slipping in her mouth, his quick hands already freeing the silk from her shoulders as she held on to him.

His mouth released her only for a heartbeat before he was kissing the bare skin of her shoulder, her collarbone, her neck.

His fingers worked the sash around her waist loose and eased off the last layers of her robe. Silk whispered on silk as it fell away. He lowered her to the mattress and she pulled him down with her. She fumbled at his vest, then the edge of his tunic.

'Let me do it,' he said.

Raising himself up on to his knees, Ryam reached around her hands. The span of his chest blocked the light from her, casting him in shadow as he pulled the tunic free. She lifted herself and wrapped her arms around him, digging her hands into the sculpted muscle of his back.

It was beyond wonderful to have him like this, with no more boundaries, no more false promises to keep them apart.

He sank his weight on top of her and took her mouth again while reaching for the ribbons of her bodice undergarment. It was a sensuous struggle, both of them striving for the same end, but too blinded to find the quickest way there.

Her heart was beating so dangerously fast. She kissed his throat and the saltiness of his skin lingered on her lips. Their chaotic dance halted when he finally removed the diamond-shaped swath of cloth that covered her breasts.

He lifted himself and let the lamplight fall onto her skin, breathing hard as he raked his gaze over her. His hand curved a reverent path from her throat down the valley of her breasts.

'Beautiful,' he murmured.

She was completely bare to him, every inch of her offered to his eyes and his touch. It didn't matter what she had been taught all her life. This moment could not be meant for a stranger. It was meant for Ryam.

He slid back onto one knee at the edge of the bed and stood to remove his belt and trousers until he was all bronzed skin and hard muscle before her. Holding her breath, she let her eyes trail down his chest to the shadowed area below his hips.

Ryam watched as she took him in with her eyes, giving her the moment to see him fully before coming back to the bed. They stretched alongside each other and she was stricken with a moment of shyness, only a moment before he surrounded her again, his hands pulling her close, his mouth tasting her neck, her breasts, filling her with sensation until her head swirled.

Her hands roamed over him, aimless and unknowing. He responded by tilting his hips against her, pushing his jutting arousal against the softness of her inner thigh. She exhaled sharply and bit down on her lip in shock.

His mouth descended to her ear and he took the lobe into his mouth. The wet suction lanced tendrils of heat down her spine. Moaning, she threaded her fingers into the coarse strands of his hair, clutching the back of his head to hold him to her as her hips lifted. The length of him brushed against her, a liquid caress that had her crying out his name.

She didn't know what she wanted, but she wanted. So much that every part of her ached with it. Her hands clung on to his arms and her lips searched for him desperately even though he was right there, pressed tightly to her. He captured her mouth and lowered his hand between them.

The first stroke of his finger into her sent her arching from the bed, her breasts flush against the hard plane of his chest.

'*Yes.*'

She squeezed her eyes shut as he circled and teased the sensation from her. She tried to reach for him, caress him in the same way. Her fingers brushed his heavy length.

He broke from her mouth with a gasp. 'I need you now.'

Her voice was strange, hoarse. 'Yes, anything.'

His arm stole beneath her, lifting her to him. He buried his face against her neck, his jaw hard against her cheek.

'This is going to hurt,' he said through clenched teeth.

'You couldn't hurt me.'

She was floating, soaring, every inch of her alive with awareness and energy. All the while Ryam held on to her. She lifted her knees to cradle him and he groaned.

'I'll try—' He swallowed forcibly, reaching between them. She felt the blunt tip of him press against her. 'I'll try to be careful.'

He gathered her into the shelter of his arms, one hand tangling gently into her hair. Even in the haze of desire, with her senses laid open and raw, she had the impression of being cared for and protected. She hooked her arms around his shoulders just as he started to push into her.

The sensation of being stretched and filled took over her entire body. With a startled cry, she dug her nails into the back of his neck. The dull throb inside her grew nearly unbearable as he sank deeper.

He grew still, every muscle constricted as he held himself over her. 'Are you all right?'

She peered at him through her lashes, unable to focus. She was pinned, anchored by his weight as her flesh tightened around him. It was pain and not pain.

Finally she found his eyes. He watched her as he pushed past a point of resistance within her. Then he slid down endlessly until he was seated fully inside. His harsh breath escaped through parted lips. She shifted beneath him as her body adjusted. Her inner muscles stretched and moulded to him.

'God.' He shook his head, eyes closing as he laid his forehead against her shoulder. Then he murmured her name as he lifted himself and nudged deeply into her once again.

She gasped as another shock streaked through her, curling her toes. He repeated her name, his forehead damp against her skin as he curved a hand around her breast. Touch reflex, she thought dimly. They were learning each other's bodies, action and reaction. She wrapped her legs around him as he began to rock into her, angling himself in a slow glide against her core.

She found his mouth as the pleasure built in tingling spirals within her, radiating from where they were joined. His movements became harsh, his fingers digging into her where he held her, but all of it welcome, all of it wonderful. She bit into her lip as the sensation crested. Her awareness curled in on itself, narrowing in on Ryam and the rhythm of their bodies, the pulsing of her flesh around him.

He placed his fingers between them, his lips against her neck. His fingers circled, rubbing at the point of pleasure just above where they were joined. She writhed against him. It was too much and it was exactly what she needed. His thrusts shortened, became more powerful.

'Soon, Ailey,' he gritted out.

She shook her head, not understanding. Cry after cry escaped her lips, the pleasure sharpening to a honed point until the world went black and her body clenched tight, jagged euphoria crashing in wave after wave over her.

Ryam cried out as she climaxed around him. Taking hold of her hips, he pushed fully into her, seeking every last bit of sensation. Then with the tense cradle of his arms around her, his control shattered, his body racked with spasms as he spilled himself into her womb.

He held on to her afterwards, his body sated and heavy. Gradually she regained control of her breathing. It was the first reminder that she was still alive and here in this world.

'You were speaking in Chinese,' Ryam said.

'Hmm?'

Ailey was curled up on top of him, her hair tickling against his chin with an arm draped across his chest. Soft and pliant and his.

For the moment.

His hand tightened on her shoulder amidst his languid exploration of her back. He waited for serenity to descend upon him. Another sort of drunkenness that followed sex. But his mind churned with a tangle of thoughts. Most of them about having her again. That would keep the other thoughts at bay. The dangerous thoughts. The pointless ones.

Her fingers played along his ribcage. 'I don't know what I was saying.'

'I think I understood every word.'

Her nails had dug into his neck so hard he could still feel their imprint. He loved that he had done that to her, driven her to the brink and beyond.

'We call it the clouds and the rain.' Her voice was muffled against his chest and drifting.

'Poetic.'

'We probably have other words for it, but I don't know them.'

He probably did, the baser ones at least. He lifted his head to enjoy the sculpted beauty of her back: strong, agile and feminine all at once. It had been heaven to have her long legs wrapped around him, all trace of bashfulness gone. But now, Ailey had her face buried against his shoulder and refused to look at him.

God's toes. He looked to the flicker of the oil lamp. The orange light danced over the butterfly swords. He was in her home, in her *room*. Once the shock of this wore off, would she be torn apart by shame and regret?

He rolled her on the bed and turned so he could look at her.

'Are you hurt?'

His stomach lurched in the seconds it took her to answer.

'I'm happy.' She opened her eyes and looked at him shyly. 'I'm glad for this. I'm glad that it was you.'

Her tiger's eyes glowed in vibrant gold and green. A surge of possessiveness clawed at him, like talons around his heart. He had wild thoughts about taking her with him. They could keep on running, accountable to no one but each other. She'd never have to marry a man she didn't want.

But that was what his life had always been. Ailey needed more. She needed honour, tradition and family. Yet she'd chosen him. She'd given herself without reservation. The knowledge stunned him. It made him believe that he could be more.

He kissed her. It was the only way to stop thinking. He was never a thinking man anyway. He kissed her again, then released her lips to move his mouth over her breast, sliding his tongue over her nipple, sucking gently until he could feel her squirm beneath him.

He ran his hands over her satiny skin until her breath caught and she whispered his name, her breath fanning soft against his ear. He had never gone hard so quickly. When he entered her moments later, she closed around him and he moved within her, lifting and lowering as he waited for the dark pleasure to overcome him.

But it wouldn't. Not completely.

Through the slick heat and the unbelievable tightness gripping him, Ailey was there. When he shut his eyes, he saw her face.

Mine, he thought as the blood rushed through his skull. For as long as she would have him. To the ends of the earth if she needed him there.

He was a fool.

Chapter Fifteen

Ailey bowed to him from across the stone courtyard, swords in hand, her silhouette a perfect form in the distance. Resilient and strong, yet soft in all the right places. Any moment now, she would come rushing at him, out for blood with two sharp blades. Ryam couldn't wait.

His head wasn't right. It was filled with memories of waking up beside Ailey with her arms tangled around him. He raised his sword with a grin, feeling pretty damn near invincible.

He held back and waited, rolling his shoulders to let his muscles warm beneath the midday sun. Ailey watched his every move. From her look of grim determination, no one would have known that they were lovers and not sworn enemies.

'Should I tie one hand behind my back?' he taunted.

He detected the ghost of a smile before she was upon him, swords flashing as the clash of her blades rang through the courtyard. She deflected his strike, blocking edge on edge, but the force of it pushed her back.

'You seem a little slow today,' he mocked, breathing hard. 'Did something keep you up late last night?'

'You talk too much, barbarian.'

She sprang at him again, more than comfortable with

remaining the aggressor. Up close, she could take away his size advantage, jam his movements while she carved him to pieces. He appreciated the differences in their training. Her lightning style was truly akin to art, thoughtful and precise. Ailey didn't have the strength to go for the quick kill against a larger opponent, so her strategy was to disable. She aimed for weak spots, joints and tendons. He could see what they meant by death by a thousand cuts.

One of the blades broke through his guard. He evaded at the last moment as a sword whistled by his ear.

She lifted an eyebrow. 'Nothing to say?'

'You missed.'

Time to show her he wasn't without technique. Against her precision he had to tighten his attack to avoid leaving any opening. She frowned, her wrists straining to fend him off before she backed away.

'You were holding back when we first fought,' she accused.

He could almost hear her thoughts. *Dishonourable.*

His father hadn't been some ambling mercenary, a brute with a sword. Ryam had a couple of tricks to show off when he needed them. He smiled as Ailey wiped her brow with her arm. Her eyes narrowed as she analysed him. She was irresistible, radiant.

He circled and tried to figure out how to put a quick end to this fight so he could take her in his arms without getting his fingers sliced off.

'You giving up?' he asked.

'Never.'

Her feet flew lightly over the stone tile. She used both swords to twist his blade aside just enough to slip in close and drive towards his centre.

Not bad. The quickest line of attack was always the straight one, but it was risky.

He dodged and his arm shot out to hook around her back and pull her towards him. She gasped and dug her heels into the ground. Before he knew what was happening, her forehead smashed against his jaw. A snap like the breaking of a branch echoed in his skull.

'God's nose, woman—'

It was some consolation to see Ailey reeling from the blow while he blinked away the black spots clouding his vision. A wave of pain radiated from the point of impact.

'Scoundrel!' Ailey had a hand pressed to her temple. 'No one would do that in a real battle.'

He wasn't done swearing yet. He spat out another stream of curses.

'I told you I can fight dirty,' she said.

The tip of his tongue reached out to swipe at the corner of his mouth. He tasted blood. 'I fight dirty too,' he said, his tone low and dangerous.

Her eyes grew wide when he tossed his weapon aside. It clanged against the stone floor and he charged before she could recover her guard. With a shriek, Ailey tried to scramble away, only to be scooped up over his shoulders. He held on to the back of her knees as she dangled helplessly over him. She slapped at his backside with the flat of her blade.

'You are the worst bully ever!'

Laughter erupted from him, welling deep from within. He wanted to throw his head back and feel the wash of the sun over his face. This was how it felt to stand at the centre of the universe.

Ailey squirmed on top of him, demanding to be let down and threatening him with all sorts of death. He spun her around before setting her on to her feet. The front of his tunic brushed against her as he leaned in to gloat. 'I think I won.'

She pointed her chin at him defiantly. 'You didn't win.'

'You're not fighting back any more, which means I win. Where's my kiss?'

His arm stole around her waist. Playfully, she twisted her face away as he lowered his mouth.

'Never.'

'You struck me so ruthlessly and now you won't even kiss it better.'

He brushed his lips against her fingertips as a small consolation prize, and sensed the shiver that ran through her. She grew still then and for the next long seconds, they simply looked at one another, taking their fill.

'You're bleeding,' she said.

His hands lowered to settle on her hips as she touched the corner of his mouth gingerly. Then a sharp voice rang through the training yard.

'*Shen Ai Li.*'

Ailey fell away from him, startled. A man in padded armour stood in the portico of the main house. His hand gripped the hilt of the sword by his side and his black eyes glittered with a growing fury.

'Huang.'

She choked out her brother's name, but he didn't seem to hear. His eyes stabbed a line towards Ryam as he strode forwards. He scarcely resembled the brother she remembered. Huang had grown a moustache and beard and looked almost a stranger.

'What are you doing with this unwashed, no-name bastard? Have you forgotten who you are?'

Her face grew hot. It was fortunate Ryam couldn't understand the stream of insults her brother flung at him.

'You don't know anything about him.'

Ryam came up behind her, speaking her name gently. She tried to draw strength from his closeness as she positioned herself between the two of them.

'Where is your husband?' Fifth Brother demanded.

'I have no husband.'

Huang's expression hardened and suddenly, she saw how much he resembled Father. 'What have you done, Ai Li?'

'I won't marry that bastard Li Tao. What he did was unforgivable.'

She needed to find a way to explain about Ming Han and the warlord's schemes. Fifth Brother knew her better than anyone. If he didn't take her side, then she was lost.

Her brother was more interested in Ryam than her explanations. Huang looked him up and down, his face twisted in disdain. 'What is this *Bái guǐ* to you?'

'I have done nothing wrong.' Her voice faltered.

She'd sacrificed part of herself to be with Ryam. That was undeniable. But what she felt for him was the only thing that seemed untainted while her ideals of honour and family were torn away.

'Little sister, this is unforgivable.'

His formal way of addressing her made her go cold. Where was the cheerful brother who had always been her ally? Huang was only three years her elder. Out of the entire lot of them, he was the only one who had never bullied or lorded over her.

'I have always stood behind you,' she said fiercely. 'Remember the weaver's daughter?'

Huang went pale. His voice cracked, and for a second he was her brother again. 'I told you never to talk about that. And this is much more serious.'

Ryam took hold of her shoulder and Huang's eyes narrowed dangerously at the sight of his hand on her.

'Let me speak to him,' Ryam said. The sound of the foreign language in the midst of their argument seemed to be the most vulgar breach of propriety, a glaring reminder of the gap between their cultures.

Huang refused to speak to Ryam. He directed his next accusation to her. 'He has shamed you.'

She could see her brother's pain beneath his anger.

'I love him,' she whispered.

The sound of the words, spoken in her native tongue, resounded in her ears. Across from her, Huang froze and his frown grew even deeper.

She hadn't realised what she was saying. Ryam's hand tightened on her shoulder and she wondered if he understood her words. She prayed he didn't.

Huang's hand gripped the hilt of his sword, his mouth

clenching into a grim line. The look on his face made her heart plummet. He stared through her as if she wasn't there.

'Draw your sword, barbarian.'

'He doesn't understand you,' she said desperately.

'The barbarian understands.' Huang switched to the Western tongue. 'Are you going to hide behind my sister?'

With that, he drew his weapon. The hiss of the blade sent a chill down her spine.

She glanced over her shoulder into the cold steel of Ryam's eyes. She knew that look. It was the deathly calm before a battle, cold resolve.

'Don't do it,' she begged him.

'You'd better move aside.' Ryam freed his sword and held her away. 'Everything will be fine.'

Ailey's brother watched every look between them, his eyes growing colder. She finally stepped back, having no other choice. Her fingers knotted together so tightly that her knuckles grew pale. He was going to have to do this without hurting her brother. Perhaps he could manage to disarm him. It was much harder defeating someone when he had to be careful.

'She chose you,' Huang muttered. 'Worthless.'

Ryam figured he deserved the look of murder the man cast on him. Hours earlier, he'd been in Ailey's bed with her naked beneath him.

There was no backing out now. Exhaling slowly, he raised his sword. It was greater in length and width than the sword Huang wielded. He imagined Ailey's brother would rely on speed, the same way she did. He would have the same skill and agility, but with more experience and greater strength.

Huang raised his arms, blade high and glinting in the sun. With a battle cry he charged, hefting the blade downwards as if wielding an axe. Ryam jumped aside easily. Huang swung again and Ryam blocked with the flat of his blade.

This was unexpected. Fifth Elder Brother was really bad.

Huang was overcautious, pausing for a fraction too long before making his moves. He signalled the direction of his intentions so clearly with his eyes that he might has well have been shouting them aloud. Ailey's older brother had the same aggressiveness, but none of the precision and strategy that marked her fighting style.

Huang charged again, swinging in earnest. With every movement, Ryam could see the errors and openings. Huang locked swords with him, pushing forwards with a snarl.

Huang glanced beyond the cross of their blades to his sister. She watched them wide-eyed, hugging her arms to herself. Her brother had to do this. Honour demanded it. Ryam effected a retreat and wondered how he was going to disengage without getting either of them killed.

Ryam attempted a war cry of his own, checking his attack as he swung. It was a challenge to make the fight look respectable, but somehow Ryam knew that he needed to. Sweat poured down Fifth Brother's face. He gritted his teeth in concentration.

'There are better ways,' Ryam tried to say. He sidestepped and cringed when Huang overcommitted and stumbled.

'Quiet!' Huang panted. 'You deserve death…or at least…a good beating.'

They crossed swords a couple more times with a spectacular clash. Huang's thinner, sharper blade rang against his broadsword.

'Please stop!' Ailey cried. 'Both of you.'

'Enough.' Fifth Brother stepped back with a short bow. 'Anyone can see you are a great swordsman.'

Ryam exhaled with relief and bowed awkwardly in return. 'Thank you for being easy on me.'

Ailey ran to him. 'Are you hurt?'

Ryam made a face at her. Huang's blade hadn't come within a foot of him.

'The barbarian fought well,' her brother conceded.

Ryam struggled to keep a straight face. 'It was an honour.'

Ailey broke the formalities by punching her brother in the arm. 'You need to think before you start a fight, Six.'

'Well, Seven, you should think before looking at a man like that in front of your brother.'

Apparently, he wasn't absolved yet.

Huang sheathed his sword and then looked Ryam squarely in the eye. 'This white demon and I have some things to discuss.'

Ryam stared at ten white porcelain cups laid out in a row before him. Huang faced off against a similar array over on his side of the table. Did Huang really think he could beat him in a drinking contest? The man was only a foot taller than Ailey.

'All in!' Huang lifted the eighth cup high. The others before it had been upturned on to the table top.

Ryam mirrored his movements. He knocked back the shot of rice liquor, then slammed the open end onto the table. After three rounds of this, he had the ritual down.

'Eight!' Huang chimed. He wiped his mouth with the back of one hand.

The sweet acid burn of the liquor emerged, not entirely unpleasant. He watched Huang warily. He'd been waiting for the true purpose of this 'discussion' for an hour.

'*Gānbēi,*' Ryam said dutifully.

That had Fifth Brother slapping his palm against the table top with glee. 'Listen to him!'

There was a frantic knocking at the door of the salon. Huang shouted in its general direction and Ailey snapped back with something equally strident.

'I told her it was going to be a while,' Huang said. 'I must thank you, barbarian, for that bit out there.' He made a sword-brandishing motion. 'No one knows what it's like to be born with the heart of a poet in a family of warriors.'

'Why do you call her Seven?' Ryam asked. It was time for a break between shots.

'It is an ordinal ranking in the household.' Huang blinked, as if he was doing some ancient calculation in his head. 'Father is one, you see. I'm six. Ai Li is a daughter, she doesn't get a rank, but we call her seven. We used to say—' His head swayed precariously.

The alcohol spoke through Huang in a jumble of languages.

Ryam nodded and nodded. To his surprise, it was actually quite easy to follow.

'Ai Li should have been born in my place. I never took to the sword like the rest of the Shen line. I was destined for other things.'

Huang picked up the ninth cup, tilted his head back, then stopped to stare at Ryam's cup, which still rested on the table. Mumbling an apology, Ryam lifted the shot and tossed the contents down.

Huang coughed, and counted the number of overturned cups, pointing them out with his finger. Then he counted again. He eyed Ryam suspiciously. 'Are you falling behind?'

Ryam threw open his hands. 'I wouldn't do anything so dishonourable.'

Huang reached out to slap him on the back, apparently pleased with his response. Then immediately he grew serious. 'There is only one reason you're still here. Ai Li was the only one who ever looked at me as if I was worth anything.'

'I understand you completely.' Ryam knew what that look could do. She trusted him more than he'd ever trusted himself.

'No one else understands.' Huang stood without warning, jarring the edge of the table. Liquor sloshed from the two remaining cups. 'I have memorised all the classics,' he boasted. 'Shall we trade verses on duty?'

Ryam stared at him. 'I don't even know what you're talking about, Fifth Brother.'

Huang burst out laughing, his finger wagging in Ryam's direction. 'I like you, foreigner. Shall we finish number ten and declare ourselves brothers?'

He took the last drink standing, most of the liquid ending on the floor. Ryam stood to help Huang back into his chair. He had been worse off than this many a time.

'You are not a bad fellow,' Huang said. 'I apologise for insulting you.'

'Don't worry. I couldn't understand what you were saying.'

'I called you a no-name bastard. I apologise.'

Huang's mention of the honour play they'd enacted sobered him up. Ailey was in enough trouble without him in the picture. No-name bastard was exactly right.

'Do you know I studied for the civil exams?' Huang said. 'But when I asked permission to go to Changan, they all taunted me, First Elder Brother on down to Fourth Brother, for wanting to be something better than I was. They were all warrior heroes.' He grew serious again. 'Fourth Brother died the way a Shen should.'

'Ailey was very affected by his death.'

'In glorious battle,' Huang said bitterly.

'She learned his death was not an accident.'

Ryam felt inadequate trying to explain, but he needed to protect her. She'd already done the unthinkable by choosing to be with him. And he'd let it happen because he wanted her too much to turn away.

'What will happen?' Ryam asked.

Huang's expression darkened, the corners of his mouth turning downwards. 'Ai Li came to me for help. She must think I can talk to our father, that he'll listen to a fifth son.' He sighed, looking down at the table. 'I care very much about my sister.'

'I care very much about her, too.'

Huang's head shot up. 'Brother, brother...' He slapped Ryam's back again, choked with sudden emotion. Apparently Fifth Brother was a moody drunk. 'She chose you. You can't be so bad. Do you know there is a tradition of lucky devils in our family? Our grandfather won himself the most beautiful bride in the province. And he was nearly as ugly as you are. My sister paints a picture of someone right away. Right or wrong, she decides very quickly.'

Shifting uncomfortably, Ryam rubbed a hand over the back of his neck. There was no getting around it. When they met, Ailey had been alone and scared and he'd helped her. He was the luckiest bastard in all the empire, but he had no idea what he needed to do to make things right for her. The consequences, the thoughts he'd been blocking, came to him again. She could be pregnant with his child. She could be banished from her family.

'I'd never hurt her,' he told Huang.

'I believe you, barbarian.'

'I want her to be happy.'

Fifth Brother dropped his head down into his arms. 'She came to me. I will think of something. I must think of something.'

Head buried, Huang stayed still for so long that Ryam thought he'd passed out. It wasn't until he stood to go that Huang mumbled his parting wisdom.

'Any man can be better than he is.'

Chapter Sixteen

She'd told her brother she loved Ryam.

The words had spilled out of her. It was a wonder Huang didn't demand Ryam's death then and there. They had been locked away for over an hour, leaving her to pace like a madwoman outside.

She loved him.

Every glimpse of Ryam filled all the empty spaces in her heart. She had fallen before Changan, but hadn't allowed herself to believe it. Leaving him in the market square had cut out a piece of her and she had prayed that they would be able to meet again in another life.

Maybe this was her other life. She had changed during the journey. As youngest daughter, she'd always been sheltered. The first important decision she had ever made was to run away from her wedding. It was the right decision, no matter what her family insisted.

Ryam had given her a taste of what it meant to desire something for herself—happiness and peace and freedom. She couldn't fill her soul on duty and sacrifice any longer.

What were they doing in there for so long? She banged on

the door again and this time it swung open. Ryam stepped out
and shut the door behind him.

'Everything's fine,' he answered before she said anything.

'What happened? What did Huang say?'

'All sorts of stories.' He was looking at her oddly and something in his expression frightened her.

'You allowed Huang to save face. Thank you for that.'

'He'd be horrified to find out you knew.'

'Everyone knows. Huang never practised. Even when he
went out to the training yard, he would pretend.'

Every word had to be coaxed out of him while she babbled
on.

'Have you been drinking?'

He made a face. 'Hardly. Huang might be sleeping it off for
a while, though.'

They were standing so close, but he held himself back. Ryam
was always reaching out to tuck back a strand of her hair or
run his hand along her back—little touches that always made
her breath catch and brought her thoughts back to him. But not
now.

'What's wrong?'

Ryam came away from the door to stand before her, a silent
tower. 'Your brother cares about you. Your entire family cares
about you very much.'

She shook her head. 'Not after what I've done.'

The sharp pang in her chest came without warning.

'They won't turn you away no matter what you've done.
Even I can sense that.'

'Why are you talking like this? Did Huang say something
to you?'

He shook his head. 'Your father will kill me the moment he
sees me and I would deserve it.'

'He would have to kill me first.'

'Don't say that.' He turned away, one hand rubbing at
the back of his neck in frustration. 'You can't be that blind,
Ailey.'

'I am not blind,' she said, her voice rising.

He could accuse her of anything but ignorance. For the first time in her life, she could see clearly. Her parents had always been icons of authority and respect to be obeyed without question, but she knew them now to be human, with the same flaws and weaknesses as anyone else.

'Are you going to leave?'

'If you want me to stay, I will.'

Pride kept her from asking it of him. How had it come to this after all the things they had said to one another, skin to skin in the darkness? Her heart shattered into pieces with his next words.

'I can tell your father I seduced you, that none of this is your fault.'

If his words were meant to be noble, they failed their purpose. She couldn't look at him after that.

'He'd kill you.'

'Maybe I deserve it.'

'You didn't seduce me. I came to you willingly because—' her eyes stung and she blinked furiously '—because I wanted to.'

He shut his eyes, raking a hand through his hair. 'I need to clear my head.'

He walked past her, ignoring her when she called after him. It was the first time he had ever done that.

'I'm going for a ride,' he said, his back turned to her as he retreated.

She let him go.

If things could only have remained the way they'd been yesterday: no one but the two of them, hidden in the safety of Longyou with nothing to worry about beyond the next moment together. But she still needed to convince her family. She needed her father to understand the extent of Li Tao's ruthlessness.

Grandmother had believed there was a way to set things right, but that was before she'd given herself to Ryam. She refused to regret what they'd done. Ryam was her only bastion of happiness since she'd escaped from Li Tao. He believed in her. He'd always protected her.

Yet, in all of their conversations Ryam had never mentioned the possibility that she could go with him when he left. He never spoke of any future, for himself or for the two of them. It made her wonder if there were words in the barbarian language to speak of such a thing.

Ryam rode out through the wild grass, aiming a line for the distant ridge. The pounding of the hooves against the plains drummed out his thoughts and he revelled in solitude as the shadow of the mountain engulfed him. Once he found a pass through these mountains, Yumen Guan was less than a week's journey away.

He stared up at the stone peaks as his horse paced in a restless circle. The animal was bred to run. He tugged on the reins to turn them back around and, before he knew it, the day was done.

By evening, he lay in a room that had belonged to one of Ailey's brothers, warm and secure with a roof overhead. The cicadas buzzed their incessant trill outside in the trees. He was completely out of place. Anyone could see it. Anyone but Ailey.

He had wandered all his life. No particular place held any pull for him.

He expected the knock on the door and knew it was Ailey from her silhouette through the paper panes of the window, a willowy shadow cast by the evening lanterns.

She slipped inside and shut the door behind her with barely a sound. Her dress shimmered in the lamplight. It was always a breathtaking sight, the sinuous drape of silk on Ailey's graceful form.

'Where did you go?' she asked quietly.

'To the mountains.'

He pushed himself up to sit at the edge of the bed. She stayed just inside the door, her hands folded in front of her. For seconds, the only movement was the rise and fall of his chest and the play of the lanterns on the walls. He knew what she risked to come here. Every moment she had spent with him since they met had been a risk. And she had so much more to lose than he did.

'I found a trail that leads high up into the rocks,' he said.

'Sometimes the men will go into the mountains to train.'

Yes. Talk of nothing. This he could manage.

'It's beautiful up there. Pure,' he continued absently.

'Even prettier in the spring.'

She spoke calmly, her voice soothing like cool water. His hands rounded over his knees, itching to hold her, but he tortured himself by holding back. Spring was nearly a year away. The mention of time nicked at his heart, a tiny flesh wound that stung more than it deserved to.

'I thought of you.'

Even though it was the truth, the words felt clumsy on his lips. He had thought of her the entire time away, as much as he fought against it. She came closer. Her eyes wandered to his bare feet resting against the floor.

'For a moment I thought you had left.' Her words plunged through the space between them like a stone into a dark well.

'I wouldn't do that.'

But he had thought of it. He had considered what it would mean to leave. When he looked back, the mansion had grown small behind him and the mountains loomed above.

'I wouldn't betray you like that,' he said, stronger this time.

'I knew you wouldn't.'

Did she? He saw the lingering doubt behind her eyes.

'I will need to go some time,' he began. 'My people don't know what has happened to me.'

She silenced him with her fingertips. Fear clouded her expression as it reared its black head full force. It was a look he could do without seeing ever again. He opened his legs and settled her into the enclosure between his knees.

Tentatively, she braced her hands on to his shoulders, at once beautiful and vulnerable. He searched hard for something to say, to be able to promise to her and felt like a beggar when there was nothing. Words had never escaped him before when it came to women, but they had been empty and sweet. Not real words at all.

Ailey saw how he struggled. Her eyes lowered as she reached up to pull the ivory pin from her hair. 'Tell me more about Yumen Guan,' she said as the dark strands fell about her shoulders.

'Marshland and desert. Not nearly as beautiful as here.'

'Your friends are there. You are loyal to them.'

He couldn't think. Her hands reached behind her back while he continued to hold her. He watched in a trance as she pulled her sash free in one long motion.

'Are there beautiful women there?' she asked. Her hands paused at the edge of her robe as she waited for his answer.

'No.'

She ran her hands over her shoulders and the silk followed the motion of her fingers down, baring honeyed skin and sculpted flesh.

'You're lying.'

The layers of her dress slipped down her hips, pooling on top of his knees.

'No, I'm not,' he said with conviction.

He stared at the smooth hollows and rounded shapes of her body. Strength held itself so differently in a woman. Ailey was stunning to behold, not a line, not a curve wasted. There were no other women in the world.

His hands itched to help her with the ties of the embroidered bodice, but he waited with forced patience despite the way his erection strained against his trousers. The entire day had been like that, one test of will after another.

'You've seduced many women, haven't you?'

He shook his head in denial. It was a lie. With a deep breath, she pulled her bodice away and let it drop to the floor. His mouth went completely dry, his mind churning.

She leaned even closer to run a hand through his hair, the gesture possessive. 'But you didn't seduce me,' she whispered. 'Seduction implies deception.'

Her breasts rose and fell before his eyes, ivory skin tipped with dusky coral. No, this wasn't seduction. Ailey was going to bring him to his knees with an open assault, right down his centre. Unable to hold back any longer, he pressed his lips to the hollow beneath her breasts and then his arms closed around her as he lifted his head to draw her nipple into his mouth.

With a shuddering sigh, Ailey leaned into the caress, her hand digging into the back of his head. He ran his tongue over her hard peak and licked at the surrounding softness, feeling her melt and mould into his embrace.

She grasped his tunic, the linen bunching in her hands as she pulled it away. He raised his arms to help her and then they returned to each other, skin to skin. He captured her other breast, the nipple swelled against the wet caress of his tongue. Using his arm across her back to arch her into him, he feasted, scraping his teeth against the tender underside of her breast. He drew the swell of it into his mouth until she gasped and clutched at him and crushed him to her.

No other women. They had never existed. He could spend the rest of his life exploring her alone.

With one hand he parted her thighs and found the glistening well at her centre. Bending his head low, he put his mouth there, his tongue caressing a deep, savouring path. With a strangled, startled cry Ailey tensed her legs. He was holding on to her and she was holding on to him as his mouth circled and tasted. She moaned wonderfully for him. He couldn't help but delve deeper, thrusting his tongue into her smooth heat.

Suddenly Ailey's grip tightened on him and he was being pushed onto his back. She tugged at his trousers and he moved to help her, lifting his hips as she freed him of the last of his clothing. He ran his hands over the swell of her thighs, appreciating the graceful strength in them as she straddled him. His beautiful warrior girl.

The sight of her over him with her skin flushed with arousal banished all thought from his head. He strained against her, unable to push inside, growing hard and heavy against her flesh.

'Ailey,' he groaned, amazed by her boldness.

'I've seen this in books.' Her voice was a soft purr in her throat that made him throb.

'Must be better books on this side of the world,' he laughed.

He reached between them, guiding himself to her. With a shift of her hips he was sliding into her depths, hot and wet and incredible. His head pushed back into the mattress, neck corded.

She held on to his shoulders, her nails cutting into hard muscle as she sank lower onto him with excruciating slowness. He opened his eyes, needing to see her. Digging down with his heels, he thrust into her, embedding himself deep with an upward motion of his hips. Her face tilted in a grip of shock and pleasure. Shadows danced over the slope of her breasts and her stomach.

'God's breath, Ailey,' he said through his teeth.

His hold tightened on her, his fingers gripping her thighs as he urged her to move on him. And she did, rising and falling, slow and then faster with her eyes held shut to focus on the pull of him inside her. Watching her stripped him bare, leaving him raw and open. Defenceless.

She took hold of his wrists, her fingers slender and cool, circling him and trapping his arms to the bed. Her breasts pressed against his chest as she laid herself over him. All the while she rode his hips, tugging the pleasure from him in wave after wave.

Hands captured against the bed, he craned his neck to search for her mouth in a haze of hunger. He grasped for her tongue while he kissed her, all finesse gone. Ailey writhed into him, searching for the rhythm that would take them both into oblivion.

'I never knew it could feel like this,' she panted, her breath feathering against his throat.

His head dropped back onto the mattress as he felt her inner muscles clenching around him, pulsing, drawing him deeper. He gripped her in his arms, fingers splayed against her back, and tried to absorb every last silken ripple of her body into him before letting go. His release poured into her while he continued to drive his shaft deep as if there could even be more, more than this.

She sobbed out his name and he wound his hand into her hair to anchor her against him, closing his eyes, breathing her in. Ailey pressed her lips to his neck again and again. Soft kisses in stark contrast to the storm that had taken them.

He had thought about leaving that day. Known it was the right thing to do. But as he looked into the cold, dark canyon through the mountains and felt Ailey's presence slipping away behind him, he had turned his horse around and ridden back faster than he'd left.

She'd brought him along from the beginning, thinking she needed a protector, but he was the one who needed her. The moments without her had been frighteningly empty. He had nothing to fill his thoughts but the shadow of all the mistakes he'd made. There was nothing awaiting him in the future but disgrace and death.

His arms closed around her, squeezing tight. He knew now what would cause a man like his father to waste away for a woman, even the memory of a woman. Blind sacrifice must be in his blood. It was all he had to offer, as little as it was worth in the end.

Ryam woke with the coverlet tangled about him, the scent of sandalwood lingering among the threads. He reached out, searching for the familiar touch of Ailey's skin, but she was gone. Rolling onto his back, he blinked at the milky light flowing through the translucent window panes.

Ailey always woke up early, eager for the day. A shame. If she had lingered, he could hide her beneath the covers and get her to tell him more about those intriguing books she had mentioned.

A knock on the door startled him from his reverie. With a muttered oath, he threw the quilt aside and struggled into his clothes. The knocking came again, more insistent the second time. He righted himself and opened the door to find Huang standing there, his complexion ashy. He appeared younger without his armour.

'Did you rest well?' Huang asked tonelessly.

'Uh…yes.'

It was a damn good thing Ailey had slipped away. Ryam inspected Fifth Brother's belt and was thankful to see he was without his sword.

'Come with me.'

'Now?'

Huang nodded. Dark circles hung below his eyes. The pallor of his complexion made him appear corpse-like.

Ryam shoved his feet into his boots and tried to right himself, raking his hands through his hair several times before giving up. Their footsteps creaked against the floorboards as they made their way to the front hall. Huang led him to a set of double doors and pulled them open, directing him to enter with a nod.

The sharp camphor smell of incense clung in the alcove. Ryam faced a raised altar set with flickering candles and plates of fruit and rice. Offerings for the spirit world, as he understood it. A fan of joss sticks stood planted in a ceramic urn at the centre. Wispy fingers of smoke curled up to the ceiling.

Huang stepped past him and stood before the altar, head bowed. After an uncomfortably long silence, he stepped back until his shoulders lined up with Ryam's.

'In memory of our ancestors,' he said. 'I have tried to explain who you are.'

Ryam stared at the wooden plaques, each one etched with a column of black characters.

'I don't understand any of this,' he began.

'I thought very carefully all night. When Father arrives, he will demand your death for dishonouring my sister. I have no doubt you are not afraid to die, but Ai Li will be sad when he kills you. She will never forgive him.'

Ryam pressed the heels of his palms over his eyes. Huang was being brutally forthright. Another trait he shared with Ailey.

'You are a talented warrior and the Shen family has always valued such skill. My father may come to understand one day why my sister chose you. You must ask for our ancestors' blessing and then you must go.'

'With Ailey?'

Huang frowned. 'Of course.'

It was early and Fifth Brother was staring at him with an expression both haggard and serious.

'You must know that both Li Tao and our father will be hunting for you. Take Ai Li as far as you can. One day, you may be able to return once this is over.'

'What is happening here?'

Ryam turned at the sound of Ailey's voice. She stepped into the alcove and their eyes met. He couldn't control the flash of heat that crossed between them.

Huang addressed her formally. 'I may not be able to convince our father, but I will speak on your behalf. I will stake my honour as well as yours. If your swordsman proves worthy,' he added grimly.

She tried to place herself between them. 'This is not his custom.'

Huang ignored her protest and directed his words to Ryam. 'Kneel before my ancestors and tell them the honour of your intentions. In life, they did not speak your language but, as spirits, if you speak in earnest I am certain they will understand.'

Ailey's brother was talking about ancestors and vows and Ryam still wasn't clear what he was swearing to. The tiny altar room became stifling as his mind tried to make sense of what was going on.

'This is between me and Ailey.'

As soon as Ryam spoke, he knew he was wrong. There was no Ailey without her family.

'My sister holds you in high regard. Is she wrong to do so?' Huang challenged.

'Stop it, Six.'

Ailey tried to take Ryam's arm. 'You don't have to do anything.'

Her hand trembled against him as she searched his face. Was she afraid to demand anything of him because she knew he could only disappoint her? Anger followed by shame burned hot beneath his collar. He removed her hold on his arm.

'I'm sorry,' he said quietly and turned to leave.

The suffocating perfume of the incense followed him as he stepped out into the open air. He didn't know what he was apologising for. He'd sworn to Ailey in the past, to protect her, to treat her honourably. But there were things she needed that he could never understand. He had to get out of there, far away from the solemn gravity of the family altar and the judgement of their invisible ancestors.

'He is not worthy of you.'

Huang's jaw tensed, his mouth tightening into a hard line. Beneath his anger, she sensed his concern for her. It tore her in two.

'You don't understand.'

'I do understand. You have fallen in love and you will not listen to anyone, but you came to me and I am trying to help you.'

'I didn't come to you for this.'

The altar loomed before her and the haze of incense was making her dizzy. It was so hard to sort out her emotions after spending the night in Ryam's arms. She had fled to Longyou because she wouldn't marry Li Tao and because she wouldn't stand by as Father shattered their family honour to pieces. But when Ryam touched her, she forgot about all those other reasons. She was safe and wanted, and the feel of him beside her became her only purpose.

'You have lost sight of who you are, little sister.'

He echoed her own troubled thoughts, and it only made her angrier. 'I know who I am. It is Father who has lost sight of who we are.'

'Is this what that barbarian has done to you? A dutiful daughter would never speak like that.'

'Ryam has nothing to do with this.'

Huang stood over her, his face twisted into harsh lines. She had never seen her sentimental brother so angry.

'Our father has no daughter.' The moment the words left her lips, she crumbled inside.

Her brother stared at her, his eyes wide with shock. 'Ai Li.'

This was the worst betrayal, the coldest, blackest thing she had ever uttered in her life. Honour and duty held them together. They each knew it from birth. To denounce her father, their family—hot tears burned in her eyes, but she couldn't swallow the words and remain silent. She knew in her heart that everything she trusted was breaking apart and she couldn't keep it whole. Not even here in Longyou.

She turned and fled from the altar room. Huang shouted after her, but she couldn't stop. His words rang through the central courtyard.

'Why are you chasing after a man who would not swear to you before your ancestors?'

She was going to Ryam, but not for the reasons her brother believed. She couldn't stay after saying those unforgivable words aloud. Her insides shrivelled, leaving a hollow pit where her heart would be. If Father could ignore everything he had taught them about honour, if he could sacrifice their mother to secure the throne, then it all meant nothing. She could turn away as well.

Her footsteps echoed through the emptiness of the main hall. The Shen family was gone. There was nothing left but ghosts. If she stayed and married Li Tao, she would be a ghost as well, a meaningless phantom for the rest of her life.

She left the house through the side door and went to the

stable, stepping around the mud near the entrance. From behind her, she heard her name in that slightly mispronounced way that was becoming so familiar.

'Ailey?'

Ryam stood with his sword strapped to his side. Just the sight of him beat back the loneliness that had settled over her in her own home.

'You thought I'd run.' He folded his arms over his chest and indicated the stable with a tilt of his head.

'You would never betray me like that.'

She was using his words, the words he had spoken to her the night before when he had held her and loved her. She went to him and his arms folded around her. She let herself sink against him, inhaling his masculine scent as she tightened her hold on him.

'I wish I could be everything you needed me to be,' he said against her hair.

She silenced him. 'You are.'

While she held on to him the world stopped spinning. Ryam was the only one she had left, the only person she could trust. The memory of what they had shared flowed through her veins like quicksilver, emboldening her.

'I'll go with you to Yumen Guan,' she said.

He turned to stone in her arms. The top of her head brushed against his chin as she glanced up at him. 'We can't stay here. I won't stay here.'

His jaw tensed. 'Ailey...'

She knew that tone. She had heard it all her life from her brothers and her parents. It was the warning tone that was meant to remind her she was too young, too impatient, too brash.

He let out a breath. 'Are you certain?'

'I'm certain.'

She had been holding her breath as well. She had denounced her family before her ancestors. If Ryam refused her, then she had no one left in the world.

'We should go now, then,' he said. He smiled at her surprise. 'Once you have your mind set, you'll go with or without me.'

That wasn't true. She saw a new path in front of her, one she had never envisioned, and it was with him. She would never escape from the burden of her family while she remained here.

'Wait here,' she said. 'I won't be long.'

She ran back to the house to get her belongings and Ryam called out to her.

'There's more to this than you not wanting to marry Li Tao, isn't there?'

He looked so solid and strong standing there in the light. Even if there was no Li Tao, she still couldn't stay in Longyou any longer. There was so much to explain, so much she didn't yet understand, but she knew it was right.

'Yes,' she replied. 'There's more.'

Chapter Seventeen

Within days they cleared the shelter of the mountains and rode into a land where the grass grew coarse and yellow before it disappeared completely. The span of the desert plains had always seemed a great emptiness to Ailey in the map room, but now she saw how the roads of the empire stretched on. The route was overgrown with thistle and wild crabgrass in places, but faint traces of the path would reappear as they continued.

Ailey had woken up that morning with Ryam beside her and the sky above. Even the most common things had seemed different. Maybe that was what she needed to do, transform herself into something new. Her father and mother had done it. Why not her?

The settlement ahead was too small to be considered a town. There were no permanent structures to be seen. It consisted of a series of wells lined with rocks. Traders gathered around the watering areas. The nomads and stragglers of the empire bought and traded goods in these border markets, never needing to venture into the cities of empire.

She wiped her brow with the edge of her scarf, leaving a smudge of dirt on the cloth. Once again, she'd traded her dress for a plain tunic. Silk had no place out here. The western frontier was an arid zone of dust and rock littered with the occasional oasis.

Ryam walked beside her as they led their horses around the edge of the settlement.

'Look mean,' he suggested with a grin.

She made a face at him.

She disliked the look of this market even more than the gambling den and the drinking house. Her butterfly swords were strapped at her belt for quick retrieval. In these lands, men wore their weapons openly. They were at the edge of the empire, an unknown place with a mix of people who spoke so many different dialects it was impossible to decipher the chatter.

Grandfather used to travel these lands in the days when the empire had sought to expand and reclaim the area controlled by previous dynasties. He had been called a vagrant and a barbarian at times, before becoming one of the great generals of the empire. She sought comfort in that part of her family history.

This was the first time she had set foot outside the boundary of her father's rule. Out here, she could decide for herself what the future would hold. She had to keep on reminding herself of that as they roamed the unruly marketplace.

They stopped beside a shallow cistern to water the horses. Ryam hitched the reins to a post. His sandy hair was tossed and dusty from the wind. It somehow made his eyes appear bluer, like cool water in the desert plains.

'Yumen Guan will be three days through the northern route. We'll need water and food.'

'Do many trade caravans from the empire go through there?'

'Quite a few, though trade has been waning over the last year.'

It was impossible to be completely free of the empire. At any moment, she expected the imperial army to march through the plains to retrieve her. But Huang hadn't chased after her and she was both relieved and saddened. Her brother knew that there was no way to bridge the rift she had created by refusing to marry Li Tao. He himself had told her to hide away until he could find a resolution. But she'd have no help any more, not from Huang or from her grandmother.

Ryam looked concerned. 'How are you?'

She must have been doing a poor job of hiding her fears. 'I've seen more of the empire in these last few weeks than I have in a lifetime.'

'Don't worry. Gansu isn't as dangerous as they say.'

'Let's go quickly then.'

He wound her braid around his fingers and gave a small tug before letting go. She often wondered in the last few days whether she had insinuated herself into this journey. As a sixth child, she was adept at getting her way. But Ryam always managed to give her an unexpected look or touch that would immediately reassure her.

The next several days stretched open and empty, leaving too much space for her to wonder about Mother and Father and the imperial palace. The nights were easier when Ryam held her. He'd hold her and whisper stories in her ear about the places he'd been. A chill would set in the air once the sun dipped behind the mountains and the wind rushed between them, making a lonely sound. She'd burrow closer to Ryam's warmth and knew this was where she belonged.

On the third morning their horses plodded through the rubble of the gravel desert while Ryam pointed out the structures of mud and clay built into the cliffs that overlooked them.

'Guard stations and forts,' he explained. 'The imperial army used to have garrisons far out into this pass during periods of expansion.'

'Do you think my father will end the truce with the lost legion now? The shipment of weapons may put you all in danger, unless Father is convinced that Li Tao was the one to blame.'

'Ailey.' He pulled his mount closer to her. His leg brushed against hers. 'Having you here is more likely to anger Emperor

Shen than some skirmish with imperial soldiers. You're going to need to make peace with him some day.'

She looked down. 'What if there can be no peace?'

He had no answer for her, but she didn't expect him to. She wanted to forget the complications of the empire out here, not wallow in them.

'I have heard of this place in poems,' she said, looking to the mountains. The peaks loomed to the north, austere and coal black, unlike the lush mountains of Longyou. 'Yumen Guan is at the edge of the world, the last trace of civilisation before the road winds into barbarian lands of the desert.'

'Trust me. There is a whole world beyond it.'

'The land where you came from?'

'And many other lands.' Thankfully, he obliged her and stopped speaking about her father. 'It took us over a year to reach the empire. We travelled across the lands of the Saracens, the Khazars, the Tibetans, fighting for our lives the entire way.'

'You're fortunate to have made it so far.'

It felt like fate for her to be here with Ryam. She'd always be thankful for the forces and accidents that had brought them together.

The Jade Gate emerged ahead, a great block of sandstone rising from the barren plain. The walls were made of rammed earth that had hardened to stone in the sun. A tower rose in several levels above the barricade. Ailey wondered if there had ever been other villages and settlements around the fortress as there were at other military passes throughout the empire. Yumen Guan was surrounded by marshland that teemed with reeds. A lone white bird lifted from the shallow water and took flight.

'I didn't think I'd make it back here before getting myself killed,' Ryam said.

Something about his tone upset her. 'Are you happy to be returning?'

'It will be good to be back around familiar faces, though I don't know if I'll be welcomed after what's happened.'

Ryam had grown tense the moment the fortress came into view. Did he consider the barren rock and marshland of the corridor to be home? She couldn't stop the wave of homesickness that hit her.

Ailey spied the figures at the top of the battlements as they came closer. Other than the patrol, the fortress stood solitary and in ruin, a remnant of a past time when the empire had stretched its hands into the corridor and traded freely on the north and south roads.

A cry rang out as they reached the shadow of the walls. She heard Ryam's name called and was shocked to see other men like him. The guards on top of the wall were also pale with the same rough features, though their hair was darker.

As she directed her mount across the threshold she couldn't resist looking up. The legendary jade over the battlements was gone. Nothing decorated the walls of Yumen Guan but dust and time.

A deep voice rang across the bailey as they entered.

'You didn't get yourself killed after all.'

A mountain of a man came towards them and Ryam dismounted to greet him. His hair was coal black and his skin tanned. This was the barbarian prince they spoke about. He gripped Ryam in a brotherly embrace. She didn't think anyone could appear imposing next to Ryam, but this man matched him in height, and his broad shoulders held the look of a warrior.

Adrian slapped Ryam across his back. 'We thought you were dead.'

'I thought I was too.'

The dark-haired barbarian looked towards her and grinned. 'Well, nearly getting killed hasn't changed you a bit.'

Ryam faced the other man with his spine rigid, unable to share in the spirit of the reunion. 'The men under my command…you trusted me with them. I'm sorry.'

Adrian frowned. 'They returned several weeks ago.'

'Returned.' Ryam's jaw remained clenched tight. 'That's good. That's good to hear.'

Adrian also seemed taken aback by Ryam's sombre response. 'No one knew what had happened to you.'

'There was something I had to see to.'

The two men looked to her and she dismounted as they approached. She would have expected Ryam to be relieved that his men were safe, but his expression appeared distant and strained.

Soon the western prince was towering over her. His look wasn't unkind, but she was suddenly intimidated in the presence of this warrior. This was truly a den of barbarians. She stood among men who held no loyalty to the empire.

She had chosen this, she reminded herself. She'd chosen to be with Ryam. She could handle whatever happened next as long as he was beside her. It would take time, that was all.

'This is Ailey,' Ryam began.

'You do have the devil's luck.'

Adrian punched Ryam's shoulder and Ryam ran a hand over his neck sheepishly. They truly did seem like brothers.

'Let me practise.' Adrian surprised her by breaking into proper Hakka. It was the formal dialect of the court, spoken by ministers, scholars and nobility. 'I am Adrian, family name Valderic. You honour us with your presence.'

In another land, he would be of equal class and standing as she. Ailey clasped her hands together in front of her, bowing low as required.

'Shen Ai Li stands humbled before you.'

He paused, eyebrows raised. 'Shen?'

The barbarian commander was an intelligent man. Legend had it that he had crossed swords with her grandfather, that he had marched on Changan alongside her father's troops. With his immovable stature and the air of confidence, he reminded her immediately of the *jiedushi* who led the defence commands.

His scrutiny intimidated her and she launched into a long litany, telling him that she knew of his reputation and how honoured she was to be his guest and how she did not wish to bring any ill fortune upon him with her impertinent decision to come to Yumen Guan.

Adrian looked over to Ryam at a loss. 'I'm going to need my wife to translate.'

'Actually, Ailey understands everything you're saying.'

Adrian's gaze fixed on a point behind her and Ailey turned and found herself face to face with the woman who was responsible for putting her father on the throne.

Princess Miya was looking at her curiously. 'What do I need to translate?'

She had expected a dragoness. A sharp-tongued, formidable shrew like Mother. Princess Miya was a slender, elegant woman who moved with effortless grace. She wore an elaborately embroidered silk robe as if she still held court in the imperial palace. Ailey had seen her only a handful of times at court and once at Longyou when they were children. Their fathers knew one another well, after all.

It was said that Miya never forgot a face. True to her reputation, her eyes widened with recognition.

'Ai Li?'

The inescapable urge to bow tugged at Ailey's neck.

'Princess,' Ryam interceded.

Miya glanced at him, a cynical smile on her lips. 'Which princess do you mean?'

The Jade Gate had once functioned as a garrison for the soldiers guarding the nearby segment of the Great Wall before it was abandoned to the elements. Ryam walked beside Adrian to the fortress tower and into the chamber they used as a war room. Not that there was much war to be planned once they'd made a truce with the Emperor.

It had been months since he'd seen Adrian, the man to whom he'd sworn loyalty. They'd spent years side by side, first defending the borders of their homeland and now fighting for survival in the frontier.

'Did the men return unharmed?' he asked.

'We lost two.'

They both fell silent. Two more gone. Ryam was grateful that the others were alive, but he couldn't absolve himself. It was a failure that he even had to ask about them. He had been put in command. He was responsible.

'They were imprisoned under imperial jurisdiction,' Adrian continued. 'Miya had to intervene.'

'She probably wasn't happy about that.'

'Neither am I. Every time the empire realises Miya still has influence in Changan, we all become targets. Tell me about your princess,' Adrian said.

His princess. As if Ailey could ever belong to him. 'I didn't realise who she was at first. She was hiding from a warlord.'

And when he had learned the truth, they were both in too deep to turn away. There was no way to explain that to Adrian. His ties to Ailey had nothing to do with reason or duty or survival. He simply needed to be near her.

Adrian looked grim. 'That weapons shipment nearly sparked a war. The empire is wary of all its alliances right now. It looks bad for us with Shen's daughter here.'

'It's not as if she's our prisoner.'

'Shen won't see it that way.'

'Then I'll take her somewhere else. Somewhere safe.'

It took Ryam a moment to realise what he'd suggested. Could he abandon the legion now, after all they'd been through? It was his actions that had turned the empire's attention back on them. He had pushed their fragile peace to breaking point.

'I'll fix this,' Ryam said. 'I don't know how, but I'll figure this out. If you force her to return to Emperor Shen, she'll flee. I know that already.'

'I wasn't going to force anything,' Adrian replied. 'I can see what she means to you.'

He stared at his friend. What choice did they have? Ailey couldn't stay here with a mismatched band of barbarians and nomads, but she had nowhere else to go.

The situation would come to a head soon. Family and honour meant everything to Ailey. Her anger would inevitably cool and she would want to reconcile with her father. Ryam didn't know if he had it in him to do the right thing when the time came.

He wondered where she was. Miya had thrown a protective

arm around her and led her away, glaring at him as if he'd ransacked the imperial palace.

'Well, you returned to us just in time. Regardless of Shen's daughter, I need to make a decision quickly.' Adrian never showed any sign of weakness, but suddenly he looked as if he hadn't slept for a month.

'What is it?'

'I'm sending a scouting party into the Tarim basin. We need to find another stronghold. Some place further away from the border and the politics of the empire. It's becoming too danger-ous here.'

'We're going to leave the Jade Gate?'

'It may come to that.'

The news stopped him cold. His first thoughts were of Ailey. He could already see how she became more withdrawn the further they journeyed from her home in the mountains. The Tarim basin was a desert wasteland dotted with oasis settle-ments. Ailey would wither away.

'The scouting team leaves in three days. The nomad has agreed to lead them. After that it may be weeks until we move. Months at most.'

Ryam shook his head in disbelief. 'I could have come back to find this place abandoned.'

He had been Adrian's bodyguard for over a decade. They owed each other their lives. For the first time, he considered that their paths might separate them.

Adrian must have been having similar thoughts. 'The others may not agree. We're no longer an army. No one is sworn to follow me.'

'The men look up to you. They'll go where you tell them.'

'They look up to you as well.'

'What are you trying to say?'

'I'm doing this for Miya's protection. The empire is too interested in her. But the men have their own families now. Some may wish to stay and they'll need someone to lead—'

'Look what happened last time I took the lead.'

'It could have happened to anyone,' Adrian said.

Ryam couldn't accept that. It was only by accident that the blow to his head hadn't killed him and that the entire party wasn't dead. Luck couldn't keep him alive for ever.

'We need to keep the legion together,' Ryam insisted.

'And what about Shen's daughter?'

'I'll think of something,' he muttered.

There were hardly enough of them left alive to call themselves a legion any longer. Ryam had a duty to the men that remained. But then there was Ailey.

Already he missed having her by his side, but even if she agreed to go with them, he didn't know if he'd allow it.

'In any case, it's good to have you back.' Adrian started for the door, but turned before leaving. 'Don't get killed again.'

Ryam threw him a grin, but it faded as soon as Adrian was gone. They would be on the run again, struggling for survival until they found another safe haven. This time, they'd be skirting the edge of the Taklimakan desert, the abandoned place where people fought to the death for the tiniest scraps of food and the faintest trickle of water. He couldn't put Ailey through that. It wasn't the life she deserved.

The thought of leaving her cut even deeper than he had expected. He needed her warmth and the thoughtful way she took in everything around her. She could soothe him with a single touch. She made him aware of a world he'd never considered. Without her, he would be biding time until death came. He had never expected more than that until Ailey had put her faith in him.

But he couldn't forget how she'd floated through the hallways in Longyou. Her face lit up like a festival lantern when she spoke of her brothers. That was the life Ailey deserved, surrounded by the protection of her family.

He had hoped that when they stopped running, he could give her some fragment of that sort of happiness. But he didn't know the first thing about family or swearing to ancestors when he didn't have any. He knew Ailey's heart was pulling her back to her beloved mountains and further away from him.

Chapter Eighteen

Miya led her to a chamber located at the far corner of the fortress. Ailey followed her inside and found herself in a furnished salon. Painted scrolls hung from the walls and a rug had been laid out at the centre of the floor. If she hadn't journeyed through the marshlands to get here, Ailey might have thought she was back in the capital city.

'Gifts,' Miya explained. 'From trade caravans and ambassadors.'

Ailey seated herself across from the former princess and folded her hands in her lap. They had only met a few times in the comings and goings of the imperial court. The princess had even come to Longyou as a child, but now that Ailey was sitting across from the young woman who once held the same title she did, she was at a loss. The only interaction she'd ever had with the imperial princess was to greet her and then back away and disappear.

Miya smoothed out her robe with graceful hands Mother would have envied. 'How are your father and mother?'

'They are well. The princess is kind to ask.'

'You are very far from home, Ai Li.'

'Not as far as the princess.'

Miya smiled, her lips curving like an orchid petal. Ailey glanced away, disconcerted by the woman's gaze. Miya was only her elder by a year, but she had been born imperial princess and crowned as Empress at one point. She exuded a quiet, natural power.

'The swordsman Ryam, what is he to you?'

The princess was also uncommonly direct.

'He's always treated me with honour,' Ailey said hastily. She had the feeling that Miya might give an order of execution if she misspoke.

'Has he?' Miya's eyes narrowed sceptically.

Ryam was more than honourable towards her. He cherished her and treated her as if he needed her more than anything, but all the world would see was her disobedience and shame. She started to explain to Miya, but stopped herself. She didn't have to justify anything out here in the frontier. Her life was her own now.

'The princess herself married a barbarian,' Ailey said.

She hadn't intended to sound so defensive, but the princess merely laughed. 'It is quite arbitrary who we call barbarian, is it not? Our great empire is such a blend of people. I am actually glad that you're here. It is so good to hear my native tongue and see someone from our land. Sometimes I get quite homesick.'

'I feel the same.' The quickness of her response surprised her. Ailey found herself longing for any connection to the home she knew and she had only been away for days. 'Is it difficult for you to live here?'

'There was nothing for me in the empire but death and deceit. Here, I have life. I have my husband and a future. In many ways, this was my only choice.' Her expression grew serious. She leaned in close and took Ailey's hand. 'But tell me why you've come here.'

Ailey looked down at the way the princess's ivory fingers laid over hers. Her own nails had become worn and ragged from the journey. Despite their outward differences, it was easy to sense a bond between them. Miya knew the Shen family and its generations of service to the empire. She understood Changan in all of its glory and treachery.

Ailey found the story spilling from her lips. 'My parents arranged a marriage for me to Li Tao. Father insists I go through with it even though he's betrayed our family.'

For the first time, she was able to explain everything about Li Tao and Fourth Brother and why she had no choice but to run away.

Miya listened calmly. Ailey had been surrounded by men all her life: her father, her brothers and uncles. She had never had another woman to confide in. Mother barely understood her and Grandmother always forged her own path, listening to no one.

'Governor Li Tao,' Miya repeated the name slowly. She frowned and Ailey caught a glimpse of the careful calculation everyone spoke about. 'Li Tao is a very powerful man.'

'It is dangerous for you to shelter me here, isn't it? I should go.'

'Nonsense. I just need some time to work out what to do when Emperor Shen comes for you.'

'My father has an empire to rule. He doesn't have time to chase after a worthless daughter,' Ailey said bitterly.

'Shen An Lu is protective of his family. He would never let any harm come to you. And he would never sacrifice you to a man he didn't trust.'

'You're wrong, Princess. Father has changed.' Ailey thought of her father's plan to make Miya his empress and the wound in her heart reopened. 'He's forgotten all of us.'

'He hasn't forgotten. Family is everything to Emperor Shen.'

The bravado drained out of her. She had been in denial the entire journey, fooling herself into thinking her father would disown her and forget he had a daughter. It was what she truly deserved for disgracing the family name.

'Li Tao is a formidable enemy. I have no bargaining power with him. Your father, I may be able to speak to.'

'No, Princess. I won't let you take this burden. This was my choice.'

There was a look of determination on the princess's face. 'You are Shen An Lu's daughter, so you must know about debt. It could be said that I owe your family a great debt for all they have done to protect me. Perhaps this is how I can repay it.' Miya stood then, exuding command in every inch of her slight frame. 'But first I need to speak to my husband about Emperor Shen and, more importantly, about Li Tao.'

Ailey rose to follow the princess. The moment she left the room, she was once again transported to the starkness of the fortress. Miya led her to a set of stairs formed against the wall. They climbed the steps to the battlements and a view of the pass emerged. Beyond Yumen Guan, the empire truly did disappear into a stretch of empty land and sky. In the distance, Ailey could see the remnants of the Great Wall, a dark line against the horizon.

'Gansu is not as desolate as I first thought,' Miya said, coming up beside her. 'There are tribes that live in the mountains and roam all around the plain. Very different from Chang-gan, isn't it?'

A patrol passed by them to take their places at the watchtowers at the corners of the battlements. Legend told that these men came from a land far west, where the sun set. Ta Chin was believed to be a kingdom of tall, fierce warriors. Legends had a way of growing with each telling, but from what she could see there was some truth to it.

More men had gathered in the bailey. Of all the things that could have reminded her of home, it was the ring of swordplay in the training grounds that made Ailey think most of Longyou. Part of her wished that she could be revelling in her grand adventure surrounded by these exotic people, but all she could think of was her family.

Ryam was easily recognisable below by his crop of blond hair. He walked around the perimeter of the training grounds, observing the sparring matches. Her heart leapt at the sight of him.

'He doesn't look like the others,' she murmured. The other men of the lost legion were darker in colouring like their leader.

'Ryam was a wanderer in their land as well. My husband was impressed by his sword skill,' Miya explained. 'He also needed a bodyguard as assassination is a threat in any part of the world.'

Ryam looked up and his gaze found her. The rugged beginnings of a beard covered his jaw. It reminded her of how he had looked when they first met: primitive and masculine. He raised his hand to wave at her in a boyish gesture and she smiled.

'What do you see in him?' Miya asked.

Down in the training grounds, Ryam stopped to instruct one of younger soldiers. She could see the sense of brotherhood among these men. It was the same as the bond between her brothers and the men they commanded. Her answer came easily.

'He fought for me. He was in danger and he didn't know me, but he fought for me without a thought.'

'And that was all you needed,' Miya said gently.

It sounded so simple, but it wasn't. Her heart overflowed with light whenever she looked at Ryam. Her feelings grew stronger towards him every moment they were together, even while she couldn't help feeling a sense of growing loneliness as they journeyed away from the empire.

She couldn't begin to explain this feeling to the princess or her family. Any words would fall short, they would fail her.

'When I look at him, I know,' she said.

Miya nodded and, for a moment, Ailey felt what it must be like to have a sister to confide secrets to.

'I must write to your father to inform him that you're safe,' Miya said.

Ailey's heart plummeted. 'I suppose it is only right to do so.'

'I could put in a good word for Ryam.' Miya gave her arm a squeeze, making everything sound easy. 'He is a talented swordsman. Your family honours the warrior tradition.'

'Father would never understand. My brothers would line up to demand Ryam's death.'

The princess wouldn't back down. 'Ryam fought alongside your father's troops when they secured Changan. If he's proven himself worthy, Shen An Lu could be reasonable.'

Ailey closed her eyes. Just the thought of how unreasonable her father had become brought out all the anger again. 'I thought so once.' She let out a breath and then turned to the princess. 'There is another reason I don't wish for you to communicate with my father. He plans to make you his first wife and Empress in order to strengthen his hold on the throne. As if Mother didn't exist.'

Miya laughed. 'Wen Yi will have my heart cut out.'

'My mother is willing to go along with his plan. She is happy to sacrifice herself for the sake of the empire.' Ailey's throat constricted and frustration poured from her anew, bitter and vile. 'If this is what duty demands of us, I don't want any part of it.'

Her vision blurred as the powerlessness sank in. She tore her gaze away to stare out over the distant plains.

'Marrying me would not help Emperor Shen. There are as many people who hate me as love me. And I'm already married.'

'Everyone listens when you speak. It's not the same for me.' Ailey wished she didn't sound so hopeless. 'No one would listen to my protests. There was nothing I could do but escape.'

They fell silent as the swords rang out in the yard below.

Miya finally spoke with her usual steadiness and confidence. 'There was an insurrection in the palace and Adrian and his men came to rescue me along with your father's army. Shen saved my life and I made him Emperor.' Her lips pressed together cynically. 'Punishment by reward. When you are Emperor, no man is a friend. Everyone is a conspirator.'

Ailey had never thought of it like that. Her father had taken on a duty greater than he had been born into. He had taken on that monumental task because he had always served the empire. Her anger began to fade. She couldn't find the fuel to sustain it.

She had hoped to forget the pain of leaving her family behind, but now she knew that she couldn't.

'Do you miss Changan?' Ailey asked.

'Every day. But there is nothing left for me in the empire.'

'If you had the choice, would you return to the throne?'

Miya's expression brightened as Adrian entered the yard. 'I made a choice and I have never regretted it.'

She admired the princess. Even in exile, Miya had created her own place with the man she loved. She was happy and in complete command of her surroundings.

Ailey found Ryam again. She followed him with her gaze, her heart beating faster just looking at him. He was back among his men, his family. Could she stay here with Ryam and forget that she was Shen? She could make a new life and be happy with the man she loved, just as Miya had done.

As soon as she thought it, the spirit of her homeland reached out to her. Grandmother, Mother and her brothers were still within the empire, protecting it as they had for three generations. Her grandfather had sacrificed himself for the empire.

She couldn't hide in the marshland for ever. There was no way to remain loyal to her family, yet still be true to her heart. The two parts of her battled with one another. She could have honour or love, but not both.

The packed dirt of the training grounds lay firm beneath Ryam's boots. The men still trained every day. The sword had kept them alive and allowed them to claim this patch of land from the bandits that roamed the corridor. For many years, the fortress had provided security. They'd become allies with the surrounding nomadic tribes and received payment for providing protection to the caravans that came through. They were scavengers, but life wasn't bad when they fed off the scraps of the wealthiest empire in the world.

He hadn't realised how it would feel to finally know a place, from the feel of the ground beneath him to the taste in the air. Something inside him had refused to believe he belonged anywhere. He had sought out the promise of adventure. That was why he'd agreed to go back into the empire. No one had forced him to take that command. It had been his own restlessness pushing him to it.

He observed the men as they sparred and instructed them after each match. His father had put a wooden sword in his hands when he was five and this sort of training came naturally to him. That was the one thing he was good for, keeping his comrades alive as long as he could.

A figure moving along the battlements continued to lure his attention away until he had to look up. It was a compulsion to see her, to know precisely where she was and that he could go to her if needed. His Ailey. The curve of her waist and the slope of her hips took hold of him and he went hot all at once, his body tightening instinctively.

This was the first day they hadn't spent every moment together and it was a long day indeed.

'A princess, of all people.'

Ryam followed the familiar voice to see Dako shaking his head in disbelief. The tribesman wore a fur-lined jacket and cap over his head as was common among the *Xianbei*, the nomads of the frontier. A sword hung from his belt with a curved dagger tucked beside it. Ryam was never certain of the nomad's age. His skin had been darkened and worn by exposure to the sun and the wind.

'A descendant of warriors and generals,' Dako drawled. 'You astound even me. How is that hard head of yours?'

The nomad's dry humour took him by surprise. The last they'd seen of each other was during the fight against the imperial soldiers.

'You left me for dead, you son of a dog,' Ryam accused lightly.

'What? You left us, barbarian.'

The nomad took special pleasure in calling him that. Dako had lived part of his life in Changan and spoke the court dialect, yet he was considered as much a barbarian as the pale westerners of the legion.

'You had blood pouring down your face and you were still

fighting like a madman. Apparently nothing can kill you, ghost man.'

Ryam grew serious. 'I heard several of your tribesmen were lost. I should have stopped it.'

'Enough. It is done.' Dako embraced him and lowered his voice. 'Who else could have known, barbarian? We checked that shipment together. The men I lost, I took care of myself.'

'What do you mean?'

'They took payment.' Dako made a cutting motion with one hand. 'So I paid them as well.'

Betrayal. Adrian was right. The affairs of the empire were bleeding into the frontier.

'What do you think about this plan to leave Yumen Guan?' Ryam asked. Adrian wouldn't make such a journey without consulting the leader of the tribesmen.

'A wise idea. We're not an army and this area will soon be in the middle of a war zone.'

'War?'

'War with the neighbouring kingdoms. They know the empire is weak. Tibet is gaining strength and there are many other kingdoms along the western border waiting to take a bite. Your prince thinks ahead.'

'And you leave in three days?'

Dako nodded. 'They say no one returns from the Taklimakan, but that rumour is only there to keep foreigners out.'

He laughed again, which meant that he was nervous. They returned to the centre of the yard and Dako gestured towards the battlements. 'So does she know how to use those butterfly swords she carries?'

'She can cut you to ribbons blindfolded.'

'Then you know what part of you she's going to cut off if you cross her.'

Ailey was speaking to the princess as they looked over the bailey. At that moment, her eyes met his and held across the span of the training yard. The thought of leaving the legion left him empty. But the thought of abandoning Ailey seized him by the throat and squeezed tight.

Dako had to raise his voice to get his attention. 'Her grandfather, Shen Leung, was a great man.'

'He was.'

'Honour is everything to the Shen family.'

'I know,' Ryam said.

'I owe Shen a debt.'

Dako's message was clear. Though he had been cast out of the imperial court, his loyalty ran deep. Apparently Ailey didn't even need her brothers to bully Ryam into behaving properly. Her family name was enough to draw strangers to her aid.

With his threat delivered, the nomad's mood lightened. 'So how did you manage to charm her?'

Ryam looked up again. The sun was behind Ailey, casting her face in shadow. The wind caught the edge of her robe and it fluttered around her. If she could only stay.

If she could only stay.

'Hell if I know,' he murmured. 'I beat her in a sword fight.'

Chapter Nineteen

Shadows flickered from inside Ailey's room and light spilled through the tiny aperture in the earthen wall into the courtyard. Oil for lanterns and candles were scarce at the Jade Gate. Pride told Ryam that she had left the lamp burning for him, even if it wasn't true. Having someone waiting for him was a comfort he had never known.

He called at the window. 'Ailey, it's me.'

A moment later, she appeared in the doorway, her silhouette framed by the lamplight. Her pale, long-sleeved robe fell just past her knees. It must have belonged to Miya, who stood a hand-span shorter than her.

With an expectant look, she captured her unbraided hair and wound it to one side. He was stricken by the purity of her.

'I missed you today,' he said.

'I missed you, too.'

The last time they had made love she had moved on top of him, riding him to ecstasy with her face radiant. At that moment he wanted to do more than make love to her again. He wanted to hold her, make her laugh if he could. If he reached out his hand a few inches, he could touch her.

'You look beautiful tonight.'

'I am leaving tomorrow.'

Her hands twisted tight in her hair as she watched for his reaction. Straight for the throat, that was Ailey's style. It took a moment for the coldness to set in.

'Tomorrow,' he echoed. 'All right.'

'I've told the princess,' she said with a calmness that was almost eerie. 'She has arranged everything.'

Her voice carried steady and soft over the pounding in his head. He found himself nodding, his body leaden. She was going as he had always known she would. The blade was falling quickly and he could do nothing but watch its plummet.

Ailey held her breath as she fixed her clear gaze on him. 'Come with me.'

'Of course.' So he had a moment of mercy, just a touch. 'I'll make sure you get home safely.'

'That's not what I meant.' She took a step closer before bracing her hand against the doorframe to stop herself. 'Come with me and stay with me.' She paused then. When he said nothing, she went on. 'If you won't stay, I would rather you did not go at all.'

He knew what he wanted. He wanted to make love to her until she lay exhausted in his arms and then blindly tell her yes to anything she asked of him. But that would have been another mistake, a mistake he could prevent for once. It was time to open his eyes.

She read his answer in his hesitation. A faint tremor crossed her face. Sadness and regret.

'I've always gone where I'm told,' he began.

'Because you are loyal.'

'Because I didn't know any better,' he bit off harshly. How could she continue to defend him, even now? 'I can't go with you.'

'Why?' She straightened and faced him with her chin raised, so stunning it hurt that he couldn't have her.

Even if he could find a way to stay with her, Shen would never allow his daughter to spend her life with a barbarian.

Certainly not with a man who had nothing, not even a name to offer her.

He crossed his arms over his chest. 'It would be a mistake. I'll only hurt you in the end.' He could see he was hurting her now, but it had to be done. 'I can't be who you need.'

She folded her arms as well, mirroring him. Her expression transformed to steel and fire. 'What is it I need?'

Ailey spoke softest when she wanted to cut deep.

'You need your family. You need honour, tradition, love.' He spoke the momentous words as if he had some inkling of what they meant. 'You need someone who can give you everything.'

'And you cannot?'

'No.'

'You don't want to.'

He knew Ailey wouldn't retreat so easily, not when she had committed. She was forcing his hand.

He fixed his jaw. 'No, I don't.'

The last answer was a lie. It hung between them, stark and final. The first sign of tears gathered beneath her lashes. He was making the right decision. He would say and do whatever it took to make it happen.

His gaze traced over every curve of her face, the rich darkness of her hair and those eyes of a colour he'd never seen anywhere in nature. He tried his hardest to commit her to memory before she closed the door and extinguished the light.

'What are you doing up here?' Adrian stared down at him.

Ryam reclined against the watchtower and shook his wineskin in response. Their banner flew above him. It flapped in the wind like the wings of a great, black bat.

Adrian stepped around his outstretched legs and sat down beside him. 'I think I'll have a drink with you.'

'This grain alcohol will knock your teeth out.'

He handed the skin over and Adrian took a long pull before passing it back. Ryam caught his friend's grin.

'Why are you in such a good mood?'

'Miya's pregnant.'

Ryam sputtered.

Adrian's grin widened. 'I know.'

For a moment the drink was forgotten in his hands. 'How is she?'

'Scared, but she doesn't want to show it.'

'Well, that's…that's wonderful.' Ryam drank again, grateful for the distraction.

They passed the skin back and forth for a couple of rounds. This far into it, the alcohol no longer burned down his throat, but it hadn't yet dulled the memory of his parting words with Ailey.

Adrian eyed him as Ryam downed the rest. 'Isn't it going to take more than that?'

Ryam swore under his breath. The last thing he wanted to do was talk. All he wanted to do was get too drunk to go back to her. She was still so close, just down below. By morning she'd be gone.

'I heard you volunteered to be in the scouting party,' Adrian went on.

'Due west,' Ryam declared. 'Nothing but sand and thorns between here and there. Even I can't mess this up.' His mouth twisted with wry humour. 'I suppose my decision got easier.'

The wineskin was empty. He tossed it aside and it slid to the edge of the wall. Adrian stared straight ahead. He did the same.

'I thought we could find another place,' Adrian said after a long time. 'A safer one, far from the influence of the empire. But nowhere is ever safe. We've been through enough to know that.'

'What do you mean? Now we're staying?'

'I mean we've been worried about survival for so long. Maybe survival alone isn't enough.' Adrian looked directly at him. 'You've saved my life more times than I can count. You don't owe me anything. Go with her.'

Ryam rubbed his hand over his eyes and wished desperately that there was more wine. 'I can't.'

'You said your decision got easier. You didn't make one. You had it made for you.'

'God's hairy—' he searched for an appropriate body part '—nose.' He wiped his mouth against the back of his hand and glowered into the darkness. 'I don't understand what she's talking about half the time. Everything is about honour and duty.'

'You're different with her.'

Ryam sank his forehead onto his knees. 'Did Miya put you up to this?' he asked.

'Do you love her?'

'Yeah.'

The answer spilled out of him. He kept his head down. The liquor must be getting to him.

Adrian was relentless. 'I would have thought you'd fight harder than this.'

'I'm going to disappoint her. Better to do it now.'

'Sounds like fear.'

'Shut up.'

Ailey belonged in Longyou and he belonged nowhere. Nothing would change that. She'd made her choice and he'd done what he had to so she could go freely.

'What makes you so unafraid when there's a sword in your hand?' Adrian asked.

Ryam whipped his head up a little too fast. The stars blurred before his eyes. 'That's different,' he grunted.

For one thing, cutting someone open with a sword was usually a clean end to things. There was no clean solution for Ailey other than for her to go and forget about him. He'd never forget her—God's breath, this was why he came up here. To *not* think these things.

He was drunk enough to try to get into a brawl with Adrian, who would probably bash his head into the tower. It would give him something to do with the anger he had inside that he was going to have to let her go. He considered it for a moment before what little reason he had left won out.

Ryam let his head fall back to stare at the sky. 'Just let me enjoy the quiet for a moment, will you?'

Ailey deserved the world and someone who could give it to her. He had slipped and admitted he loved her. Love was an uncompromising, unyielding beast that led to nothing. So, yes, he loved her. Ailey had got to him like a dagger in his heart. When it was removed, he would bleed out.

Chapter Twenty

It took all of her will for Ailey not to look back as she rode out from the still fortress of Yumen Guan the next morning. She hadn't expected Ryam to come to see her off after their parting the night before, but she had held out a glimmer of hope. Now even hope was gone.

Miya rode beside her, surrounded by an escort of guards. The princess had been kind enough to offer to accompany her part of the way that morning through the corridor. Dako and his men would escort her the rest of the way home. Twenty men riding through the frontier for her, because she had been stubborn and impulsive.

'I thought he would go with you,' Miya said quietly.

Ailey had nothing to say to that. Ryam had fought to protect her so many times, but in the end he had given up this battle without a struggle. She had been wrong about him, about the both of them. That was the part that hurt the most.

'Give him time,' Miya soothed. 'Not everyone can be as confident of the world as you are.'

A tight, pinching sensation hovered at the bridge of her nose. 'He should be confident about something like this.'

'I will write to the Emperor on Ryam's behalf.'

'There is no need. He has made his decision.'

Miya could not fix this, no matter how much influence she had. Ailey stared down at the rocky earth from her saddle. Her chest constricted with each step forwards. No matter how far away she travelled, it would still hurt like this, sharp and raw and open.

She still loved Ryam, still wanted him more than anything. But she had to bury this emotion in her heart. Fate without destiny, that's what they were.

The ride took them through mud-caked marshland and yellowed grass. Long-beaked birds swooped through the reeds, their white-tipped feathers brilliant in the sun. High against the mountainside, the ruins of earthen watchtowers marked the distance.

'I am sorry to see you go,' Miya said as they reached the bend. 'Please say you'll return. I think I'll want to have a "little sister" by my side.'

The princess's hand rested over her stomach. Miya had told her that morning of the news. Ailey wanted to be nothing but happy for Miya, but she couldn't help feeling the ache of regret. She would never have the same happiness or freedom for herself.

Miya reached over the saddle to take her hand in farewell, but her grip tightened suddenly. Hoofbeats pounded in the distance, growing louder by the moment. Dako halted the entourage and reined his steed in.

'There's too many to be a trade caravan,' Ailey murmured.

Dako's mouth pressed into a grim line in agreement. A cloud of dust rose around the bend, billowing higher in the wake of the riders. Ailey glimpsed patches of red on black.

Her fingers went numb. 'Li Tao.'

'Protect the princess,' Dako commanded to his men, positioning himself at the head of the party.

'Go, Miya,' Ailey urged. 'Get to safety.'

Li Tao's soldiers had come for her, but they would change tactics if they knew the exiled princess was within their grasp.

Miya calculated her odds before she broke away, digging her heels in as the escort surrounded her to race back towards the fortress.

Ailey brought her horse alongside Dako's as she stared at the approaching storm. They were outnumbered more than two to one from the looks of it. Miya wouldn't be able to make it back unless they bought her some time.

'The Shen bloodline flows strong in you,' Dako said, lifting his sword high.

The riders thundered closer. All around her, the tribesmen prepared for battle, steadying their mounts. She freed one sword into her right hand. The hilt slid against her sweat-slicked palm. With her other hand she clung on to the saddle, wishing she had some training for fighting on horseback.

'Stay close,' Dako shouted and then the fight was upon them.

The riders surged around them in a wave and the dust rose in a choking cloud. Her horse gave a snort, clomping backwards against the onslaught of riders. The first connection of her sword against another blade vibrated up her arm and nearly knocked her from the saddle. From the shouting, she knew she'd been recognised.

Ryam would not allow fear to set in if he were there. They had fought Li Tao's soldiers once before, side by side. His presence had given her courage, but he was no longer with her. She willed herself to breathe, attempting to control her heartbeat, trying to let the energy flow through her as she had been trained all her life.

The black swarm circled closer. Dako positioned his mount to cover her back. Behind her, the clash of his blade rang out again and again while she concentrated in front. One of the mounted soldiers galloped alongside her and tried to grab the reins. She slashed at him, her blade slicing through skin and jarring against bone.

Her horse turned itself to face the next approach, rearing to hold the attack at bay. The animal knew what to do better than she did. She hugged her knees against its sides. Without a centre to sink into, her sword swiped through the air without power. She might as well have been waving a silk scarf at the soldiers. They ducked away from her before charging forwards again.

Metal clashed all around and the air grew thick with dust and the sour smell of sweat. Her horse tossed his head in protest and strained to break free from the battle. She had to fight for control of him, slashing at anyone who came close as her body jerked around violently in the saddle. Her heart threatened to explode and it seemed the shouting around her would never end.

Out of the corner of her eye, she glimpsed the leader of the attack. His broad shoulders towered over the field as he galloped astride a coal-black stallion. Beneath his cloak, Ailey caught the glint of studded armour. His face was hidden by a helmet. The long cast of his shadow fell over her as he singled out the strongest threat. Dako. He raised the broadsword overhead and the cry of metal jarred the heavens as he struck.

Her horse broke into a run at the impact, separating her from the pack. She grabbed at the reins and found herself holding off two attackers. She cut again and again, hitting nothing as her frustration built. She needed to use both her arms. She needed to be able to manoeuvre.

There was a cry to the left as the broadsword bit into Dako's shoulder. The nomad twisted to the side as he fell and Li Tao's captain dismounted for a killing blow.

Ailey shouted and brought the reins up hard to direct her horse back into the fight, kicking her heels to drive him in between them. The leader stared at her as she rode close. He lifted his sword calmly. The gleaming blade looked as big as she was.

With cold determination, he swung in a deadly arc towards the horse's neck, his arms straining with the force. At the last moment she lost her resolve and pulled aside. The sudden motion threw her from the saddle.

She landed against her shoulder, her arm flung protectively over her head. The impact knocked the air from her lungs and left her gasping, struggling for the next breath that would not come. She rolled onto her knees, moving sluggishly. Her horse twisted back onto four legs, safe but shaken. He bolted from the battle, leaving her tormentor looming over her with the sun behind him. Her hands closed around dust. Her sword had been torn from her hands.

He didn't come any closer. Instead, he waited for her to recover. Arrogant bastard. Her sword lay inches away in the dirt and she reached for it, the sharp gravel biting into her knees. Slow. She was slow and stiff and aching. With great effort, she staggered to her feet. Her entire body throbbed with pain, but everything moved when she told it to. She wasn't broken.

She unsheathed the other sword and felt a surge of strength as she found her balance and lifted them. Dako stirred on the ground just beyond the fearsome warrior before her.

This was the fight of her life. She would need all the skill she could summon. For some reason, her adversary held back. She didn't.

She darted in, breathing through the motion, drawing from instinct and muscle memory. He moved to counter, but the broadsword took longer to bring around than the butterfly swords. Her eyes focused in on his elbow to watch for his next attack as her feet brought her within striking distance. Her leading sword cut across his forearm and the trailing sword struck high across his cheek.

He fell back cursing with a hand pressed to his face. She'd connected, but not deep. She needed to attack again while his momentum was broken. He thrust at her. She tried to deflect, but it was like shoving against a stone wall. The blow knocked her back with hardly any effort and his blade flew at her in unrelenting lines. She blocked each attack with one sword and then the other as she tested for a shift in his energy, searching for any opening. There was none. His balance was frightening and soon her arms ached from holding him off.

She couldn't keep up the fight much longer. It was then that she made her mistake, growing reckless. In desperation, she lunged at his blind side, aiming for his throat. One swipe of his broadsword was all it took to wrench the weapon from her grasp. Her fingers screamed with pain. Disarmed and off centre, she had no choice but to block his next strike by bracing her hands against his sword arm.

The energy flowing through her came to a shocking halt as she was shoved to the ground. She managed to shield herself from the blow. The second sword was knocked from her hand. Dark spots loomed before her vision as his fingers clamped around her wrist to haul her to her feet. Then, she experienced her first taste of the terrible strength in him.

Blood poured from the side of his face. Black eyes glittered beneath the helmet and the hard lines of his mouth loomed close as he dragged her against him, twisting her arm so hard she thought it would break. Ailey gritted her teeth to stifle a scream. She wouldn't give him that satisfaction. With the last of her will, she snapped her forehead against his nose.

'She-demon!' he cursed and shoved her back.

Her head rang from the impact and tears poured from her eyes. The soldiers surrounded her and dragged her back to her feet. She tried to search for Dako, but her arms were forced roughly behind her. They tied her before throwing her over a saddle like a sack of grain.

The soldiers whipped the horses into a gallop. Their hooves kicked up a shower of gravel and dirt and a rough hand held on to her as they thundered through the corridor, back towards the empire.

Yumen Guan was in a blur of motion the moment the escort returned with the princess. Ryam cut through the swarm of men as they hurried to their assigned stations. There were hostile soldiers in the corridor. Princess Miya had just returned with only half of the armed escort that had ridden out with her. Dako was unaccounted for.

Ryam shoved past the men surrounding the princess. 'Where is Ailey?'

'Li Tao's soldiers have taken her,' she said. 'Wait! I don't think they'll hurt her.'

'I can't take that chance.'

Ryam was no longer listening. He'd stood back while it happened. Ailey had been left alone to face the man who'd killed her brother and was intent on forcing her into marriage.

'It's suicide to rush in like that. Give me time to think. I can appeal to Emperor Shen,' Miya implored.

She thought in terms of diplomacy and negotiation, but there could be no negotiation with this warlord. Ryam started towards the gate.

'Get me the fastest horse.'

He ignored the throbbing in his head. His entire body ached from the last dregs of the grain liquor he'd consumed, but he willed the pain away.

'You can't go alone,' Adrian said.

Ryam stopped and looked towards the men gathered in the bailey. Already several of them were stepping forwards, waiting for his command.

He turned back to Miya. 'How many were there?'

She looked pale. 'I don't know.'

'How many?' he growled.

'I'm not certain. Twenty.'

'Archers?'

'No.' She closed her eyes as she tried to recall. 'Riders with heavy armour and swords.'

He gave the princess some credit. Miya was shaking, but she remained lucid and observant. He'd have to trust her assessment. He turned to Adrian.

'Take them,' Adrian said before he could ask. 'Go quickly.'

He assembled fifteen of the volunteers and sent the others to ready the horses. Yumen Guan couldn't afford to spare more than that and they would have to ride quickly. What they didn't have in numbers, they'd have to make up in skill and organisation. The Gansu corridor was their territory. They knew its terrain like the back of their hand.

'They have half a day on us,' he told his men. 'We'll need to ride through the night.'

His orders met no protest. They were ready to follow his lead.

He saw Adrian and Miya standing just outside the gates as he mounted. For a moment, Ryam thought of how it had always been Adrian who'd led them into battle. He banished it immediately. He'd fought by Adrian's side in every engagement and this was his fight. The warlord's soldiers had Ailey and they were dragging her back to him. Li Tao would punish her. He could kill her for defying him.

Ryam would take on ten of them with his bare hands if that's what would free her. Death didn't scare him; failure did. He should have never let her go on her own. The mistake that he had been afraid of making was right before him, looming large and threatening to drag him down to the ninety-nine hells the Chinese spoke of.

With a final salute, Ryam dug his heels into his steed and urged it into a gallop. The regiment quickly took their positions. They weren't an army any longer, but they had been for many years. It was the only thing that had held them together.

There were more soldiers stationed further down the corridor. Her captors shoved her into the back of a wagon. They tied her ankles as well as her wrists and then rode for hours. The rope cut into her as the wheels jostled over rocky terrain.

The commander ordered them south through the Qilian mountains. They would lose any pursuers in the trails that snaked through there. Ailey tried to sit up and look behind them, but it was impossible as she tumbled against the wooden slats. She hoped Miya had returned in time to send help for Dako. There was no hope that they could reach her.

At dusk, the wagon rolled to a stop. They had reached the foothills. Their leader came by the wagon to give her a cursory glance as she sat propped up against one side. An angry cut slashed across his cheek, below his left eye. Someone had stitched it closed and the blood had begun to dry over the wound. It gave her petty satisfaction knowing she had put it there.

'Untie me.' She repeated her demand louder as he walked by, but he ignored her.

He stood apart from the rest of them, turning her butterfly swords over in his hands as he inspected them in the waning daylight. Then he hooked both of the swords into his belt as if they were trophies. Of course Li Tao would send mindless brutes like this to do his bidding.

The next time they stopped the wagons, it was to rest for the night. She watched as they unhitched the horses. Yumen Guan was not that far away. If she could get free of her bonds and steal a mount, there was a small chance.

She could hear the commander barking orders from the other side of the camp. No fires would be set for the night. They didn't want to risk being discovered. Once the guard detail was set, he positioned himself beside the cart and drew his sword, resting it across his arms.

He remained nearby while she was given food and water. She wanted to spit it at him, but she needed her strength and she was still shaking from the battle. He probably slept standing up with his eyes open, she thought ruefully, as she slumped down in the cart. With a rough motion, he threw a coarse blanket over her shoulders.

She cradled her sore arm close, thankful it wasn't broken. A matter of nights ago she had been with Ryam, probably for the last time. It had ended so abruptly, cut to the quick. She couldn't stop thinking of how they hadn't said farewell to each other. They hadn't said anything at all.

Sleep took a long time in coming, but when it did, it dragged her down into a murky exhaustion that spread bone deep.

She hadn't stirred at all until the beat of hooves jerked her awake. The dingy light told her it was just before dawn.

The sound was faint, but it grew steadily louder. From the cadence of it there were multiple riders approaching. A faint hope rose within her. The morning watch stirred and shouted to the others to rise and take arms.

Li Tao's head man found the direction of the sound and

moved to the front of the camp where he stood waiting, feet apart and shoulders squared.

It was Ryam. He rode at the head of a band of the western barbarians. She let out a startled cry. The soldiers surrounded her, spilling into the wagon to grab her and force her back down as she tried to rise.

Ryam looked half-crazed. He must have ridden through the night to find her. His face was haggard, his complexion grey. What could he do against fifty armed men? They were going to be slaughtered.

'Go back,' she pleaded.

He found her with his eyes and she was stricken cold with fear.

He had come there to die.

Two thoughts entered Ryam's mind. They faced much more than twenty men. A quick scan over the swarm of black-and-red uniforms told him they'd be outnumbered more than three to one. The second thought was that it was too late to turn back.

He signalled to the men and they pulled into a tight formation as they advanced. They knew the scenario. When you were outnumbered, stay close. Separation meant death.

Ailey stared out from the throng of soldiers. Her arms were bound and she looked as if she'd been beaten. Rage coursed through him until his body overflowed with it. Someone would die. All of them, if he had his way.

'Ryam, you shouldn't have come.'

The sound of her voice sent a surge of strength like quicksilver through his limbs. It wouldn't last. They had ridden with little rest and barely a drink of water, let alone food. His single aim had been to get to Ailey.

He drew his sword and kicked his steed forwards to lead the charge. Li Tao's forces hadn't saddled up yet. His men needed to strike before the enemy could mount a defence. They rode through the centre of the camp, scattering the soldiers before them.

He kept his sights focused ahead on Ailey. If he could cut a path to her—once he had her secured within his grasp, he'd deal with the rest. To his left, the clang of steel told him they'd hit resistance. After the initial attack, the soldiers formed their defence on the ground, swords drawn. Ryam took out a foot soldier on his right with a strike to the head. Another swipe of his sword sent another man to the ground.

This wasn't about defeating the enemy. He needed to keep moving forwards. He tried to urge the steed ahead, only to be surrounded by the bastards. His men cut through the throng. Their swords were heavier, able to inflict enough immediate damage to push through the crowd. It wasn't long before the laboured grunt of a horse filtered through the shouting. One of the riders was being taken down. The impact beside him shook the earth.

Ryam cut through two more soldiers before the man at his right flank was dragged from the saddle. Hands grabbed on to his bridle. More took hold of him from the right, shoving him off balance. He kicked at them.

Numbers. There were too many. Once the right guard broke, the enemy surged between them.

His ride was going down. Ryam freed himself from the stirrups and attempted to control the fall. Gravel bit into his shoulder as he struck the ground. A cloud of dust crowded his lungs. He rolled and then dragged himself to his feet. His body ached from the impact.

He was better on the ground anyway.

But visibility was gone. Through the thick of the battle, he saw a few of the men were still on horseback. A few fought on foot.

An imposing warrior in armour stood at the edge of the throng. His sword was drawn, but he stood apart, watching. Their commander. The sight of Ailey's butterfly swords hanging from his belt added insult to injury.

Ryam trained his gaze on him and the warrior never moved. His underlings skulked forwards, a pack of wolves closing in on an injured animal.

He'd lost sight of the others in the dust storm. A vague thought came to him: death ground. He was on death's ground and there was nothing to do but fight. It was how he'd survived when the imperial soldiers had outnumbered them. It was how he'd rescued Ailey when they first met.

His strength was fading. He swung his sword in an endless volley. He didn't know how many he took out. It didn't matter. When the sword was knocked from his hands, he resorted to his fists. He could hear Ailey crying as he was wrestled to the ground and the sound of it broke him. The jagged gravel bit into his shoulder blades as he continued to struggle.

Something hard and blunt slammed against the side of his head. With his last thread of sight, he saw his father's blade lying fallen in the dirt. Then everything went black.

Chapter Twenty-One

Ailey stopped fighting her captors during the long journey back to the southern defence command. There were too many of them and they watched her as if their lives depended on it. They would return her to their master and she was powerless to stop it.

The soldiers had taken Ryam and four of his men prisoner and left the rest in the corridor to die or flee. They didn't seem to care. For the first days, she had pleaded and bargained with their leader to release them. Each time, he presented her with the back of his head. He and the others must have had orders not to speak to her unless necessary. After that, she sat in the wagon and watched as the mountains and wild plains faded into the dense forests of the south. She needed to be calm and think of what she would do once she was returned to Li Tao.

The warlord wanted to kill Ryam himself. That would be the only reason they kept him alive. They kept him imprisoned in one of the other wagons, refusing to let her see him. Her last sight of him had wrenched her heart. He'd been slumped over, his face to the ground, broken and bleeding. Unmoving.

Ryam had charged into battle as if he were invincible. It seemed he would always come for her, but only when she was in danger. It was another thing entirely to be willing to stand beside her, to stay with her.

The commander rode by to check on her, the cut below his eye making him seem even more vicious. He regarded her tears with a hard expression, eyes narrowed. Lifting her chin in defiance, she glared back at him, not caring if he saw her crying.

By the time they reached the edge of the bamboo sea, she had retreated into herself. It was a rare day when she spoke more than two words aloud. The sea was a wide expanse of bamboo that was known to sway and lilt in the breeze like a verdant ocean. The towering shoots engulfed the party in shade, but the natural beauty couldn't touch her. This was supposed to be a place of tranquillity and peace, but for her the dirt path cutting through the forest led to the executioner.

Li Tao's home was a military compound much like hers. As they arrived, there were soldiers assembled in pockets around the grounds, practising sword strikes against thick columns of bamboo and sparring against one another. Her father's soldiers were trained to fight in the mountains, Li Tao's to fight in the woods. Even if both Ryam and she were armed, they wouldn't be able to escape against so many.

The wagons pulled around to the back of the mansion. The compound was protected from the rear by a wide gorge, the walls of grey stone cutting deep into the earth. As the wheels came to a halt, the soldiers cut her bonds. She tried to see where they would take Ryam, but they dragged her into the house and left her to the servants.

At first the household hovered about, uncertain of what to do with her. They addressed her politely as their mistress and would not meet her eyes as they spoke to her. A grey-haired woman who reminded her of Amah took her by the arm and led her into a private chamber. The old woman had a bath drawn as she clucked over the ugly bruises on Ailey's arms and the rope burns at her wrists. The unexpected sympathy was a sharp contrast to the roughness of her capture.

'Where is your master?' Ailey asked. She wasn't going to waste any time speaking to anyone but Li Tao.

'Master Li will be back shortly.'

The servants assisted her in her bath, carefully washing around the nicks and bruises from her fight, which had been given enough time to grow dark and brutal. They dressed her in a sapphire-coloured robe and sprinkled her sleeves and collar with perfume, filling the dressing room with the scent of orange blossoms. She wanted to tear the heavy silk from her. She was being prepared as a new bride to be welcomed into the household. The thought sickened her.

The old serving woman who called herself Auntie Jinmei led her out to the sitting room and directed her onto a couch. Auntie's thin hands worked efficiently, her touch not unkind as she smoothed out Ailey's skirt and arranged the long sleeves over the discoloured patches on her arm. When she was finished, she backed out of the room in small steps without saying a word.

No more running. Ailey clasped her hands together to keep them from trembling. Li Tao had full rights to her since her parents had agreed to the marriage. Now that she was in his hands he could lock her up, he could beat her for her disobedience. He could do anything he wanted to Ryam. She sprang to her feet at the sound of footsteps in the outer hall.

'I demand to see the Emperor,' she said, turning to face the door.

'I have already summoned your father.'

The calm reply cut through her anger. She staggered back as Li Tao stepped into the room. Her stare fixed on to the wound that slashed over his left cheek. He came to stand before her, stretching to his full height. His armour had been replaced with a nobleman's robe, but he was no less intimidating.

'You're Li Tao?'

His mouth twisted into a smile that did not reach his eyes. 'And you are Shen Ai Li.'

She had never considered the governor would come for her himself. The expanse of his shoulders and chest loomed before her, forcing her to abandon the assumption that he would be old and soft. She knew he was just over twice her age. His hair was cut short and jet black, threaded with silver at the temples. He hadn't been this close to her since they had fought. His nose was raised like an eagle's, his features well defined, starkly handsome.

'Shen An Lu told me his daughter trained with swords. I didn't imagine a woman would have the patience to acquire such skill.'

His disrespect lashed out endlessly. He insulted her in the guise of faint praise and called her father by his name instead of Emperor.

Li Tao traced the line of the cut across his cheek with a finger. 'Since you are the one who marked me, you should have no complaint about having to look at this every day.'

She finally found her voice at his intimation. 'I'm not marrying you.'

'You will.' His response was immediate, uncompromising. 'You were promised to me and I have gone through considerable effort to find you.'

He came even closer, backing her up until her legs pressed against the edge of the couch.

'I have known since you were born that I would marry you.'

There was no sentiment in his statement. His gaze fixed on her with feral intensity. She tried to meet it and was reminded of their swords locking in combat, her arms straining to hold up against his power.

Survival instinct had her searching the edges of the room for escape. Her heart pounded against her ribs, but she would not let him intimidate her.

'Are you plotting against my father?' she demanded.

He laughed, a punctuated bark. 'I have fought alongside Shen An Lu in many battles.'

'You did not answer me. I was told about your schemes.'

He turned his back to her, dismissing her accusation. This had been his method for the entire journey when he chose not to answer. She refused to back down. Treason was a serious accusation to make of a man like Li Tao and she had staked everything on her conviction.

'I know about the shipment of swords you smuggled into this province. You're building an army against Changan. If you are truly a man with nothing to fear, then admit it.'

He swung around. 'Those doddering ministers in Changan think they can control this vast empire. The *jiedushi* already rule this land, if they don't destroy it first.'

'Those were your weapons.'

'They were,' he replied calmly.

Despite her suspicions, it still unnerved her to hear the proof from him. 'You want to break up the empire.'

'It is already broken.' He loomed closer. He lowered his voice until it rumbled deep against her spine, unnerving her. 'There was no need to run to your father. I will tell him myself. I *have* told him. I can be his greatest ally or I can be his fiercest enemy.'

Li Tao was even more fearsome than she imagined. He wasn't a simpering politician, grasping for power. He was a warrior like her father. Looking into his eyes, she truly believed he was capable of killing in cold blood, if it served his purposes.

She had to know. 'Did you have my brother killed?'

Her hands were trembling and she clenched them into fists. She watched the warlord's grim expression for any telling signs. He gave nothing away.

'Shen Ming Han was young and brash. Reckless.'

Always that word. 'You never answered the question,' she said.

The way his gaze skimmed over her face set her heart pounding. If Li Tao had ordered her brother's death, she would have to demand his life in return. But she already knew she was no match for the warlord.

'Does it make sense that I would kill one of the Emperor's precious sons? For what purpose? Your brother shouldn't have rushed into battle like that. He was trapped in that valley. Many men were killed.' Li Tao shook his head. 'No one will ever know what happened there. But I will tell you this—if it had been me, I wouldn't lie about it.'

His denial gave her no comfort. She couldn't sense anything behind his motivations but cold logic and it frightened her even more than his reputation for being ruthless. 'A man like you will never be loyal to anyone.'

'Your ideals about honour are ghosts of a dying era,' Li Tao declared without apology. 'No one but Shen holds them any longer and that will be his downfall.'

'I could never marry a man with no sense of honour.'

'You speak of honour.' He lowered his face to hers. 'The barbarian who fought so valiantly for you—how honourable were his intentions after you gave yourself to him?'

A flood of heat rose up her neck. He was standing too close. She would have shoved him away, but that would mean touching him.

'You were promised to me and you let him put his hands on you,' he said through his teeth. 'I should kill him for it.'

The blood drained from her face. He would do it. He was within his rights as her intended husband.

'If I marry you, will you let him go?'

The thread of control snapped in him. She tried to move away, but he crowded her, blocking her escape and she fell back onto the couch. He placed his hands on either side of her, caging her in.

'You may carry swords, but you are not a man and this is not a negotiation. If I do not kill this barbarian with my own hands, your father will execute him for the disrespect he has shown for both of us. And for you.'

The anger radiated from him in dark waves that made her tremble. For the first time she had a sense of the power Li Tao wielded: enough power to challenge the Emperor. She was a mere woman, a disobedient child. She already belonged to this man according to law and custom.

'If you touch him...' her chest rose and fell with each breath '...if you hurt him, I promise you will never have a moment's peace in your own home. You will never enjoy your marriage bed. I will put a knife in your heart. It may be tomorrow, it may be fifty years from now. I swear it. I am Shen An Lu's daughter and I will make good on my word.'

She glared up at him, challenging him to do anything, say anything to counter her. He could strike her or threaten her, but she meant every word.

His jaw tightened. 'They said you were beautiful.' His gaze slid over her face, lingering on her mouth. 'They also said you were obedient.'

He straightened slowly, his eyes remaining on her the entire time. When he turned and strode from the room, she sank into the couch, finally able to breathe again.

The next morning, Ailey emerged from her sleeping chamber to see a gown of red silk laid out like a tongue of fire in her dressing room. On the bodice, tiny pearls had been sewn into the wings of a phoenix. The coloured threads hurt her eyes, they were so vibrant. Gold and silver and the purest green like a bamboo leaf shining with morning dew.

Auntie Jinmei stood beside the dress and touched the pearls with a reverent brush of her fingers. 'Master Li told us you would need to be fitted for wedding clothes.'

Ailey grabbed a fistful of the red silk and marched out to the balcony, the only portal she had been allowed to the outside world. The old woman gasped as she tossed the dress over the wooden railing and leaned over wickedly to watch it fall.

'Ungrateful child!'

'Tell Li Tao he can spare the expense of buying me clothes. I am waiting for the Emperor to take me home.'

'You will make master angry,' Auntie muttered, shuffling out of the room.

Good. Ailey stared at the splash of crimson on the white stone courtyard below. A breeze rippled the silk. Perhaps the wind would drag the wedding dress into the chasm.

Li Tao had left her alone after their brief encounter the day before. Armed guards stood outside her door and the balcony was too high to escape. She was a prisoner until Father arrived.

If Li Tao had his way, she would be a prisoner for the rest of her life.

Alone in the dressing room, Ailey put on a plain grey robe and ran a comb through her hair. Memories of Ryam took hold of her. She closed her eyes and imagined him burying his face into her hair as he kissed her neck. No one would tell her where he was. She pleaded with the servants, but they only averted their eyes and fell silent.

She returned to the balcony and breathed deep to take in the fresh, damp scent of cypress and moss. When Father came, she would swallow her pride and beg that Ryam be freed. She had to find a way to convince him, but nothing came to mind. Father would be angry at her for disobeying. He would be ashamed of her.

He would certainly demand Ryam's death.

Her parents believed Li Tao to be a good match, yet he spoke proudly about treason and spat on honour as if it was a disease. He didn't even deny that he was using her for his gain. She couldn't live each day with contempt, distrustful of her own husband.

Ryam didn't have power or wealth, but he cared for her. When she spoke he listened, curious and willing to learn. He treated her as if she was important, not a worthless woman. But what did all the concern in the world matter when he wouldn't allow himself to be with her?

The wooden planks creaked behind her. She'd been too absorbed in her thoughts to hear Li Tao enter.

'Ai Li.'

The mere sound of her name seemed like a command from him.

'You and I are not familiar enough for you to address me so,' she said, staring straight ahead.

'Lady Shen,' he amended easily. 'You are quite disagreeable. Not what I would expect from the daughter of An Lu and Wen Yi.'

She hated the reminder of how well he knew her parents. 'Break the engagement, then,' she demanded.

'Your temperament does not matter to me. It does not even matter that your virtue is no longer intact.'

She turned and found herself staring at his chest. He stood close, his hands by his sides.

Her gaze shot up to his face. 'Marry a wooden puppet, then.'

'I would if her name was Shen.'

She glared at him hatefully. 'You are everything I thought you would be.'

He crossed his arms. This was how he must look before his army. An unyielding warlord, his face a mask.

'Look down below.'

The way he said it put a chill in her heart. She looked back over the railing.

Soldiers dragged Ryam into the courtyard with chains clamped on to his wrists and ankles. It took three men to subdue him. They grabbed on to his arms and shoulders and forced him onto his knees. She gripped the ledge, her nails digging into the wood as her heart plummeted to her stomach.

Ryam struggled against his captors to look up. Frightful bruises marred his face.

'I'll kill you,' he growled at Li Tao.

The men holding him staggered against the force of his weight as he thrashed and twisted. They finally managed to force him down, shoving his face against the ground.

'You've been torturing him,' she cried.

'I am not a monster,' Li Tao said in disgust. 'He fights my men at every chance. They might be forced to kill him in defence.'

The quiet threat nearly broke her resolve. He was testing her bold declaration from the day before. He came forwards to stand beside her. The raw edge of his scar showed clearly in profile. She steeled herself against whatever threat he was about to make.

'Marry me and I will release him.'

'And the others?'

'The others as well.'

She was beginning to see the sort of man he was. Emotionless and unpredictable.

'You refused such an offer before,' she said warily.

'It is offensive to me to let your lover live.' He stared at Ryam with contempt. 'But I do want sons and I will not force my own wife. And I do not relish the thought of a knife in my heart from a woman who is quite capable with swords.' His gaze returned to her. 'Marry me willingly and I will let him go. I rarely compromise.'

'You'll kill him anyway.'

'Only the weak need to lie,' he replied and she knew he meant it. There was no reason for him to lie to her. He had the higher ground, all the advantage, all the power.

Ryam continued to fight even while forced to the ground with a knee pinned on his back. She withered inside to see him taken down. He would fight to the death. That was the one thing he knew how to do.

'When your father comes, he will take my side in this,' he said with cruel reason. 'Do you think he will feel any sympathy for the man who defiled his precious daughter?'

Ailey pressed a hand to her stomach, trying to force out the ache and the hollowness that ate at her.

Li Tao circled for the kill. 'You were alone when I found you. You were returning to the empire without him.'

It was true. She had laid herself bare and asked Ryam to go with her and he had refused. She had already lost him.

Her throat tightened unbearably. 'I will marry you if you let him go.'

She couldn't feel her fingers any more or her feet. The weight of her body left her. She would need to remain without feeling for the rest of her life to survive.

The men still held Ryam to the ground. Every time he tried to lift his head, they shoved him down. He bled from a cut in his mouth. This was the last she'd see of him, broken and bleeding.

Li Tao reached up and gripped the back of her neck. She fought the urge to shake him off.

'Swear it to me, Ai Li,' he said with razor softness. 'If you swear it, then I know your word is good.'

She hated him. She hated herself for being unable to fight back.

'I swear it.'

Slowly he released her. He rested his hands on the rail beside hers. The signet ring given to him by the August Emperor gleamed on his second finger.

'Go down to him and tell him what is to happen.'

Li Tao's warning followed her as she retreated from the balcony.

'If I see him touch you, I won't be able to restrain my temper. He will die, our agreement be damned.'

She went down alone. With each step she knew Li Tao would be watching from above.

The men let Ryam up when she stepped out into the courtyard. He straightened, the iron chains hanging from his wrists. Ailey's heart cracked open when she saw how pale he looked. The hollows of his cheeks were sunken and mottled with bruises. Behind his ravaged face, his eyes shone bluer than ever.

Ryam looked her over, his face full of concern. 'How are you? Are you hurt?'

He would think to ask about her when he looked so battered. She almost broke before him.

'I am well.'

He started forwards and she recoiled from him. Confusion clouded his expression.

He was still so beautiful to her. She bit hard into her lip, but the tears came anyway.

'You are going home and I am going to marry Li Tao.'

'No.' Ryam glanced up to the balcony. 'That bastard is forcing you to do this.'

He pushed away the guards and surged towards her. The guards hauled him back and shoved a blade against his neck. At that moment she would have done anything, sworn anything to save him.

'Stop,' she begged. 'Please stop.'

'You don't have to do this.' Ryam strained against his captors, ignoring the sword at his throat. 'My life isn't worth anything.'

'It is to me.'

The chains rattled. He would not stop fighting. 'I'm not going anywhere.'

'It is your nature to seek death, but it isn't the only way, Ryam.' She closed her eyes to shut away the pain and anger on his face and willed herself to walk away.

She had to go before he got himself killed. It would happen some day. He would rush into some situation without thinking and it would be the end of him. But today she needed to know that she had sent him home safe.

'I'm not going anywhere,' he shouted after her. 'Ailey! Do you hear me? I'm not going anywhere.'

The chains scraped against the stone floor as they dragged him away.

Chapter Twenty-Two

Ryam flew at the door of his prison and pounded against it until the wood dented and his knuckles were scraped raw. Then, for good measure, he rammed the door with his shoulder. It shook, but held. What he wouldn't give to go face to face with Li Tao with a sword in his hands. The bastard's soldiers would get him, but not before he cut the man's throat. But his hands lay empty. His sword had fallen from his grasp and lay forgotten on the gravel of the Gansu corridor.

His father's sword. The sword that had kept him alive as they'd fought their way across the desert.

Ailey didn't have to do this. She didn't have to sacrifice for him, not after she had fought for so long. He was destined to die lying in the dust with a knife in his ribs anyway. A pointless death. He'd always known it. Ailey was the only one who had ever asked for him to be anything more.

He dropped his forehead against the door. He wasn't going anywhere. The moment they released him, he'd come back. He would be inviting death, but the thought of death, of nothingness, didn't bother him. Not when he had nothing left to lose.

He stared around the hut for something, anything to use as a weapon. There was nothing but damp earth and bare walls.

He wouldn't allow himself to think of odds. Rationality would only invite doubt and if he doubted himself for a second he'd lose.

The only way he was leaving without Ailey was when they carried his carcass out of there. Except getting himself killed was the one thing Ailey had begged him not to do.

Slowly he sank to the ground. It came to him then. Ailey had been wrong. He wasn't a courageous swordsman in the least.

He had never been brave for a single moment. All the times he had rushed into battle, saving Adrian's life, Ailey's life—none of it. He could only be fearless with a sword in his hand because he had never cared whether he won or lost.

His father had wasted away needlessly for the woman he loved. Ryam claimed to never mourn his parents, but he had been doing the same, bit by bit. What Ailey thought of as courage was simply his own way of searching for that final drunken duel that would kill him. He had been chasing the falling blade his entire life.

Death couldn't be the only way, Ailey had told him before turning away. She had carved his name into her beloved tree in a language he didn't know. There had to be another way to sacrifice and another way to love. She knew how, and he didn't.

He sank onto the wooden bench that had served as a bed in the cramped enclosure. He needed to conserve his strength instead of spending it in rage. It was time to fight a battle that mattered.

He wasn't going anywhere. He had meant it when he told Ailey that. He meant it even more now.

Ailey didn't recognise her own reflection as she sat before the mirror. Her face had been dusted with a sheen of powder and her lips painted cherry-red like the silk of the wedding dress. Red for good fortune, for fertility, for happiness.

'Everything that you desire, young princess.' Auntie murmured blessings as she smoothed back Ailey's hair with careful fingers. 'Everlasting joy.'

A shadow blocked the door as Auntie bent to slip a pair of pearl earrings into her ears.

'You shouldn't be here,' Ailey said.

Li Tao remained at the entrance. By tradition a groom wouldn't see his bride until they were alone in the wedding chamber. Husband and wife would look upon each other immediately before they became one. After all that had happened, those customs meant nothing to them.

'Your lover is being released,' he said coolly. 'Do you wish to see evidence that he has left safely since I'm a man without honour?'

'You gave your word. I believe you.'

But she would never trust him.

'I was watching you with that barbarian.' His mouth turned down with scorn.

'Do not talk about him.'

She stiffened as he came close. Auntie continued tucking flowers into her hair, undaunted and invisible in the usual way of servants. Li Tao motioned the old woman aside and stood by the chair.

'It occurred to me you might consider taking your own life to avoid this marriage.'

The sleeve of his robe brushed her shoulder, sending a shiver down her spine. How could she endure their wedding bed? Whenever he was near, Li Tao purposefully used his size to intimidate her and throw her off balance. He claimed to have no honour, but took no issue using honour to his advantage.

'You have my promise,' she said bitterly.

A low rumble came from outside, growing louder by the second in a pounding rhythm.

'Your father is here.'

Both of them knew the sound of marching troops. Li Tao left to greet the Emperor. More than a month had passed since the day she had left home in her wedding procession. She was going to marry Li Tao as her parents expected. Outwardly nothing had changed, but she had travelled to the edge of the empire and back. She had fallen in love.

A crier announced the Emperor's arrival. Taking a deep breath, she went outside to see him standing in the courtyard, his expression grim. The imperial dragon bared its talons on his armour. She went to him, all the while searching his face for a sign of disapproval and disgust.

'Let us walk,' was all he said.

Her father clasped his hands behind him as they strolled through Li Tao's garden. She followed dutifully by his side while a train of attendants shuffled behind them.

'How is Mother?'

'Heartbroken.' Quiet anger vibrated through every fibre of his body.

Swallowing, she bowed her head to acknowledge her part in her mother's despair. To say anything, to make any excuse would have been disrespectful.

'Your brother worries every day for your safety. Your grandmother blames herself for your foolishness.'

She nodded and nodded, feeling selfish and unworthy. When she had decided to return, she knew there would be consequences for her act of rebellion.

Father continued, 'What is this I hear about a foreign swordsman named Ryam?'

Her stomach wound into a tight coil. 'He saved my life. He's a good man.'

'Princess Miya speaks highly of him.'

He gestured and an attendant ran forwards with a letter. Her fingers closed around the thin rice paper. She didn't open it. Miya was kind to intervene, but it made no difference any more.

'He is gone. I will never see him again,' she said in a small voice.

'We are fortunate Li Tao is generous enough to accept you as his bride despite what you have done.'

'Generous?'

Her biting tone earned her a sharp look.

'Yes, he is a powerful ally,' her father continued. 'Li Tao is accomplished. He is a capable leader. He fought along with me as well as the August Emperor in battle.' His voice rose. 'He is able bodied, not too old. Wealthy. What more could a daughter hope for?'

'I was trying to protect you,' she blurted out.

He shook his head impatiently. 'Your mother was so happy we had made such a good match.'

'You don't need to be angry any more. I've agreed to marry him.'

She stared down at her feet. The butterfly pattern of her slippers peeked out from the hem of her robe. Butterflies for love, red for happiness. She was clothed magnificently in one lie after another.

'Your mother was very upset when you left. She thought she might have said something to you to make you run away.'

'Mother?' She looked away. 'It was not Mother.'

Her father nodded. He was satisfied with her answer, but she wasn't. She stopped, no longer able to walk dutifully beside him.

'It was not Mother,' she echoed, her voice rising. 'It was you.'

He raised his eyebrows. She fortified herself for what she needed to say. What good were all her acts of protest if she couldn't speak now?

'Father is asking our family to go against all that it has lived by.' She fell into formal address in her anger. 'He is asking us to go against honour.'

'Are you saying that you do not wish to marry Li Tao?' he asked quietly.

She shook her head, feeling the desperation. He still didn't understand.

'You were planning to take Miya as your Empress,' she said.

'There were reasons.'

'There can be no reason.'

The words caught in her throat. Her father had been a giant to her all her life, larger and stronger than anyone. But for once, he was just a man, as fallible as any other.

'Mother is a good woman. She has given you five sons. How can you listen to advisers and take that away?' she demanded with more boldness than she had ever dared. 'You cannot buy respect. You cannot negotiate for it.'

He raised his hand to stop her and she feared she had gone too far.

'And one daughter,' he added.

She looked at him, puzzled.

His hand tightened on her shoulder. 'Five sons and one daughter.'

A gong signalled the tenth hour. The wedding was to begin soon.

'Do you want to marry Governor Li?'

Ailey stared up at her father. The creases deepened at the corner of his eyes as he waited for her answer. He'd never asked her about what she wanted.

Did it really matter what she wanted? Ryam hadn't wanted her enough when it mattered and she had sworn to marry Li Tao willingly. Fourth Brother's spirit no longer called to her. It was her own heart calling now, buried deep as she swallowed her sorrow.

Duty before all else.

The gong sounded again. Auntie hovered nervously, afraid to interrupt the Emperor.

'I have been sworn to Li Tao by my father, my mother and by my own word.' She fought to keep her voice steady. 'The Shen family honours its promises.'

Chapter Twenty-Three

The soldiers led Ryam out of the hut and prodded him towards the forest. Four of his men in his regiment stood beside the road. It was the first time he'd seen them since they were captured. At one point, he'd considered that they might already have been executed. The warlord could still execute them now. No one would ever find a band of barbarians tossed into the thick of the bamboo forest.

Ryam approached his men in a silent parade with a pair of soldiers on each side. The chains weighed down his wrists and ankles. The men were similarly shackled, but he saw immediately that they hadn't been mistreated. The only injuries evident were ones they'd sustained in the fight.

He wasn't able to talk to them, but he was brought to the front as they marched down the dirt road. The crash of cymbals came from the direction of the mansion. The wedding procession was beginning. Ailey had bought their freedom with her life.

Part way down the road, the captors stopped to unlock their chains. All of the schemes Ryam had considered through the night came back to him. He'd attack the soldiers with his bare hands. He'd disarm them and take their swords to fight his way back. Desperation would give him the strength to do it.

The cymbals grew louder, accompanied by the sound of drums and horns. His men were watching him carefully. They'd fight if he told them to—unarmed and outnumbered, hundreds of miles from home. Thousands of miles, in truth.

He realised then that all of his daring plans would come to failure.

'I'm staying,' he said.

Li Tao's soldiers tensed when he spoke, not understanding. But he was addressing his men. He turned to the veteran among them.

'Bertram, take them back to Yumen Guan.'

'If you stay, we stay.'

And they'd die. This was brotherhood beyond blood. 'You've done enough. This is my fight now.'

The guards reached for their weapons.

'*Róngyù,*' he declared.

The captors paused. He repeated in case his inflection was all wrong the first time. This was no plot. Just a decision he'd finally made.

Róngyù. Honour.

They frowned and looked at one another. He'd learned plenty from fighting alongside Shen An Lu's soldiers in the palace rebellion. Begging for your life made you an unredeemable coward, but demanding to die the proper way was always taken seriously.

'Go,' he said to the men who'd fought with him.

They didn't like his command, but they obeyed it. They had fought well in the corridor when he'd brought them against insurmountable odds. He wouldn't let them sacrifice their lives for him. Ailey had once told him she'd rather die than marry Li Tao. He wouldn't let her sacrifice herself either.

He gave one final nod to Bertram before they disappeared into the bamboo. The captain of the guard shook his head at him, appalled that a barbarian would try to mimic their traditions. But they led him back towards the mansion.

Li Tao's defence command assembled in the front square along with a regiment of imperial soldiers. At the centre of the congregation, four servants lifted a bamboo sedan carrying a woman in red silk. The soldiers tried to drag him around the back of the house, out of sight.

Once the wedding was done, it would be too late.

'Li Tao!' he shouted. And then he shouted his one-word challenge again. Honour.

The captain struck him with the back of his hand.

A murmur snaked through the crowd and the woman pulled the cloth from her face. Ailey. Her mouth fell open, her lips painted scarlet.

She tried to rise and the sedan lurched as the carriers struggled for balance. Li Tao stood on the front step. His soldiers poured out onto the square like a swarm of black ants.

'Stand down.'

The command came from a man in dragon armour standing beside Li Tao. Emperor Shen stared him up and down before beckoning him forwards.

Ryam moved warily past the gauntlet of drawn swords and bowed to the Emperor. Li Tao's black eyes looked as if they could pierce armour.

A look of recognition crossed the Emperor's face. '*Bái xiá*. What is your business here?' the Emperor asked calmly.

Being referred to as white warrior was a bit better than white demon. Ryam glanced down at his ragged clothing. He hadn't expected to do much talking. 'I am here for your daughter.'

'Take him,' Li Tao ordered in disgust.

'Wait.' Ailey scrambled from the sedan. 'You promised to release him.'

She stepped between them and faced Li Tao, forming a barrier with her slender form. His warrior girl, still trying to protect him. Li Tao fixed a possessive look on her that made Ryam want to plant a fist in the man's face.

Ryam stared at the flowers pinned in her hair. 'I should have said yes,' he said quietly.

She glanced back at him. Her lips parted to speak.

'Swordsman.' The Emperor's voice rang out over the assembly, cutting off Ailey's reply. 'You are disrupting my daughter's wedding.'

'I swore myself to Li Tao,' she whispered brokenly. 'There is nothing you can do.'

He had no command of the language to say what he needed to say to the Emperor, but he couldn't go quietly.

'I'll challenge Li Tao for her,' he said loud enough for the entire assembly to hear. 'For her freedom.'

Ailey grabbed hold of his arm. Her touch was enough to reassure him. How did he ever think he could let her go?

'I told you I don't want you getting yourself killed for me,' she said.

'This is different.'

He couldn't explain it to her, but it was different inside.

'I accept the challenge,' Li Tao replied calmly. 'If that is the simplest way to resolve this, then I accept.' He came down the steps and called for his sword. His dark gaze locked on to Ryam with disdain. 'Let us put an end to this.'

Ryam removed himself from Ailey's grasp and directed her away. He rubbed at the raw marks on his wrists from the chains.

'I don't have a weapon.'

'Use mine, Swordsman.'

Emperor Shen held his sword high and tossed it towards Ryam. The blade arched through the air, landing at his feet. A pulse of energy filled him as he gripped it. Once again he had a sword in his hand. He bowed his head briefly in the Emperor's direction, thanking him.

Ailey looked over the bruises and scrapes on his face. Her eyes danced with colour, reflecting frustration, hope and fear.

'I love you,' she said.

He nodded. 'I'm going to win.'

The disrupted wedding party moved towards the rear of the compound with him and Li Tao at the lead. Ailey and her father trailed behind them, followed by the rest of the assembly.

He and Li Tao walked side by side, neither of them looking at the other. The warlord was nearly as tall as Ryam was, with broad, bone-crushing shoulders.

'You have no right to her,' Li Tao rumbled beside him as they neared the battleground.

'You don't own her,' Ryam retorted.

He caught the way Li Tao's knuckles tightened on his sword. In the short walk to the courtyard he picked up an array of signals about his opponent: the familiar way he held his sword, the steadiness of his gait. If he was worth anything as an opponent, Li Tao would be doing the same.

They took to opposite ends of the courtyard. Ryam swung the blade, testing its weight. Double-edged and straight with a dragon etched near the hilt. They called it the *jian*, the sword of gentlemen. Its light weight belied its deadliness. He had faced them, but never wielded one.

'Everything you've got,' Ryam murmured, keeping his line of sight on Li Tao as he bowed.

Li Tao's eyes flashed cold like a viper before the strike. Ryam didn't know if he understood, but he returned the bow.

In the stillness before the fight, he searched for Ailey. She stood beside her father, a scarlet beacon as a cool wind drew up from the depths of the canyon to stir the air around them. This was no drunken brawl. This was the one fight that mattered. She had chosen him once. He would have to convince her to choose him again.

In the next heartbeat, Li Tao rushed forwards. They engaged, swords crashing in a grip of lightning and thunder.

Li Tao took no quarter. His sword sang with deadly purpose. Ryam managed to slap it away with the flat of his blade only to have it flash back, stinging across his forearm. First blood, and not two seconds in.

No time to think about it. Li Tao was on him again. Ryam's blade rang from the blows. He was using his weapon wrong and he could feel the dissonance in his arms.

Li Tao met his gaze without any satisfaction. 'I am glad you returned so I can kill you.'

Ryam swung at him and Li Tao dodged easily. They locked blades crosswise.

Ryam tried to push free and drive back, but Li Tao answered with a slice across his shoulder. He felt the burn of it without ever seeing the blade. Before he could back away, Li Tao's sword cut again. He jumped back, but not before taking a glance against his ribs.

He did his best to fend off Li Tao's attacks, but the warlord drove him back relentlessly. Ryam found himself edged against the gorge, its wide mouth ready to devour him.

Li Tao raised his sword, the steel stained red with blood. Ryam's blood. He was being carved up piece by piece. The man was better than him, at least with this sword. With a shout, Ryam charged. When Li Tao parried, Ryam twisted his blade free and continued forwards. Too close for blade work, he struck the hilt of his sword against Li Tao's breastbone, forcing the breath from his lungs. Then he came in hard, striking at soft targets. He sent the heel of his hand into Li Tao's throat and brought his knee up to strike·his gut. Li Tao's sword clattered to the floor. Instead of bending to retrieve it, he tackled Ryam and they toppled to the ground.

The back of Ryam's head struck against stone, blotting his vision with spots of light. Li Tao was still gasping for breath from the blow to his chest, but he wasted no time. He balled his hand into a fist and drove it down against Ryam's jaw. Ryam surged past his pain to reply with his own fist, striking out wildly until he connected against flesh and bone. Li Tao fell back and Ryam stumbled to his feet, grabbing on to his sword. He swiped his tongue over the salty, metallic tang of blood.

Li Tao had been a street fighter at some point in his life. Ryam would swear by it.

'Pick up your sword,' Ryam taunted. 'Let us settle this like gentlemen.'

He waited while Li Tao stooped to retrieve his weapon. The last exchange had taken a lot of the venom out of Li Tao's bite. The area over his eye swelled and he bled from the corner of his mouth. Wiping the blood away with the back of his hand,

Li Tao glanced once at Ailey and then faced him with a look of determination so fierce Ryam knew at once it was more than male rivalry. Li Tao believed in his heart that he was defending Ailey's honour and that she belonged to him.

Breathing hard, Ryam switched tactics. He held a precision weapon in his hands, not a strength one. Small efficient movements, he reminded himself. Keep to the centre, energy forwards.

Li Tao broke into a series of attacks, each advance chained effortlessly to the previous one. This time Ryam parried with a pure harmony of steel strike. He was finding the rhythm, sensing the intention through the blade to anticipate the angle of the next strike.

With a flick of his wrist, Ryam cut through Li Tao's defences. The sword grazed the warlord's midsection, the sharp edge tearing through fabric to draw blood.

Ryam had been in many fights in his life. Most opponents backed down after a wound, but Li Tao knew how to take a blow. He barely winced before resetting his guard to form a new attack. Ryam was going to have to kill this man or beat him into submission.

This time he let Li Tao come in close. Ryam watched the leading edge of the attack. The sword bit into his free arm as the gleaming steel sheared past him. Ignoring the burning pain, he followed the motion, waiting until the moment when the strike was most committed. Then he grabbed Li Tao's arm and wrenched it opposite the joint, locking it. Ryam lashed out with his sword arm.

His blade stopped an inch from the warlord's throat.

'Surrender.'

Ryam knew from his dark glare that Li Tao would never do it.

Ryam's grip tightened on the hilt of his sword. He didn't want to Ailey to see this, but it would be an insult to demand Li Tao's surrender a second time. It would be an insult if Ryam let him go. But Li Tao hadn't wronged him enough to murder the man. If he killed him, Li Tao would be the hero and he the scoundrel.

Emperor Shen stepped onto the fighting grounds. 'A worthy battle. The foreigner has won.'

Li Tao showed no signs of relenting when Ryam let go of him.

'Do not plead on my behalf, Shen,' Li Tao spat.

'The Emperor has no wish to lose a loyal ally.'

Ailey came up behind her father and said nothing as she looked between the two of them. Li Tao fixed his gaze on to her and his hands clenched. 'I release you from your promise,' he said finally. He switched his gaze to the Emperor. 'And to you I promise nothing.'

He turned to stride back into the mansion without a proper dismissal. The household followed and his soldiers retreated to their posts, leaving the Emperor and his entourage in the courtyard. It was over.

Ailey rushed to him. 'You are hurt.'

She pressed her silk handkerchief against his arm with trembling hands. It seemed like for ever since she was by his side, with nothing between them. If his chest swelled any more, it would burst.

'You look good in red.' He smiled.

He must look like a nightmare, bruised and bleeding while Ailey stood next to him smelling like springtime, her cool touch on his skin. She held his hand in both of hers, turning his palm over to inspect the cut on his knuckles.

'Look at you! Getting yourself cut up like this,' she scolded gently, eyes lowered.

'I was bleeding for you and you were going to marry him anyway.' He couldn't help but be a bit disgruntled about how she'd hesitated, even after his victory.

His *glorious* victory.

'But I swore to him.' She looked at him through her lashes. 'There is a way that things must be done.'

One of the Emperor's soldiers came to bind his wounds.

Ryam had to wait for him to finish before he could speak to Ailey again.

He leaned close, lowering his voice. 'If I swear myself to you, will you help me around those ways should I get confused?'

The answer came from the Emperor. 'You had better swear to her, swordsman.'

Ailey jumped back at the sound of her father's voice. Ryam grinned. The fierce little swordswoman was afraid of her parents. She started to explain, but her father silenced her.

Taking a deep breath, Ryam faced Emperor Shen. The fight with Li Tao might have been the easier part of the day.

'Thank you for lending me your weapon.'

Ryam held out the sword and the Emperor tucked the dragon sword alongside his arm.

'Finish what you were saying to my daughter,' he said. Ryam didn't fail to notice that Shen hadn't put the sword away.

'I was going to swear—' He cursed himself for never learning proper Han. He looked like an unwashed barbarian and definitely sounded like one. 'I was going to tell her I love her.'

Ailey's face grew bright and she straightened, ready to rush into his arms. The Emperor thwarted her.

'Walk with me,' he commanded.

She made a sound of protest as they turned and took the path away from the compound. A spark of amusement lit the Emperor's eyes at his daughter's impatience.

'You fought well.'

Ryam pictured Li Tao and him on the ground, rolling and exchanging punches. Not exactly brilliant technique, and probably not quite honourable either.

'The Emperor is generous with his praise,' he said, rubbing at the back of his neck.

'You displayed great sword skill. Tell me, how did you learn?'

'From my father.'

The Emperor nodded. 'That is the best way.'

Shen reminded him of Ailey. He could see the roots of her

quiet strength and her ability to accept. Walking beside the Emperor filled him with a solid sense of purpose. The stone pathway gave way to dirt as they made their way back into the forest. The Emperor's train of attendants and soldiers fell into position around them.

Ailey walked a respectable distance behind them, her hands clasped together nervously as she strained to hear the conversation.

'This is why we arrange marriages.' The Emperor shook his head. 'Look at the two of you. Completely blind. How would one ever make a good choice?'

'I…uh…' Ryam stammered for words. 'I know I don't deserve her—'

Shen raised his hand impatiently. 'My daughter does not like self-doubt. When she makes a decision, she holds on to it.'

He held the sword out between them, showing the dragon insignia. 'You recognise this?'

Ryam nodded. 'It belonged to the great General Shen, your father.'

'My father,' he echoed. 'And now it belongs to you.'

The Emperor held it out to him, balancing the blade against his arm.

'It's an insult to refuse,' Ailey whispered over his shoulder. She was staring at her father with surprise and adoration. Ryam recognised that look from her. He hoped he'd get to see it often in his lifetime. Humbly, he wrapped his hand around the hilt. The weapon was lighter than the one he'd carried all his life. It moved with more freedom.

'The glory of our family was built on honour and loyalty. You will serve that tradition well.'

The Emperor beckoned Ailey over with a nod. Ryam curved his arm around her as she fitted herself against his side, soft and radiant and perfect.

'My fifth son will be joining me in Changan. His talents will be better served there. I need a capable warrior in the north-west frontier to administer the lands, train our soldiers and protect the border.'

Ryam frowned. The court dialect was extravagant, verbose. He couldn't quite follow the Emperor's meaning. Was Shen actually suggesting that he install himself at Longyou?

'This humble...I mean, I don't...'

Shen clasped his shoulder in a paternal gesture. 'None of us deserves the things we have been given. We can only spend the rest of our days earning them.'

With that, the Emperor walked away, taking the lead of the assembly of attendants and soldiers. They followed him en masse.

'He says yes,' Ailey explained breathlessly. Finally alone with each other, she snuggled close and wound her arms around his neck.

'How do I tell him I accept?'

'You already have.'

She searched his face for a spot that wasn't battered. Carefully, tenderly, she kissed the corner of his mouth. He laughed and tightened his arms around her to hold her against him. The aches and pains of the day faded away.

Chapter Twenty-Four

They travelled together with the Emperor's escort through the forest and back to Longyou. Ailey watched with pride as Ryam rode alongside her father, learning about the empire from the Emperor himself.

During the journey, she asked Father if he regretted breaking his alliance with Li Tao over her. His only reply was that it was already broken long before.

Ryam fell back beside her as they came upon the family home sheltered in the embrace of the mountains.

'This is more responsibility than I've ever had,' he said with a deep breath.

'You are not afraid?'

He grinned. 'Never.'

'Mother hasn't seen you. Or Grandmother. They'll want to come by. And my brothers.'

He stopped her. 'Now I am getting scared.'

'You may have to fight my brothers,' she said with complete seriousness. 'And maybe Grandmother.'

He blinked. 'I had better practise.'

Her father rode forwards, tall and proud in the saddle as he looked on their home. It was how she felt returning there.

Father would return to Changan to reign as Emperor, but she never had belonged in the imperial city. This was her home in the silent mountains, as the youngest daughter in the honourable line of the Shen family.

Ryam didn't look at all like her father or her brothers, but he was the same. She had known it before he had known it. She had known it from the moment they had crossed swords.

'This is a long way from your home,' she said.

'No.' He shook his head. 'This is the closest I have ever been.'

* * * * *

REQUEST YOUR FREE BOOKS!

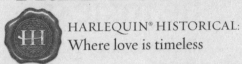

HARLEQUIN® HISTORICAL:
Where love is timeless

2 FREE NOVELS PLUS 2 **FREE GIFTS!**

YES! Please send me 2 FREE Harlequin® Historical novels and my 2 FREE gifts (gifts are worth about $10). After receiving them, if I don't wish to receive any more books, I can return the shipping statement marked "cancel." If I don't cancel, I will receive 6 brand-new novels every month and be billed just $4.94 per book in the U.S. or $5.49 per book in Canada. That's a saving of 20% off the cover price! It's quite a bargain! Shipping and handling is just 50¢ per book.* I understand that accepting the 2 free books and gifts places me under no obligation to buy anything. I can always return a shipment and cancel at any time. Even if I never buy another book from Harlequin, the two free books and gifts are mine to keep forever.

246/349 HDN E5L4

Name _____ (PLEASE PRINT) _____

Address _____ Apt. # _____

City _____ State/Prov. _____ Zip/Postal Code _____

Signature (if under 18, a parent or guardian must sign)

Mail to the **Harlequin Reader Service:**
IN U.S.A.: P.O. Box 1867, Buffalo, NY 14240-1867
IN CANADA: P.O. Box 609, Fort Erie, Ontario L2A 5X3
Not valid for current subscribers to Harlequin Historical books.

Want to try two free books from another line?
Call 1-800-873-8635 or visit www.morefreebooks.com.

* Terms and prices subject to change without notice. Prices do not include applicable taxes. N.Y. residents add applicable sales tax. Canadian residents will be charged applicable provincial taxes and GST. Offer not valid in Quebec. This offer is limited to one order per household. All orders subject to approval. Credit or debit balances in a customer's account(s) may be offset by any other outstanding balance owed by or to the customer. Please allow 4 to 6 weeks for delivery. Offer available while quantities last.

Your Privacy: Harlequin Books is committed to protecting your privacy. Our Privacy Policy is available online at www.eHarlequin.com or upon request from the Reader Service. From time to time we make our lists of customers available to reputable third parties who may have a product or service of interest to you. If you would prefer we not share your name and address, please check here. ☐

Help us get it right—We strive for accurate, respectful and relevant communications. To clarify or modify your communication preferences, visit us at www.ReaderService.com/consumerschoice.

HH10R

HARLEQUIN®

A Romance

FOR EVERY MOOD™

Spotlight on

Inspirational

Wholesome romances
that touch the heart and soul.

See the next page
to enjoy a sneak peek from
the Love Inspired® Suspense
inspirational series.

"It's okay. I'm here to help." The voice was as deep as the darkness, but Jenna Dougherty didn't believe the lie. She could do nothing but lie still as hands slid down her arms, felt the rope around her wrists.

"I'm going to use a knife to cut you free, Jenna. Hold still."

The cold blade of a knife pressed close to her head before her gag fell away.

"I—" she started, but her mouth was dry, and she could do nothing but suck in air.

"Shhh. Whatever needs to be said can be said when we're out of here." Nick spoke quietly, his hand gentle on her cheek. There and gone as he sliced through the ropes on her wrists and ankles.

He pulled her upright. "Come on. We may be on borrowed time."

"I can't leave my friend," Jenna rasped out.

"There's no one here. Just us."

"She has to be here." Jenna took a step away.

"There's no one here. Let's go before that changes."

"It's dark. Maybe if we find a light…"

"What did you say?"

"We need to turn on the light. I can't leave until I know that—"

"What can you see, Jenna?"

"Nothing."

"No shadows? No light?"

"No."

"It's broad daylight. There's light spilling in from the window I climbed in through. You can't see it?"

She went cold at his words.

"I can't see anything."

"You've got a nasty bruise on your forehead. Maybe that has something to do with it." His fingers traced the tender flesh on her forehead.

"It doesn't matter *how* it happened. I'm blind!"

Can Nick help Jenna find her friend or will chasing this trail have Jenna running blindly again into danger?

Find out in RUNNING BLIND, available in November 2010 only from Love Inspired Suspense.

FROM #1 *NEW YORK TIMES*
AND *USA TODAY* BESTSELLING AUTHOR

DEBBIE MACOMBER

Mrs. Miracle on 34th Street…

This Christmas, Emily Merkle (just call her Mrs. Miracle) is working in the toy department at Finley's, the last family-owned department store in Manhattan.

Her boss (who happens to be the owner's son) has placed an order for a large number of high-priced robots, which he hopes will give the business a much-needed boost. In fact, Jake Finley's counting on it.

Holly Larson is counting on that robot, too. She's been looking after her eight-year-old nephew, Gabe, ever since her widowed brother was deployed overseas. Holly plans to buy Gabe a robot—which she can't afford—because she's determined to make Christmas special.

But this Christmas will be different—thanks to Mrs. Miracle. Next to bringing children joy, her favorite activity is giving romance a nudge. Fortunately, Jake and Holly are receptive to her "hints." And thanks to Mrs. Miracle, Christmas takes on new meaning for Jake. For all of them!

Call Me Mrs. Miracle

**Available wherever books are sold
September 28!**

MIRA®

I looked across the street, at Tasha
Thompkins's bedroom window. I wondered
if she was stretched out on the bed crying.
That's where I'd be, if I found out either of
my brothers had been killed.

I felt a wave of grief for Tasha, and for her parents. I didn't know anything about gangs, but I thought that whoever had killed Nate couldn't have known him all that well, because he'd been a nice kid. Smart, too. It was a waste. A real waste.

I saw a curtain move. Tasha was standing in the window, looking down as the squad cars in her driveway pulled away. Poor Tasha. There was nothing I could do for her. I mean, if I had known when her father had come over that Nate was in trouble, I might have been able to find him. But it was too late for me to help Nate now.

But not too late, I realized, to help his sister.

Little did I know, of course, how my decision to help Tasha Thompkins was going to change my life. And the life of just about everybody in our entire town.